Rise of the Queen

Elvish Chronicles, Volume 1

Prudence MacLeod

Published by Prudence MacLeod, 2024.

Rise of the Queen
by
Prudence MacLeod
Book one of the Elvish Chronicles
(second edition)
Copyright June / 2016

RISE OF THE QUEEN

First edition. March 19, 2024.

Copyright © 2024 Prudence MacLeod.

ISBN: 978-1927478738

Written by Prudence MacLeod.

The Chronicles

Herein I will endeavor to record the events which brought the Elves back from the gates of extinction to rule the vast forests of Elendor. Through several twists of fate, and the rediscovery of their ancient magics they were returned, and now they inhabit and control the vast forests of northern Elendor.

It all began with the sudden appearance of the assassin...

Shadow Assassin

I n the city of Magdan, as ruled by the Geni Overlord, Ocra, the night had fallen strangely silent. It was one of those odd silences that sometimes falls for no reason, and vanishes a moment later. However, it was enough. Ariel, newly promoted to the City Watch, arose from her bed with liquid grace, stepping into her soft boots and silently sliding her sword from the scabbard hanging at her bedside.

Ariel, descended from the High Born Elves of Elendor, had managed to earn her freedom from slavery and rise to a post in the Watch. Few Elves ever managed to earn freedom; none had ever been trusted to carry a sword.

With silent steps she slipped from the building and cast her gaze about for anything that was amiss. She found it on the rooftop, a shadow in the moonlight that did not belong. A few swift and silent strides carried Ariel to the dark figure. "Stand and surrender." She spoke in a clear ringing voice as she laid the tip of her blade against the intruder's neck.

"Not tonight, little sister. Go back to your warm bed and your dreams of glory. Live to fight another day." Ariel was shocked. First, the voice was low pitched, yet feminine, and gentle, almost loving, caressing her senses. Second, the intruder had spoken in High Elvish, a language that was forbidden on pain of death. Few remained who could actually speak it.

Ariel didn't realize the figure had moved until a strong arm encircled her neck and a silvery blade caressed her cheek. Again that gentle loving voice spoke. "Go back, little sister. I've come here this night to take a life; I'd prefer it not be yours. Return to your warm bed and sweet dreams." The arm left her neck and a strong hand deftly relieved her of the sword. She barely noticed it happen.

Ariel felt the intruder step away and she turned to face her opponent. The moon broke from behind a cloud to show her a tall Elf with elaborate tattoos on her left cheek. Ariel swallowed and stepped back. "You're one of the ancient Borni tribe. You can't be real. Your people died out centuries ago."

The woman's eyes danced with merriment and her smile was radiant. "No, little sister, we did not vanish from the realms, but we did withdraw from this one for a time. Now we're returning." That voice was still soft and gentle, almost hypnotic. "I must be about the business now. I beg you, do not follow me or sound the alarm. It would grieve me to have to harm you."

The woman tossed Ariel her sword, then leaped from the roof top to vanish into the shadows of an alley below.

Without a second thought, Ariel followed as best she could. This Borni was like a wisp of smoke in the breeze. Somehow Ariel managed to catch sight of her quarry often enough to keep up yet stay back out of sight.

Her heart froze in her chest, the woman had slipped into Ocra's house, the most heavily guarded palace in the entire region.

Ariel knew she should sound the alarm. She knew it would mean her death if it was discovered that she had known of the intruder but done nothing. She swallowed hard, but before she could make a decision, the Borni slipped out of the house, carrying a sack. There had been no alarm.

"A common thief," mused Ariel, disappointed, and not knowing why. And then she saw the blood dripping from the bag. The Borni had said she'd come to take a life. By all the gods, what had she done? Ariel followed as the assassin headed for the wall that surrounded the town. With a cat-like grace the woman leaped to the top and disappeared over it, vanishing into the darkness below.

Ariel climbed swiftly to the wall and peered over as well. The assassin was sitting on a horse below, waiting for her with a huge smile. "Well? Are you coming or not?"

Without a second thought, Ariel slipped over the wall and landed beside the horse. A hand was extended and she grabbed it, swinging up behind the Borni as the horse leaped away. She could hear the alarm sounding back in the town.

As she clung to the rider, Ariel's heart beat wildly with the sudden and intoxicating rush of true freedom.

Mercenary

A riel had been born in the city, and she'd never been beyond the walls. Now she was outside in the moonlight, riding on a war horse behind a figure from legend. Her mind spun with the magnitude of what she'd done, and yet the countless new sights and smells battering her senses were intoxicating. She reveled in them as well as the power of the beast beneath her.

The huge animal seemed tireless, and the night slipped away to the rhythm of its movements. Eventually they turned from the road and into the forest, slowing to a walk. Never having been on a horse before, Ariel was now in some discomfort. She made no complaint, yet her squirming was signal enough.

"We'll rest here for a moment, and then we'll walk to rest our friend." The Borni swept her leg high over the saddle then slipped lightly to the ground. Ariel tried to mimic the move, but her muscles had stiffened, and she fell into the arms of her companion.

The Borni held her for a moment, smiling, then set her lightly on her feet. "A body unaccustomed to riding will stiffen up rather quickly, but that will pass soon enough with practice."

Ariel stepped back and watched as the woman stripped off the saddle and, seizing up a handful of sweet grasses, began to rub the animal down. The beast nickered softly and nuzzled the woman's shoulder. A treat was produced, and the horse chewed happily as the saddle was reapplied.

Ariel finally spoke as the woman tied the grisly bag onto the saddle bow. "Who are you?"

The response was filled with merriment. "I am many things to many people. Right now, I'm your traveling companion. My name is Mearith. Now, my delight, who are you?"

"My name is Ariel. Where are you taking me, Mearith?"

"Wherever I go, for as long as you wish to accompany me. Ah, ah, hush now, we have to be on the move. We'll put tonight's little adventure to rest, then there'll be time for questions, for both of us."

"Both of us?" she asked, as she set out behind Mearith and the horse.

"Yes, both of us. Ariel, your name means princess. You're as unique and exotic to me as I am to you. When the Borni left this world we believed all the High Born to have been slain, that none were left alive to tell of their final passing. Imagine my delight to see you sleeping there so peacefully amid our old enemies."

"Enemies? What? Wait, you saw me sleeping? You were watching me sleep?"

"I was. It was those delightful sleep sounds that drew me."

"You were, wait, are you saying I snore?"

With a laugh of pure delight, Mearith leaped to the saddle and held her hand out for Ariel. With a regal toss of her head and a look of pure indignation, Ariel accepted the hand and climbed to the horse's back.

The world was lighter now, and the path was easy for the horse to follow. Ariel was nearly asleep due to the fatigue and the rocking motion of the animal's gait. Suddenly they were challenged from a gate in the trail. "Halt. Stand and deliver."

"It is I, returning," shouted Mearith, her voice harsh and threatening. "I've performed my task and wish to be paid. I'll deliver your death if you don't open that accursed gate, and quickly."

"Always a pleasure to see you too, mercenary," grumbled the huge man, as he heaved the gate aside to let them pass. Ariel stiffened at Mearith's tone. These were not friends, and this wasn't a safe place.

Her hand drifted to the sword at her side. It was loosely shoved through her belt, as she had left the scabbard behind.

The Borni's hand reached back and patted hers. "Not yet, Ariel, but stay alert." They rode up to a rough looking building and dismounted. "Wait here." As Mearith stepped toward the door she sensed Ariel right on her heels. She turned to see an arched eyebrow and a challenging look. She grinned, then winked. "Stay sharp."

Inside the inn was like any other in the bad part of town where Ariel had been on patrol. The stench of stale beer and spilled wine filled the air, as did the smoke from guttering candles. One man, or something like a man, a Geni, stood out amid the squalor. He was too well dressed and too tall. Mearith strode right toward him.

"Ah, mercenary, it's about time you returned. Have you completed your errand? Have you brought my prize?"

Mearith tossed the bloody sack on the rough table. "The deed is done. Pay me."

"Always in such a hurry. Tell me, now that my enemy is dead, why should I pay?"

The Borni's sword leaped to her hand with lightning speed. "The rules are simple, Geni. I do the job, and then I get paid. Pay me now or die where you stand."

"All right, all right, no need to get all worked up," he said as he backed away from her blade. "here you go." He tossed a bag of coins to her, and she passed them back.

"Ariel, twenty-three gold coins?"

A moment passed then, "Yes. All are here."

"Then we'll be on our way."

"Not so fast, mercenary. You brought a slave out of the city while in my employ. That makes the slave my property."

"There are no slaves here," replied Mearith. Her tone was so cold Ariel actually shivered. "This woman is my companion. Show her disrespect again and I will be deeply offended. Touch her and meet your doom."

Ariel was startled at how quickly everyone looked away. The big creature lost his bluster as he realized none of his companions wanted to fight the Borni. "Be off with you then, Elf. I declare you an outlaw. Set foot in my city again and the Watch will have you."

"A pleasure doing business with you, Overlord Dorgon," replied Mearith, as she began to back away towards the door. Once outside she fairly tossed Ariel into the saddle then leaped up behind her. The horse raced away and they thundered past the rude gate, back into the forest.

As soon as Mearith was certain there was no pursuit, she turned the big horse into the stream they had crossed earlier. They rode downstream for a while then dismounted in a small clearing. She stripped off the saddle, tossed it and the bags on the ground, and then rubbed the horse down. The beast instantly began to graze on the grasses beside the stream.

"What can I do to help?"

"Rest, Ariel. We will both rest now." Mearith sat with her back against a large tree and patted the ground beside her.

Ariel sat quietly, listening to the world around her, a world she had never experienced before. She could hear the horse feeding, insects buzzing, birds tweeting, and so much more. Mearith smiled with delight as she watched the look of wonder on the young Elf's face. Suddenly a look of fear and embarrassment settled on the young one.

"What is it, Ariel?" asked that gentle voice.

"Nothing. Nothing at all."

"Never lie to a Borni, little sister. What is it that steals your joy of life?"

"It's the madness. I've been too long without the oshar. I will not long survive, but I thank you for this experience. I knew I'd die, but it's been worth it to be truly free, even for a day."

"There is much I don't understand about this, Ariel. Please help me to learn. Of what madness do you speak?"

"The madness of my people. Only by eating the oshar daily can we remain free of it."

"The madness of your people? The High Born? I've called a few of them mad from time to time, but never as a whole people. What form does this madness take?"

"It is too terrible to speak of, but it begins with the voices."

"Voices?"

"Yes, the mind snaps and you begin to hear voices on the wind."

"And you have heard such a voice?"

"Yes."

"What did it say?"

Ariel turned to give her companion a startled look. Mearith was actually smiling at her. "What does it matter what it said? I heard it clearly; the madness has begun. You should leave me here to die in peace....What are you smiling about?"

"What did the voice say, Ariel?"

Ariel didn't know what to make of her strange companion. Mearith seemed so at ease, almost delighted. Is that why she'd brought her here, to enjoy the spectacle of the madness? "It said, 'Welcome home.'"

"I thought as much. Ariel, you're not going mad, you're awakening. All Elves hear the voice of the wind."

"What? Mearith, what is happening to me?"

"You're starting to remember what it is to be an Elf. I suspect this oshar has an ingredient in it that dulls your Elvish senses. Do all the slaves eat it?"

"Of course. How else could we survive?"

"I sensed a wrongness within you when we first met. Your reactions were too slow, your stealth lacking, and yet I sensed the strength within you. Let me tell you the history as I have experienced it."

"Experienced it?"

"Yes. We Elves are quite long-lived."

"Long-lived? I've never known anyone to live beyond a hundred turns."

"That has now changed for you, Ariel, for I've lived many hundreds of turns, and fully expect to live as many more. Listen to me now. Our people were once one, but some remained within the forest, tending the lands, nurturing the trees. Others became enamored of the high magic and forgot the forest. They used their magic to build magnificent cities instead. They called themselves the High Born.

"In time we became two separate peoples, still living on and sharing the land, but from two different perspectives. However, when the invaders came and the wars began, we ended up on different sides for a time. At the end of the great war, when the world was broken, the Borni left this world for another.

"The High Born refused to come with us, remaining behind to work great magics, but they were betrayed by the alliance of Orcs and Humans. As the waves of death swept over the High Born, the Borni left this place. I was among the last to go. I'm also the first to return, and I'm thrilled to find some of my kin have survived.

"You were once of the forest, Ariel, and the living magic's as natural to you as breathing. Release yourself to it, embrace it and the joy of life it will return to you."

Ariel gazed into Mearith's eyes. A deep sigh escaped her lips, and she looked away as she spoke. "For us the tales are very different. During the great war against evil, the Borni abandoned the High Born to their fate and left the field of battle.

"In anger the great leaders brought down magic to destroy the Borni. As the mages lay exhausted, their allies placed the High Born in the care of the humans, but they were betrayed as well, and the Elves were enslaved. The humans keep us alive as long as we serve them faithfully. Fail and they withhold the oshar. When the madness comes, the Elf is executed.

"This is how my grandmother told me the tale as it was told to her by her grandmother."

"There's much here to be discovered, Ariel. For now it's enough to know that you're quite sane and healthy. Your Elvish senses are returning. Embrace them, enjoy them. Rest now and let the winds sing you to sleep." She did.

Awakening

Ariel settled down in the grass beneath the tree and sleep soon claimed her. She shivered in her sleep. "By all the powers, what have they done to her?" thought Mearith, as she laid her cloak over the sleeping girl. "Her body can't even warm itself." She slid beneath the spread cloak with Ariel to share body warmth.

Sleep didn't come to the warrior as easily as to the girl. Before she could rest, Mearith needed to clear her mind on what had happened and what she planned to do next. She closed her eyes and debated with her inner voice, the one that insisted she think straight.

"Mearith, what have you done this time? She is not, nor can she ever be, Elaith. You know this. Yes, she wears the face of your lost love, but that and nothing more."

"I know this, my conscience. I held Elaith as she breathed her last and returned to the great forest. I also know this one is of the High Born, more, she is the heir to the throne of the High Born. It was her sleeping face that caught my attention, but nothing more. I don't seek to reawaken the past."

"Then why? Why bring her with you? Obviously she'd made a life for herself among the humans. She wears no slave collar and carries a weapon. She must have arisen from the pens to a position of rank. Why destroy her life?"

Mearith actually smiled at that. "Ruined her life? With that line of thought, I should have killed her to maintain her silence while I went about the assassination. No, she came with me of her own free will. I offered her the choice to make her exercise that free will. I will do so again many times in the coming days."

"Look at the rest of it, Mearith. There'll be no rest for you until you do."

"As you say, my conscience, the rest of it. Yes, at a glance I saw Elaith's face and moved closer. I was curious only, nothing more, and then I felt the Spiritpull. I've always thought myself to be unusual, and to feel the Pull for a second time confirms it for me. I know of no other who has ever been drawn a second time, no matter what the circumstances.

"Yes, I've felt the pull of her spirit as my own embraced it, but she's the heir of the High Born, although I doubt she knows it. I also doubt she knows of, or understands, the Spiritpull. I won't force this union but will allow her freedom of choice. She must choose me above all others on her own. Now let me rest." She was smiling as she drifted off to sleep.

While Mearith debated with herself, Ariel dreamed. In the dream, she wandered vast halls with soaring arches holding the roof high above. Rain fell softly outside and freshened the air. As she passed, others nodded respectfully then returned to their studies, for indeed, this was a study hall.

Ariel moved towards a window and looked out. She was in a high tower that soared above the forest below. Suddenly the tower shook and began to sway. There were great siege engines below battering at the foundations. She saw the mages working their magic to hold the city together and repel the invaders, but the attackers had magic users as well. The air crackled with the energies being hurled back and forth.

Ariel whimpered in her sleep and cuddled closer to the warm body beside her. Gentle arms enfolded her in life as well as in the dream. In the dream she fled the tower and slipped into the forest, to the waiting arms of her lover. A love that was forbidden.

As a member of the royal house, she must mate with another of the High Born, but her spirit had been pulled to this forest runner with the facial tattoos of the warrior class. She ran through the secret tunnel and into the trees, seeking her lover. Ariel recognized Mearith's face even as the arrow pierced her body and she awakened with a start. She was held gently in Mearith's arms.

Ariel slowly brought her breathing back to normal. A dream, only a dream, but it had seemed so real. Perhaps this was another of her Elvish senses returning. If so, she would happily do without it.

She propped herself up on one elbow and drank deeply of the clear fresh air. The forest around her was now alive with sound, soft rustling, the breeze high in the branches, and the singsong of the waters tumbling over the stones in the stream filled her senses and made her smile with delight.

Ariel turned her attention to her sleeping companion, studying her face. Why had she come with this assassin? Why had she not sounded the alarm? More importantly, why was she so compelled to be near this tattooed woman? From the first moment she had heard that hypnotic voice she had been lost in the nearness of this rogue Elf. Why? It had felt the same in the dream. The dream, yes, there had been something about that in the dream, what was it?

She paused in her musings and began to study Mearith's face more closely. The finely chiseled nose and chin, the graceful up-swept ears, and the silky reddish hair, all burned their way into her memory so as to never be forgotten. The eyes that were almost cobalt blue when open were closed in repose now.

She looked closer at the markings on Mearith's face. They were colored in reds, purples, and blacks, shaped like leaves with weapons hidden within. There were symbols hidden there as well and almost seemed alive. Suddenly she was aware of the skin near the eyes had crinkled slightly. The perfect lips had curved the tiniest amount as well.

"You're awake, aren't you?"

"Yes."

"How long?"

"I felt you start in your sleep."

"You knew I was studying you. You were enjoying yourself. Admit it."

Mearith laughed then, a full and rich song of joy. "I admit it freely. It seems only fair since I did the same to you in the city."

"Why? Why did you study me in sleep? How did you find me? Why did you bring me with you? What..."

"Whoa, little sister, whoa. Yes, we have time for questions, but first I must retreat to the trees to relieve myself. The day is well along now, we'll remain here until the morrow, so we have time for questions." Mearith rose easily and fairly melted into the trees.

Nodding her agreement, Ariel rose and went in a different direction. She relieved herself then hurried back to the clearing. Mearith wasn't in sight and she nearly panicked until she heard that rich voice cooing softly. Mearith was rubbing down the horse again, singing softly to him as she worked. Ariel was shaking with relief as she approached.

Stopping a few paces away, Ariel was startled to feel her fear and unease melt away. The nearer she got to Mearith, the better she felt. Whatever magic this was, it needed explaining. "Mearith?"

"Yes?" She stepped around the horse and smiled, lighting up Ariel's world.

"Can we do the questions now?"

"Yes, let's do. I'll make a fire to heat food and we'll share tales while we share bread." She moved easily back to the spot where her cloak lay beneath the tree. She caught it up then swept it around Ariel's shoulders. "Stay warm now until the food is ready."

Ariel watched, fascinated, as Mearith gathered up a few twigs, scraped off some tinder with her dagger, then struck a flint to the steel. A moment later there was a small fire. She added a few more twigs to get it going then settled down beside it with the saddle bags. Ariel sat beside her, wrapped in the cloak.

"Ask before you burst," chuckled Mearith.

"So many question are in my mind, I hardly know where to start. Mearith, why is it that when I'm close to you I feel wonderful, and when there is distance between us I start to panic?"

"Tell me more of this."

"It happened in the city when you jumped down to the street, I was suddenly lost and had to follow. Again at the top of the wall when you asked if I was coming with you. I would have died if you'd ridden away. Still again at that inn when you told me to remain outside. I just couldn't, and again just now. What is happening to me?"

"Your Elvish nature is awakening, Ariel. This is part of your nature."

"I don't understand."

"You will come to in time."

"The time is now, Mearith. Please help me to understand. What is this feeling? Will it fade?"

"No, it will not fade, but only grow stronger. You must learn to control it for it brings many gifts if you can, and madness if you can't."

Ariel sighed and set her jaw, gazing into Mearith's eyes. "Is it possible to get a clear answer from you? Ever?"

Mearith grinned with delight. "Yes, it is. Ariel, I had hoped to have more time together before having to explain this to you."

"Oh damn, it's the compulsion, isn't it?"

"Compulsion?"

"The mating compulsion. My grandmother spoke of it. When two spirits meld the people are compelled to be together. It's the most terrible thing that can happen to an Elf."

"Why would you say that?"

"Because the masters choose who mates and who doesn't. To be so compelled and yet forced apart…"

"I understand. Yes, this is what it is, Ariel. We Borni call it the Spiritpull. It happens when two spirits are pulled towards each other. It happens only once in a lifetime as a rule."

"As a rule?"

"Apparently, there can be exceptions."

"You're doing it again. Explain please."

Mearith smiled wistfully the put her arm around Ariel's shoulders. "Long ago I felt the Pull and joined with my soul mate. We had long happy years together, then the wars came. On the day the world was broken and the High Born fell, she was taken from me. I have felt the loss of her each moment since that time.

"I saw her face in a small shelter atop a roof. She was sleeping. I moved closer as the Pull gripped me again. I soon realized this wasn't my Elaith, but one of the High Born slaves, yet she wore no collar, and a sword hung by her bedside. I was intrigued and bemused. In all my long memory the Spiritpull has never happened a second time, but there I was.

"I tried to shake it off and get back to business, but the Pull awakened you. The rest you know."

"Then why did you try to leave me behind?"

Mearith's laugh was rich and filled with the joy of life. Ariel's heart swelled to the merry sound and she smiled. "I nearly went mad making sure you could follow me through the city."

"Making sure I could, wait, are you saying you waited for me? Are you saying I couldn't have followed you if you'd tried to lose me?"

"You were under the influence of the oshar, Ariel. Today is different. Now the Pull would lead you right to me no matter where I go, or how hard I might try to hide."

"You're still grinning at me. You have far too much fun at my expense."

"Sorry."

"You're not either. So, what happens to me now?"

"What do you want to happen now, Ariel? Think clearly. The Spiritpull is an ancient instinct. It can be overcome by force of will. Your mind is clear and you have free will. What do you want to happen?"

Ariel didn't speak for a long moment and Mearith prepared herself for long years of emptiness once again. She almost didn't hear the soft voice beside her. "I really don't care what happens next as long as I'm beside you. That's what I truly want."

Mearith tightened her arm around Ariel's slender shoulders. "Then we shall face the grand adventure together, side by side. There's some daylight left; we'll practice for a while then we'll rest again until morning. Tomorrow we'll move on."

"Practice? What will we practice?"

"Things."

"What sorts of things?"

"Elvish things," grinned Mearith.

The woman's mischievous and joyful nature was infectious, and Ariel smiled at her. It was a game and she was starting to enjoy it. Suddenly Mearith moved away from her. She held up a hand to signal Ariel to remain by the fire.

"Close your eyes, Ariel. Tell me if I'm moving closer to you or moving away."

Ariel closed her eyes and felt the emptiness as Mearith moved away. "You moved away," she said, eyes closed, but turning to face Mearith anyway.

A moment later joy filled her heart. "Closer, you came closer." She had the game now. She could use the Spiritpull to locate Mearith, her direction of travel, and her nearness.

After a bit more practice she was able to point right at Mearith as well as tell when she had moved only a few paces. Suddenly her heart filled with joy then loving arms enfolded her. She returned the hug enthusiastically. "That's enough of that for now. Let's build up the fire a bit then I have questions for you."

Mearith threw a few sticks on the fire then took out food wrapped in moist leaves. Poking a stick through the Elvish bread she warmed it over the fire for a moment then passed it to Ariel. She warmed one for herself then smiled at her young companion.

"Now, questions for you. I spent many days in the city, studying my prey. I knew that the High Born had survived, yet enslaved. However, I learned of one who had reached freedom and a position with the City Watch. I found you sleeping in a small hut on a rooftop, no slave collar, and a sword by your side. How did this come to be?"

"I was lucky to, wait, you knew about me? You sought me out?"

"I was intrigued. I stayed three days longer in that city than I wanted to, but... I was compelled. Now talk to me."

Ariel blushed softly and dropped her gaze. "Master was an elderly scholar and a kind man. He bought us to keep the former master from having us killed. Mother had slipped away and mated according to the compulsion, against the wishes of her master.

"Our new owner doted on my mother and raised me more like a daughter than a slave. He educated me and taught me the sword. He had been a master of the weapon in his younger days. Master refused to have me mated and when pressed, he set me free. Overlord Ocra had his champion test my sword skills then offered me a post on the Watch. He made my skin crawl. They all do."

"All?"

"Humans, Orcs, whatever race the overlords are... the Geni."

"Why?"

"As a member of the Watch I saw the abuses they heap on my people. I swore to one day find a way to set them free, that or avenge them. I was lucky, most aren't. Oh yes, a precious few manage to escape beyond the walls, but they're hunted like animals."

"I know. I've met a few who survived. They told me of the city and the fate of my kin. That's why I accepted the job of killing Ocra. I wanted a closer look into that city."

"Mearith, there are others? You know where to find them?"

"I sent them on to Fugitive, a village of many races who flee the heavy hand of the Geni law. Come closer, we'll share the cloak and rest now. When the sun returns to the forest we'll move on." She banked the fire then settled down with Ariel.

On the Road

Ariel awakened to birdsong. It was early, not quite full light, and a heavy frost lay on the ground. She snuggled deeper into the warmth of the heavy cloak and fought the empty feeling inside her. Mearith wasn't far away, she could tell. Mearith had said she would grow accustomed to this feeling in time, learn to use it as a tool.

Ariel had her doubts about that. "Have I just exchanged one form of slavery for another?" she wondered. Yes, she had been freed from slavery in the city, but dared not leave it. Now she was free of the city, but locked to this assassin with a slave chain that was much stronger.

Mearith was moving further away, and the gloom tightened its hold on her heart. With a sigh, she arose and swept the cloak around her shoulders. She stepped into the trees to relieve herself then followed Mearith. Ariel found her by the stream, several fat trout on a string beside her.

Ariel had made no sound as she approached, but Mearith knew she was there. "We'll have fish for breakfast, Ariel." She pulled another from the stream, quickly cleaned and added it to the string. "We have enough now. Come, let's get back to the campsite and make a fire for cooking." She gave Ariel a quick hug then set out for the camp.

Ariel followed, shivering. Once at the camp, Mearith lit the fire, being careful to go slow so Ariel could follow what she did. Once the fire was blazing cheerily, she left Ariel warming herself and went to cut two sticks for cooking. Staring at the fire, Ariel knew where she went, how far, and in which direction. She also felt her return. How the joy sang through her soul as the woman returned.

They cooked the fish and ate in silence. It warmed Ariel from the inside out. Sitting beside Mearith, her belly full, she sighed with contentment and swept the cloak around her companion to share the warmth.

Mearith smiled and nudged her with a shoulder. "You're not going mad, Ariel, and you aren't a slave. Oh yes, I know what's in your mind, for I've experienced it before. The Spiritpull is new to you and extremely powerful. In time you will grow accustomed to it, know it's true power and purpose, and take joy in that, even if we're apart for a time. For now it's new, raw, almost painful at times, and it's growing stronger."

"It isn't as strong for you?"

"Oh yes, it's every bit as strong for me. I can feel you, your every movement, every emotion, and I burn with every step of distance between us. A few more days, Ariel, and the bond will be complete. After that it'll recede into the background, like your sense of smell, or hearing; there when you need it, but not overpowering your every thought. We'll remain close until that happens."

"All right, wait, what happens after that? Are you going to leave me somewhere?"

"Relax, Ariel, my delight, relax. I won't leave you, not ever. I promised to keep you with me, and I'll do just that. What I mean is this; right now, if you stay here and I go to a town for supplies we'd both be tormented into madness. A week from now this won't be a problem. You'll know where I am, how far I've gone, and when I'm returning, but you'll be able to function freely."

Ariel sighed and laid her head on Mearith's shoulder. "I have so much to learn about being an Elf." Mearith chuckled and snuggled her closer.

A moment later Ariel sat up, listening. She turned wide eyes to Mearith who smiled. "What does the wind say?"

"It says we need to seek shelter soon. Is that right?"

"Indeed so. Brother wind does indeed give us warning of an impending change in the weather. Ah well, the sun's up, we should be on our way." Mearith rose, leaving the warm cloak around Ariel's shoulders. She whistled and the big war horse trotted over to her. They were soon mounted and on their way once again.

The path followed the stream, and they took their time, chatting easily. Ariel continued to assault Mearith with questions, and Mearith happily indulged her. The sun was high overhead when they reached the road. This wasn't the main highway, but a less used back road. As they left the shelter of the trees, an icy wind sprang up from off the western mountains.

Ariel shivered and Mearith felt it. She dismounted and helped Ariel down. They walked on, letting the great horse break the wind for them. They soon encountered a covered wagon coming their way. There was a jolly fellow driving and he called out in greeting as he pulled the horses to a stop.

"Now there's something you don't see every day," he said. Ariel was surprised at how rough the common language sounded to her now.

Mearith called the man by name as she responded to his greeting. "Ho, Randall. Just what is it that amazes and entertains you this fine day?"

"It's not often I see a warrior using her horse as a pack mule while she walks beside, Mearith."

"Ah, but the wind's bitter today and horse makes a fine windbreak," Mearith replied. "It's cold up there."

He laughed heartily then spoke. "We're well met, Mearith. I'm on my way to the city with fine wares that'll keep the cold from the bones of the rich folk this winter. If you've no coin you can pay me when you find work."

"I've been busy, Randall, and there's coin in the purse. This is Ariel, my companion. We'll both need heavier woolen cloaks. Ariel will need boots, leggings, tunics, a belt, and a scabbard for her blade to begin. Perhaps daggers for her as well."

"I have these things and more in the wagon. Let's see what we can find." He climbed down then walked to the back and dropped the tailgate to climb inside.

Mearith turned to Ariel. "This man is Randall; he's a trusted friend. Come, let's get you better outfitted for travel beyond city walls."

A Glimpse of the Darkness

Ariel smiled with delight as she snuggled into her new clothes, finer clothes than she had ever hoped to own. The boots were a soft, supple leather, the leggings and tunic of the finest combed lamb's wool and the hooded cloak was heavy, made of tightly woven wool. A new sword hung at her side and a long dagger as well. She flexed her hands inside the new leather gloves, feeling like she imagined a great lady might feel.

Mearith wasn't smiling as she listened to Randall's tale of the changing times. His wagon was heavily loaded, for he had everything the village had to offer in it. No one else was willing to risk the journey to Magdan.

The roads were crawling with cutthroats, so the rumors were told. Randall had no other choice, he'd had to risk the roads, but none would ride with him. They all stayed back to protect their homes and village.

Ariel was appalled by the price Mearith paid for the goods, but Mearith only winked at her and smiled. Her smile faded at the sound of horses, several of them. A moment later six riders appeared from a bend in the road. Upon spying the wagon, they charged. "Ariel, Randall, defend the horses and wagon."

To Ariel's horror, Mearith ran right at the charging horsemen. As the first man swung his sword at her Mearith ducked his clumsy blow and caught his arm, dragging him from the saddle. She didn't stop, but continued to the next man, avoiding his blow and stabbing his horse's flank lightly, causing it to rear and throw the rider to the ground. A thrown dagger killed the next man and Mearith was instantly up into his saddle, pushing the body to the ground.

Two riders had raced past her, but she wheeled the horse and went after them, catching them as they reached the wagon. Leaping nimbly from the saddle she ducked a sword blow and pulled the man to the ground. She stabbed him with her sword as Ariel engaged the last man.

Ariel exchanged sword blows with the robber and was amazed at her own speed. She stood in the wagon seat while the man was on a plunging horse. He seemed so slow. "Leave off," she shouted as she wounded him for the second time. "Leave off or die."

The man had no time to make that decision as Mearith's blade pierced him from behind, ending his life. He was still falling as Mearith turned and ran back to the other men, making sure they were dead, then gathering the horses. She passed the reins to Randall then started dragging the bodies off the road. "Help me with this, Ariel."

Ariel hadn't moved from the wagon seat. She was still in shock, frozen with horror and revulsion at what Mearith had done. She saw Mearith rifling the bodies, taking what she found of value and callously rolling the dead aside as she moved to the next.

"Ariel!" Getting no answer, Mearith turned to see Randal gazing at her with a pitying look. Her eyes moved to Ariel who swallowed hard and looked away. Showing no emotion at all Mearith turned back to her task.

She returned to Randall and passed him the weapons, belts, boots, and cloak that she had gathered. He nodded and tossed them into the cart then returned the gold she had paid him earlier. "I'll need one of the horses for Ariel. Sell the rest." He nodded.

Ariel had climbed down from the wagon and slowly walked over to stare at the dead men. Actually, five men and an Orc. She was aware as Mearith reached her side. "I offered him a chance at life, but you slew him from behind."

"I did. Ariel, what chance would you have me give him? The chance to kill you? To kill Randall? How many others has he killed? Tortured? Maimed? Would you give him the chance to continue? He lies there before you, look at the trophy on his hilt."

Ariel felt her stomach rise up as she saw the grisly charm dangling from the man's sword hilt. The blade had broken when he fell so Mearith hadn't taken it. The charm was a child's hand. She swallowed hard and fought the rising gorge in her belly.

Mearith's voice was soft and hypnotic as she took the girl's arm and led her back to the wagon. "Come, we will join Randall on his journey to the city."

"Of course. We...wait, what? We'll do what? Have you gone completely mad?" Mearith was smiling at her with that delighted grin again. "What are you thinking?"

"How can I think at all with you so near me?"

"Stop it, Mearith. Answer me."

"If I must, but it's more fun to tease you. I'm thinking Randall needs guards to reach the city safely. I'm thinking we're out of work right now and need a job. We'll see this fine merchant safely to the city walls then back again to his home in the forest village. By then it'll be too late to cross the mountains, so he'll repay us by giving us food and lodgings for the winter."

"Mearith, we can't go into the city, and you know it."

"Yes, I know, but we can see him to the edge of the forest safely and then back home again. Ariel, I feel the turmoil within you. This realm is a hard place. Life is cheap here, and there is little room for mercy when dealing with an enemy. There are other realms. If you wish I'll send you to a realm of peace, to my people there. They will welcome you.

"No, make no answer now. Wait a few more days until the Pull settles within you, and then decide. For now I'll keep you safe as I've promised. I'll take the lead, you ride with Randall, protect him." She turned away then and mounted her warhorse. She set out towards Magdan at a walk.

Randall spoke softly when he felt Mearith was out of hearing range. "You travel with her, but you don't know who she is, do you?"

"She's Mearith, an assassin," replied Ariel, her voice flat and emotionless.

"No, she is Mearith of many names. Mearith the Mercenary, Mearith the Merciless, and others. She was there when the world was broken, when my race and the Orcs betrayed the Elves and enslaved them. She was there, holding the love of her life in her arms as the woman slipped away from an arrow through the back.

"Her name is Mearith Waleen, Champion of Combat, and sister to the Borni king, Evanseth. She's the greatest warrior the Borni ever produced. The tattoos on her face mark her as a defender of the forest. Since the death of her lover, she's wandered the realms working as a mercenary.

"You're young, and this was most likely your first battle. I tell you this as a friend. If you can't stomach the life of a wandering warrior, take her offer, and go to a safe world. Stay here and you'll surely get her killed trying to defend you. You should have slain your man and been down there helping her."

"Perhaps I should just murder you for practice," she snarled. Ariel jumped down from the wagon and disappeared into the forest. A moment later she lost the battle to keep her last meal down. It wasn't the killing that disturbed her so deeply, it was Mearith's utter cold savagery. Still, she ached inside as she felt Mearith moving slowly away from her.

When Ariel regained some measure of control of her body she returned to the road. She found a horse waiting, her new cloak, a water skin, and a food packet tied to the saddle. Ariel swept the cloak about her shoulders and pulled it close, for she was now chilled to the bone. Weakly she struggled into the saddle then realized she had no idea what to do next, or how to make the horse move.

She held the reins loosely and leaned over the beast's neck, stroking, and cooing softly in High Elvish. "I'm lost and sick in my heart, good horse. I don't know how to give you directions. I need your help. Will you help me?"

The horse tossed its head and nickered softly. "Take me to the others now, follow the wagon." With a snort the horse set out down the road. The air was colder and the sky darkening as she found their camp near a stream.

A Hard Reality

As Ariel neared the camp her heart sang with a wild joy at the nearness of Mearith. She cursed the feeling even as she returned Mearith's smile of delight. "You're mocking me again." She dismounted and began cooing to the horse as she fumbled with the saddle, trying to remove it.

Mearith reached past her to help, gently guiding her fingers to the proper buckles and straps. "I do not mock you, my delight," came that soft hypnotic voice. "I revel in the nearness of you.

"Ariel, think now. Without the Spiritpull's grip on me, do you think I'd have brought you with me? No. I wouldn't have dragged an untried fighter into this life, but I was compelled even as you were.

"Ariel, I strive to teach you the things you need to learn to survive and find a joyful life as your true self."

"You have that smile of amusement on your face again," said Ariel, as she began to rub the animal down with sweet grass. "You mock me as master used to, as Ocra did, like I'm some lesser being."

"I don't mock you, my heart. I'm smiling with delight that you managed to find a new piece of yourself and come to me without help. All Elves have an affinity for horses. We don't know why, and neither do the horses, but we do. We work well together. You convinced your new friend to bring you here. No other could have done this. My smile is a smile of pride and delight.

"Ariel, I'm not your enemy, nor is Randall. I know him, and I'm quite certain he was less than gentle with you, but I'm also certain he spoke with purpose. He's trained many warriors in his day, and

30

led many more. This world is filled with petty feuds and small wars. Randall spent much of his younger life there. I..."

Mearith got no further as Ariel burst into tears and threw herself into Mearith's arms. "Mearith, I'm so sorry. I'm sick inside and afraid. I don't know what to do."

"First, you must eat. Let me hold you a moment longer then you must eat. The food will return you to yourself so you can think clearly."

"And the holding?"

There was a near giggle in her voice and Mearith smiled with delight to hear it. "That's for me. Come now, my delight, it's time to feed you." She led Ariel to the fire and seated her in the warmth.

Randall passed her a bowl of stew and a spoon. Ariel set to with a will; she was hungry like never before. She emptied the bowl a second time before sighing with contentment, warmed from within as well as from the fire. When she finished Randall spoke again. "It's hard, this choosing of a life. Harder still when the life chooses you."

"What do you mean?" asked Ariel. Mearith smiled and settled down beside Ariel.

"Let me tell you a story," Randall began. "I was young when the Orcs attacked my village. I ran out with my father and brother to fight them, but I froze with fear. They were savage beyond all imaging. They killed everything in their path, and they were brutal about it.

"The men fought them all around me, but I just soiled my breeks and wet myself. My brother struck me upside the head to knock me away from a spear thrust at my belly. I scrambled to my feet and ran to the trees as fast as my legs could carry me.

"The Orcs destroyed the village and most of the people who had lived there. I rejoined my family when they fled the battle. That night my father told me I had to make a choice. I could join the clerics and pray for safety or learn to fight and survive.

"That hard choice has now fallen to you, Ariel. Yes, it's unfair, but it is what it is. This is the world we live in, and this is how we survive."

"Is there no room for mercy at all? No place for compassion?" Ariel asked sadly.

"Both are noble sentiments, girl, and you should practice them often. However, be careful where you practice. That one today was unworthy of your mercy. He would not have extended you the same courtesy."

Ariel was thoughtful for a while, and no one broke the silence. Finally she sighed and straightened her back. "Mearith, I failed you this day. I swear it won't happen again. If I'm ever to free my people from slavery I'll need to learn everything you can teach me. I'm ready to learn."

"Come here to me," smiled Mearith, gently pulling Ariel closer. "I swear I'll do all I can to teach you, and to help you in your quest. First we learn about survival and how to take joy from that."

"You found joy in that today?"

"Not in the battle or the deaths, no. I did, however, find joy in our survival, no injuries, and the blessing of a horse for you, new clothes, and we still have a fat purse. You learned a new skill on your own, and came back to me. Life is good."

"How is it that I feel the joy and love in you, Mearith, but when you attacked those men I saw only savagery?"

"As a member of the Watch, you've encountered men who faced you with drawn weapons, but you and your companions disarmed them and tossed them in the dungeons. You were trained to keep the peace, Ariel, and what you saw today was war. A fight, a battle, are savage by definition, there's no room for quarter when you face those who will grant none.

"If I'd waited for them to bluster and boast, the element of surprise would be lost, and we'd have faced two to one odds. By going on the attack, I managed to even the odds before they could react."

"And thereby increasing our chances of survival," sighed Ariel. "You fought for, and ensured, our survival, while I stood on the wagon playing at Town Watch."

"You did as your training guided you, my delight."

"Then I have to change the training."

"We'll start in the morning. Now is the time for rest."

"I'll take first watch," said Randall, as he rose stiffly to his feet. He scooped up a bow and arrows then limped into the darkness.

"Is it safe to sleep?"

Mearith squirmed down so she was resting near the fire, gently pulling Ariel down beside her. "It is with Randall watching. He's old, but his eyes are still keen and his hands steady. None will approach without our knowledge."

Ariel settled down, her head resting on Mearith's shoulder. "Will you truly help me free the rest of my people?"

"Yes, my treasure, I will. We must wait and prepare until the time is right, but we'll set them free. Sleep now, my delight, you've had an eventful day."

The Road

The next two days were spent on the road to the city Ariel wanted to flee. However, Mearith kept her busy practicing her riding skills and learning how to fight from horseback.

Through it all Ariel noticed Mearith's eyes always searching the road ahead and watching the road behind. She marveled at her mentor's seemingly unconscious skills. She recalled her sword master saying, "Practice every day, Ariel, until the movements become part of your being."

The sun was barely risen on the third day when they sighted the city walls. The road they were on was rarely used, but there was traffic on the main highway from Magdan to the coast. With a wave of his hand Randall set his wagon moving towards the city gates. Mearith and Ariel faded back into the forest.

They set up camp, then settled down to wait. Suddenly Ariel felt the wild joyous singing of her heart brought on by Mearith's nearness flare up, and then subside. She gasped at the sudden flare of emotion and the wave of peace that followed it. She looked up to see Mearith smiling at her. "Stay there, Ariel." Mearith fled into the forest.

Ariel felt her moving away at speed, but the unbearable ache she would have felt the day before wasn't there. Instead she felt a warm glow inside. Ariel relaxed back against a tree and opened herself to this new experience and what it could teach her. She felt Mearith going farther away. They were now further apart than they had been since they met.

Ariel smiled as she felt Mearith stop to rest then begin to circle back around to their small camp. She felt the warm glow within as Mearith drew nearer, but the burning need for her nearness was gone, replaced with a warm desire to be near her. She had food ready by the fire and a tea made when Mearith arrived.

Mearith smiled with delight as she sat beside Ariel and accepted the mug of tea. "This is what you meant, isn't it? This is the settling of the Spiritpull?"

"Yes, my delight, it is. Tell me how you feel, what you experienced as I ran away and again as I returned, what you feel now."

"The desire for your nearness is as strong as ever, but it seems to have receded. It no longer overwhelms my mind as you move away. I'm filled with joy at your return, but again it no longer overwhelms me, I can think and focus through it. It's as if it's melted into my entire being and no longer needs to hold my full attention. Is it the same for you?"

"It is. I can now sit beside you without burning inside."

"Burning inside?"

"With desire for you, Ariel, my delight."

"Mearith, why haven't you...I mean, I would certainly be willing to enjoy your touch."

"I was waiting for the settling," smiled Mearith, as she enfolded Ariel in her arms. "I wanted you to be certain of your feelings."

"But I have no choice now that we've been pulled together, do I?"

"Of course you do, and now that..." Mearith got no further as Ariel pressed her lips to Mearith's. She moaned with delight as she melted under the fire of the young Elf's kiss. Mearith was left breathless by the time their lips parted.

"Mearith?"

"Mmm?"

"Stop holding back from me."

Mearith needed no further urging. She pulled the young Elf closer and kissed her deeply. Ariel's mind floated helplessly in a roiling sea of new emotions as Mearith explored her body. She floated higher and higher, the tension within her growing stronger and stronger, until her awareness exploded into stardust. When the waves of the orgasm slowed down to a warm flush, Ariel snuggled into Mearith's arms and allowed sleep to claim her.

Three days passed in the forest camp. There was time to practice weapons, stealth, to bond with the horses and each other. Alas, all good things must come to an end. The sound of distant thunder awakened them in the night. "It'll soon be here," grumbled Mearith. She climbed to her feet and began to spread her cloak in the branches of a tree.

Ariel gathered the saddles and tack, bringing them into the shelter while Mearith moved the rest of their gear under the makeshift tarp. She moved the fire closer and built it up a bit just as the rain began. They huddled together in Ariel's cloak until the full light of day.

"Randall should be returning today. Stay here in the shelter, Ariel. I'll go watch for him on the road. I'll return for you in time for us to meet him."

Ariel nodded then passed Mearith the cloak. "I have the shelter and the fire for warmth. You'll need this more than I."

Mearith nodded, accepted the cloak, then set out for the road. Reaching a vantage point where she could see nearly to the city gates, she waited beneath a pine tree. When Randall finally appeared and slowly made his way toward her she knew something was wrong.

He was drinking heavily from a jug and singing a bawdy song about an Elf slave girl. He could be heard from a great distance. Mearith knew Randall rarely drank and not before sundown. Something was amiss. She hurried back to the campsite.

Ariel was already saddling the horses when Mearith arrived. "Something's wrong," said Mearith, as she pitched in to help. "Randall's trying to warn us about something. We must be cautious. Have your bow ready, Ariel."

Ariel smiled as she patted the bow hanging from her saddle. She had never held one before meeting Mearith, but had a natural affinity for it as she did for the horses. She swung easily into the saddle, Mearith's now soggy cloak around her shoulders and the hood down over her eyes. They reached the road to hear Randall's song and another voice from within the wagon telling him to shut up.

They huddled together for a moment then Ariel dismounted and hid behind a tree, an arrow ready for the bow, and three more leaning against the trunk within easy reach. Mearith slipped further down the road then stopped to wait for Randall.

The wagon drew nearer. Without warning of any kind, Randall suddenly kicked on the brake then leaped from the seat to the ground, landing in a forward roll that brought him back to his feet and running straight to the trees. There was a volley of curses and oaths from the wagon and men poured out drawing their swords.

"Watch Guard, halt!" called a clear ringing voice. Instinctively the men responded to their training.

One man stepped away from the rest, facing the trees and trying to brush the rain from his eyes. "Who goes there?"

"An outlaw and a thief," replied Ariel. "We have you surrounded. Drop your weapons and walk away towards the city."

"And if we don't?"

An arrow pierced his shoulder. He fell to the ground, moaning and cursing. "That wagon is ours by right of capture," called the voice. "Drop your weapons and walk back towards the city or another will fall."

"There's only one of you; you can't get us all. Rush her!" That command died on the man's lips as an arrow from another direction pierced his heart. He fell to the ground and was joined by a number of swords. The men hurried away towards the city, Mearith pacing them from behind on her horse.

As soon as they were out of sight of the wagon, both Randall and Ariel appeared and sat the wounded man up against the wheel. "You'll need a healer," growled Randall, as he broke off the arrow tip from behind the man's shoulder then pulled the shaft out of the wound.

The man cried out and nearly fainted. Ariel pressed a bit of cloth to the wound. She had cut it from the dead man's shirt. She cut two more strips, but Randall stopped her. "I have proper bandages in the wagon and strong alcohol as well." She nodded and he went to fetch them.

While Ariel bandaged the man's shoulder, Randall rigged a tarp over them to keep the rain off. By the time Mearith returned, all three were huddled beneath the shelter, waiting. She hopped down and snuggled in with them. "All right, Randall, what happened?"

"I have no idea, Mearith. The trading went well, I got a good price for the horses, I bought everything on my list, and then headed out this morning. The Watch grabbed me at the gate, piled inside, and told me to keep going. I've no idea why, but I have my suspicions."

"I'll just bet you do." She leaned over to go nose to nose with the watchman. "I see Ariel has patched you up. You're lucky it was her with the bow. I'd have killed you."

He swallowed hard and avoided eye contact. "You're the Elvish mercenary."

"I am that. Tell me why you hid inside this wagon. What were your orders? Why did you choose this wagon?"

"This man spent a tainted coin. We watched him carefully and joined him as he left the gates. We hoped he would lead us to you and Ariel. Our orders were to kill you and the merchant but to bring Ariel back alive."

"So, Dorgon paid me with marked coin, did he? There will come a reckoning for that."

"Paid you? For what?"

"Killing Ocra."

"So you admit it. Overlord Dorgon told us that you killed Overlord Ocra and dragged Ariel off with you. He wants her back unharmed. He's offered a great reward for her return."

"I'm sure he has," sighed Mearith, as she relaxed back against Ariel's shoulder. "The truth of the matter, Soldier, is that Dorgon paid me forty-five gold to kill Ocra. I did that, and Ariel followed me out of the city, of her own free will."

"Now that I do believe. I didn't think Ariel could be dragged away easily. I've crossed swords with her in practice. She's not that good, but she's slippery."

He yelped as Ariel poked him with her elbow. "Shut up, Dirk, or the next time I shoot you it'll be in the balls."

Randall chuckled at that then grunted. "The question now is, what are we going to do with him. The proper solution would be to kill him and leave him for the crows, but I get the idea Ariel wouldn't like that."

"What are we to do with him, Ariel?" asked Mearith.

"Free will, Mearith, my heart. We let him choose."

"Well, in that case, killing him is out of the question," grinned Dirk. "How about taking me with you."

"Why in the name of seven gods would we do that?" grunted Randall.

"You owe me. You shot me, but didn't kill me, so now I'm wounded with nowhere else to go. I can't go back to the city; Overlord Dorgon would kill me slowly himself for failing. I can't earn a living as a sell sword while I'm wounded, so you have to take me with you and nurse me back to health."

Mearith laughed heartily at that. "Randall?"

"Skin me for a fool, Mearith, but I'm starting to like this young buck. He can earn his keep at the village, and we can always use another sword hand if the pig men attack."

"Tell me something about your past, Dirk. How came you to be in that wagon?"

The young man gazed at the woman with the tattooed face for a long moment. He had never seen her like before, but he recognized a hardened warrior when he saw one. Only the truth would help him here, he knew. A lie would mean his death.

"I come from a farm far to the south of the city," he replied carefully. "My uncle had been to the wars and taught me the use of the sword. I left to seek my fortune, and eventually found my way to the city where I earned a place in the Watch.

"Ariel and I were taken on about the same time and trained together. I was drawn to her, but she had no interest. I looked elsewhere for companionship, and we became friends instead. That's why I was leading the troops in the wagon. Overlord Dorgon thought it would be easier to persuade Ariel to return if she saw the face of a friend."

"You seem eager enough to join our merry band, why is that?"

"What other path could I choose? I was sickened by what I saw in the city and wanted to leave, but I stayed for Ariel."

"Explain."

"I once overheard Overlord Ocra talking with the chief of the Watch. He said to keep a sharp eye on Ariel and protect her from harm, he had plans for her. I stayed, waiting for a chance to warn her, but she vanished before I got the opportunity. With Ocra dead, the Watch was always on full alert, and, as a friend of Ariel, I was being followed everywhere. I had no chance to leave."

"Ariel and I have bonded. I'd hate to upset her."

"Understood, Warrior. Ariel and I are friends, nothing more. I'll make no advances to your companion."

"It was your death that I feared might upset her."

Dirk gave a great bellowing laugh at that. "Understood and accepted."

"Welcome to the clan," grinned Mearith. She stood and stretched. "The rain's eased, fellow travelers. Shall we move along to a better campsite before we lose the daylight?"

They stopped for the night by a small stream, now swollen by the rains. The sky had cleared, and Randall built up a large fire so they could dry themselves out. Ariel lay sleeping, or so they thought. She overheard Randall speak softly to Mearith. "Do you think she knows, Mearith?"

"No, I don't think so."

"Plan to tell her any time soon?"

"Perhaps. I don't know."

"Tell her what, Mearith?"

"So, not sleeping after all, are you?" That delighted smile was there, bringing joy to Ariel's heart.

"Answer the question, you evader."

"As you wish, my delight. I have a good idea what Ocra had planned for you, princess."

"You do? What...wait, what did you call me? Princess? You haven't done that before. Talk to me, Mearith, what are you hiding from me?"

"For the past fifteen years or more," said Randall, "Mearith has had me and others looking for an Elf maid who bears that mark that you have on your shoulder."

Ariel drew her tunic closer to hide her birthmark. "That ugly thing? Wait, Mearith, what do you know of this?"

"Much. It's a long story."

"We have plenty of time, tell me. What do you know of this mark, and why did you want to find me? Did you know what would happen between us?"

"No, my delight, the Pull came as much a surprise to me as it did to you."

"The mark?"

"It's the mark of the heir to the throne of the High Born Elves. Always a woman ruled, and the eldest daughter always carries the mark. When I learned that some of the High Born had survived, and in the chains of slavery, I tried to determine if the royal house still continued."

"I see. Well, perhaps...wait, are you saying I'm..."

"The natural monarch of the High Born. Have you noticed how you always speak of them as your people? That's no accident."

Ariel sat back and gazed at the fire for a long moment. "You said you know what Ocra had planned for me. What was it?"

"You told me that your master was a scholar. If so, he'd have know the meaning of the mark, and so would Ocra."

"And that's why I was raised differently from the other slaves? You think they would try to use me? How?"

"Wars are brewing, as always. The Elves are fierce warriors when aroused. I think they wanted to control you so you could lead the Elves into battle for them. They raised you in privilege, bringing you up to be one of their own so you'd believe in the rightness of what they wanted."

"Dorgon knows this too, doesn't he? That's why he wants me back so badly."

"That's my thought on the matter," replied Mearith. "This changes things; what do you want to do next?"

"Beat the pulp out of you for keeping secrets from me," said Ariel, as she lightly punched Mearith on the shoulder. "What else have you not told me?"

"All has now been revealed, my heart. What would you like to do?"

"As I've said before, I just want to be near you, to go where you go. I'm no queen, just a former slave. You promised to help me free my people from slavery, Mearith. There's much I need to learn and do before we're ready to attempt that task. You lead, I'll follow."

Mearith sighed and put her arm around Ariel's shoulder. "One day that will change, but for now, I believe it's best."

"Mearith, you have a reason for wanting me to live as a mercenary for a time, don't you?"

"Ah-huh." Ariel poked her in the ribs. Mearith laughed and flinched away. "All right, I'll talk. You know the life of the city, but that's not what you'll face if we set them free. They'll be pursued, hunted, and worse if caught. You'll have to lead them in a rough life until they're ready to settle, until it is safe to do so."

"And I'll need to be familiar with that kind of life. I understand, my love. There is much to ponder. I'll relieve Dirk at watch. I'm far too awake for sleeping now."

For the next three days they plodded along through the muddy road. Rain came and went, but was never far away. At one point Ariel complained she was growing gills, bringing a merry laugh from her companions, all except Dirk. He was slipping into a fever and Ariel could read the concern on Randall's face. Near sundown on the third day he fell sideways and would have toppled from the wagon had Randall not caught him.

Ariel leaped from her horse and helped ease him to the ground. She threw her cloak over him to keep him warm. "His wound has gone septic. Is there nothing we can do to help him?"

"Is that your wish, Ariel?"

"Don't do this to me, Mearith, not now. Don't force me to make every decision so I become accustomed to it. I'm not ready for that yet. This man is no threat, he's a friend and an ally."

"Right now he's a burden."

Mearith's face was impassive, and Ariel was suddenly revolted. Jealousy? Now? Wait, dammit, it's a test. She's testing me. "Mearith, can you help him?"

"Perhaps, there are some herbs growing nearby, but only well enough to reach the healer."

"Please do so, for me."

Mearith's face split into a bright smile. "See, that wasn't so hard, was it?"

"Go!" demanded Ariel as she stood and stomped her foot, her arm pointing at the forest. With a merry laugh Mearith disappeared into the trees. "Everything is a test, a challenge, with that woman," she complained as she knelt beside Dirk once again.

"She'll test you for certain," grinned Randall as he built up a fire. "Like the blacksmith who heats, and then pounds the iron into shape, will she test you. As the smith beats the iron until it breaks or becomes steel, Mearith will test you.

"You were born to rule the Elves of this world, but that was an accident of birth. The choice to do so you made yourself. Mearith will prepare you, Ariel, but you will be sorely tested in the making."

With a deep sigh, Ariel let her head slump toward her chest. "Have you any useful advice, Randall? I'm in sore need of guidance right now."

Randall chuckled at that then sat near her, letting his old bones enjoy the heat of the fire. "The hard part will be to avoid being offended by what she does or says, Ariel. It's the same for any bonded couple. Sometimes people say or do something that is hurtful, but not intended to be so. She pushed you this time, and you responded well. I have great hopes for you.

"Secondly, never lose your sense of justice or your compassion. Control them, for those emotions can often be at war, but you'll need them both to avoid becoming like the overlords."

"You mean, arrogant, uncaring, brutal..."

"I see you're quite familiar with the Geni." He chuckled and so did she.

Ariel felt Mearith's nearness even before she entered the camp. She was carrying a freshly picked herb and a handful of green mold. To Ariel's great surprise she smeared the mold on Dirk's wound then re-bandaged it before passing Randall the herbs.

"Brew this into a tea, we all will need to drink it." He nodded and heaved himself to his feet then set to work. "We need to hurry," she continued. "Dirk needs the healer, and we need to get out of the rain for a while, to properly dry out. As you've said, my delight, I'm growing gills."

"Mearith?"

"Mmm?"

"When I asked you to help me free my people, you knew who I was and what that would mean, even though I didn't."

"Yes, I did."

"I'm beginning to see now the magnitude of the quest. I will rele...."

"Don't say it, my delight," sighed Mearith, as she stretched out by the fire and laid her head in Ariel's lap. "Don't even think it. We're bound together by a force more powerful than we can imagine, and I for one and happy for it. We'll face the adventure together."

Ariel gently pushed the hair back from Mearith's brow. She smiled at her love and spoke softly. "You will test and provoke me at every turn, I know. Promise you'll always forgive me when I get angry with you."

"Always, my delight. You're actually quite c..."

"Don't say it, Mearith," said Ariel. "Mearith, will Dirk recover?"

"We need to get him to the healer, but yes, I like his chances. He's young and strong. He should recover. Ariel, why'd you shoot him if he's a friend? Why not shoot another?"

"I tried. I was aiming at the man beside him, but the arrow brushed a branch on its path and it struck Dirk. That's why I moved before I loosed another bolt."

"Ah, now it makes sense. Ariel, I'm quite proud of you."

"Because I shot a friend?"

"No, silly, because you didn't scream his name and run to him when it happened. You held yourself in check until the situation was resolved."

"Mearith, you're familiar with royalty. Do you truly think I have the makings of a queen? What if I make a mistake, a bad one that costs lives, or worse?"

"Such is ever the lot of the head that wears the crown. Let me tell you some of our history. Long ago, as I've said before, we were all one people. The Elves lived in peace with the Dwarves of the mountains. The High Born began to raise up their great cities and the Borni resisted them for they destroyed forest lands to do so.

"About that time the humans arrived in their great ships, bringing their own magics and machines. The High Born welcomed them, but the Borni fought them to preserve the forests. The humans are short lived, but they breed like rabbits and their numbers increased.

"Orcs began to arrive from the south, their clans driven before an advancing army. They, too, allied themselves with the humans for mutual protection. The war was on.

"The Borni and the Dwarves joined forces to resist the destruction of the lands. All was bad enough when the armies of the Geni Overlords arrived, driving the last of the Orc clans before them.

"Like the High Born, the Geni were great workers in magic. They were also smooth of tongue. My father believed their promises of sending their hordes of Ogres, Giants, and other foul things away if we would help them against the humans. He was betrayed in the end, killed by a demon sent by the overlords.

"Soon after that the High Born locked themselves in a magical battle against the Geni. They lost. When it was over, the humans surrendered, the High Born were enslaved, the Orcs scattered, and the Borni were devastated as were the Dwarves.

"The lands were broken, new seas and rivers flowed where forests had stood. Old mountains sank beneath the seas and new ones rose high into the air.

"We few thousand Borni used the last of the old magic to leave this world for another realm. There they rested and healed as best they could. In my anguish at the loss of Elaith, I fled into the vast forests of the new world, seeking solace, refuge, release from life.

"Generation of humans passed into the mystery of time before I returned to find my brother ruling in my absence. By my own decree he continues to do so.

"Slowly I found myself again, and then returned to this world to see if there was anything left worth salvaging. I found the vast populations dead from the final battle.

"A few Geni continue to rule this world, the humans have managed to survive and thrive, the Orc clans continue, and the Dwarves, as few as they are, have begun to rebuild their cities under the new mountains.

"I tell you all this, Ariel, so you will know that royalty is not infallible. Royals make mistakes, just like anyone else. The problem is, when they do, the consequences are more far reaching. We'll be careful, and we'll live with the results of our decisions, whatever they may be."

Ariel continued to stroke Mearith's brow, slowly trying to absorb all she'd been told. At last she nodded. She didn't have to be perfect, but she couldn't afford to make rash decisions.

Mearith finally broke the silence. "Ariel, overwhelm and self-doubt are luxuries you can't afford. Sometimes events are such that decisions must be made in a heartbeat."

"I know, and you're going to teach me how to do that, even if I don't want you to, right?"

"She's got you pegged, Mearith," chuckled Randall, as he passed each of them a mug of the tea and some rations.

"So it would seem," smiled Mearith. She sat up and accepted the food. "What do you think, Randall, can we make Fugitive in two more days?"

"That's pushing it, but if the boy's up to it we should be able to make it."

"He'll have to be."

Randall's head came up at that. "Oh?"

"Snow's coming," said Ariel, as she rose to her feet. "I get first watch, you two rest." She strode into the darkness and found a post.

Mearith cocked her head to one side for a moment then grinned. She felt it as Ariel climbed into the branches of a tree. "Well chosen, my love. Well chosen."

Reaching Fugitive

D irk's fever broke in the night. By morning he was weak, but alert once again. Huddled in his cloak, he silently endured the rough bumping of the wagon as Randall pressed the horses for more speed. By sundown they reached the swamps, nothing but water and clumps of sedge between them and the forest in the distance. The road ended at the water's edge.

They set up camp and settled down for the night. Mearith and Ariel spent time rubbing down tired horses and making certain they had grain for a treat. They'd earned it that day. After a meal themselves they snuggled under both cloaks. The air had turned colder.

Frost covered the ground when Mearith awakened, alone. She stretched beneath the warm cloak and smiled. Ariel wasn't far, hers had been the last watch. At Mearith's soft bird call, Ariel returned and built up the fire.

"Looks like we may get a decent day," yawned Randall, as he appeared from the back of the wagon.

"We won't," sighed Mearith. "Look to the north." The sky was clear, but a long band of dark heavy cloud hung in the distance. Randall grunted and climbed to the ground. He nodded then walked stiffly into the trees.

Seeing Ariel's gaze follow the man, Mearith smiled. "Randall has seen more summers than most humans, Ariel. His joints stiffen with age, and mornings are often difficult for him now."

"Then why was he chosen to risk the roads alone?"

"He wasn't sent, he chose to go. The medicines and other goods in the wagon will be needed in the village before the winter is gone. He chose the risk himself."

"Why? Why would he take the risk at his age?"

"For his people. Because no other would."

"His people?"

"Randall is headman for Fugitive, chosen by the others at a full gathering. He takes the job seriously."

"There is much I can learn from him. Another reason for us accompanying him?"

"You know me too well already," grinned Mearith. She rose and trotted into the trees. Upon her return she found Ariel had prepared food and was questioning Randall about leadership. Randall was explaining how a good leader always held the welfare of his people in mind. Mearith smiled and ate swiftly, then went to fetch the horses.

Camp was quickly broken and packed up. Dirk was bundled in two cloaks as he rode in the back of the wagon. He was getting feverish again. Ariel and Mearith mounted and moved to the edge of the swamp.

"Now where?"

Mearith grinned with mischief. "We follow the road." She started her horse into the water slowly.

Ariel moved up beside her. "The road?"

"Yes."

"I see no road."

"Look down."

Ariel looked down at the water and was surprised to see what looked like a road paved in stone beneath the waters. "Mearith..."

"The High Born did many amazing things with their magics before it poisoned their minds. This bit of road is one of the remaining wonders they wrought. One day there was a well worn trail through the forest leading to the sea, the next there was a broad roadway paved in stone. It remained dry in the rain, and snows melted as they touched it. That road stayed open all year round.

"After the breaking of the world, this piece remained. When Randall and a few refugees from a losing battle, made their way into this part of the forest, he found it. They established Fugitive and then forced the streams to change course to hide the roadway."

"Thus keeping their village safe from prying eyes," nodded Ariel.

"Yes. Notice the clumps of swamp grasses. We move between them then turn towards the next pair. Enough of the old magic remain in the road to keep it clear of silt, but the waters will freeze in winter."

Ariel could see the wandering path they would take clearly now that she knew what to look for. "So, everything my people did wasn't bad."

"No, Ariel, it wasn't. As I said, at first they did some incredible things."

"But?"

"The magic is a powerful thing, Ariel, and terribly addictive to those who overuse it. Surely you have seen mages among the humans."

"I have. All hate and fear them. I've always pitied them; they constantly seek power. No matter how much power they achieve, it's never enough and they strive for more. There's no joy in a life like that. Is that what happened to my people, Mearith?"

"That was a big piece of it."

"Is all magic evil?"

"Magic is neither good nor ill, Ariel. It is merely another tool. The use to which it is put determines it's value."

Ariel nodded thoughtfully and turned her horse to keep beside Mearith. "So, you're saying it could be used for good, that my people did some good things with it."

"They did. The made safe homes, good roads, improved healing and more. However, they also tore down forests to fuel the fires of magic, conquered or drove out the peoples who lived where they decided to build their cities. As the power of the magic took them they lost their respect for all life except their own."

"A pitfall to avoid, for certain. Mearith, how can you live as an assassin and still keep your respect for life? You slew Ocra in his sleep."

"I killed one man, Ariel, and he was awake and armed when I slew him." Mearith nudged her horse to a faster walk.

Ariel urged her horse ahead to catch up. "Forgive me, my heart, I meant no offense. I'm trying to learn...wait, he was awake and armed?"

"He was." Mearith slowed her horse again. "Although I'd have killed him in his sleep had I found him so."

Ariel tightened gently on the reins and dropped back to Mearith's side once again. "You've never spoken of that night. May I ask?"

"He knew I was coming, his magic told him that. I arrived to find his rooms unguarded. He was inside, fully dressed in armor, and with sword drawn."

"What happened?"

"He laughed and stepped towards me. He started to tell me what he was going to do to me."

"A fatal mistake, I'm sure. You've said often there's no time for talk in battle."

"Yes, as he began to boast I threw a dagger at him. He popped up his magic shield, but I have fought those before. A shield is of no use when the enemy is behind you. While he focused on the dagger I moved behind him and drove my sword through his heart. I then retrieved my dagger and used his own battle axe to remove the head. The rest you know."

"Once again the lesson is brought home," sighed Ariel. Seeing Mearith's raised eyebrow, she continued. "The battle of the wagon. You attacked swiftly, gave no quarter, and cut down several enemies while I argued with a single attacker. Were you not there, I'd have been easily overwhelmed and killed, or worse."

"And the lesson is?"

"When there is no option but battle, attack at speed and show no mercy."

"Close, but not complete. Try again."

"What? Wait... give me a moment." She thought for a few minutes then spoke again. "It isn't about battle and killing at all, is it? The lesson is to recognize what action must be taken then be swift about it. It applies to every situation. Yes?" Mearith's radiant smile of delight was her answer.

"Dammit, Mearith, everything is a test, a lesson, a challenge with you. You're just lucky I love you."

"Indeed I am, my heart," chuckled Mearith, "indeed I am. Look now, we are nearing the forest, can you see the road beyond the swamp?"

"No. Wait, you did it again." Laughing, Ariel swatted at Mearith's shoulder. "All right, let me see. The path through the waters leads to that tall tree beside the boulder. The tree must be the marker for the road beyond. How did I do?"

"Perfect. You reasoned it beautifully and chose the right marker. Now, what is the lesson?"

"Think before I speak," sighed Ariel. "Mearith, you would make a far better leader for my people. Will you not take the job?"

"You were born to this, Ariel, but, just as with the Spiritpull, your mind can override that push as well. Do you wish a different path?"

"Yes and no, my love. Everyone would choose a safer path for themselves, but too many others would suffer if I do. Just like the Spiritpull, this fate has befallen me. I must make the best of it."

"That's my girl. Wait, did you just...?" Ariel laughed heartily and urged her horse into a gallop. Mearith gave chase.

Ariel was waiting by the tall tree as Mearith rode up, shaking a threatening finger at her. "Oh, Mearith, it was so much fun to finally get you back for all the teasing."

"Brat, you're just lucky I love you."

Mearith was smiling with delight and Ariel's heart sang. "These are the moments to live for," a voice seemed to whisper in the trees. "Hold them dear."

The Village

They waited by the tree until the wagon reached them. "We're safe enough now, Mearith," called Randall, as the wagon made a slow awkward exit from the water. "Go on ahead and find the healer lest my passenger depart this world for the next."

Mearith nodded then set her horse into a canter as they headed for the village. The forest soon gave way to open fields and a cluster of buildings with low mountains in the distance. Smoke was rising and sounds of battle could be heard. They urged the horses into a gallop.

Drawing near Ariel saw a strange group of beings fighting against something she had never seen before. Humans, Orcs, and others, stood back to back against smaller yet savage attackers. They had heads and faces like wild boars, yet the bodies more closely resembled those of Dwarves. They were poorly armed, but brutally savage in their attack.

Mearith's horse was bigger, faster, and trained for war. She fell on the pig men like a hurricane, blades and hooves flashing and dealing death. A ragged cheer arose from the defenders.

As Ariel arrived she saw a group of Elves cowering beside a barn. It was starting to burn. She turned towards them, shouting. "To me, Elves, to me. Get that fire out, I'll protect you." She leaped off her horse and drove her sword through an enemy charging at the unarmed Elves. "Quickly, get that fire out."

Her sudden appearance issuing orders broke their terror. They began to pull water from the well to throw on the flames while others beat at the fire with wet rags.

Ariel faced another pig man as he tried to stop the Elves. He was slow and clumsy, easily dispatched. Ariel pulled her blade from his falling body and faced the next two running at her.

Ariel easily dispatched the two, but three more appeared before her. She hurled herself at them and brought down two then heard a thud and groan from behind. Spinning around she found an old Elf standing over the third pig man, a bloody axe in his hands. "Well done, my friend." Together they faced the next two approaching.

Suddenly Mearith was there with a number of others. "Ariel!"

"See to the fire," she shouted. "Get the animals out. Mearith and I will defend you." The villagers ran to help with the fire while she and Mearith faced the oncoming attackers. She glanced at Mearith who was grinning at her. "Well?"

"Nicely done, dear heart. Nicely done. Let's make an end of this now." With that she leaped at the oncoming pig men. There were only five and together Mearith and Ariel made short work of the fight.

The last attacker fell, twitching to the ground then lay still. "I'll take two fighters with me and make certain the village and surrounding area are clear of these vermin. You stay here and organize these folk."

Ariel made no argument. She knew what Mearith was doing, and she sighed. Mearith would make her a queen whether she wanted to be or not. She was resigning herself to it. "Mearith, what are these things? Are they a people? I've never seen their like before."

"They're not quite yet a people, but they're far more than they were. These are the results of magic gone wrong. The residue of mighty workings has caused them to evolve too swiftly. They have no compassion or feeling for any other beings except themselves. They came here looking for meat."

"Meat? You mean people?"

"I do."

"Do what you must, my love. Make the village safe. I'll get the cleanup started as soon as the fire's out." Mearith grinned and winked at her then shouted and trotted towards another building. Two Orcs dropped their buckets, swept up axes, and joined her.

Ariel turned to find the Elf who had defended her waiting to get her attention. He lowered his eyes and spoke softly. "The fire is out, my queen."

"Why did you call me that?"

"Because you could be no other."

"Explain."

"You commanded Mearith and yet live, no other would dare, or could survive. She obeyed instantly. Lady, she has searched for the true queen for as long as I've known her. You can be no other."

Ariel smiled and shook her head. "I'm Mearith's bonded companion. She will obey me or suffer." He chuckled at that. "I'm Ariel, my friend. The old ways are gone. There are no queens, kings, or slaves here, only folk. What's your name, my comrade in arms?"

"My name is Olan, Lady."

"Come on, Olan, let's help the others start getting this place cleaned up."

Ariel had barely taken a step when the wagon rumbled into the village. All the villagers turned to look at her as Randall called out. "Ariel, I'm here. Where do you need me?"

"Find your healer, she has much work to do if she yet lives." She turned to the others. "Is the fire completely out?"

"Yes, Lady," smiled her friend as he knelt before her. The rest of the Elves dropped to one knee as well. Ariel blushed and signaled them to stand.

"Very good. Nicely done. All Orcs, take up weapons and help Mearith secure the town. The rest of us will start cleaning up this mess." The few Orcs grunted their approval and trotted off to do her bidding. "Someone bring a wagon so we can haul the bodies away."

Her friend trotted into the barn, signaling some of the others to help him.

Randall arrived with an older female Orc in tow. He found the villagers loading the dead pig men onto a wagon while Ariel and the Elves were spreading fresh straw on the floor of the barn to soak up the water that had been thrown onto the fire. "This is Egma, our healer."

"Tell me what you need, Egma."

"Medicines, Elf Queen," grunted the old Orc, "and a place to lay the wounded."

"Randall where would be the best place?"

"The inn. The room's large enough and it's still intact. That's it there."

"Bring up the wagon. We'll help get Dirk and the medicines inside. Olan, go with Egma and help her fetch whatever herbs and such as she'll need from her home." The old Orc grunted her approval then led Olan away.

Randall brought the wagon to the door of the inn where the rest of the Elves helped get Dirk and the cargo inside. The inn was like so many others, low slung with a large open room, heavy beams supporting the rooms above. A fireplace graced one wall and nearly filled it. The bar was on the opposite wall facing it.

The Elves pulled the tables apart and made sleeping pallets near the huge fireplace. As soon as Egma returned, Ariel led the Elves out to help find wounded and bring them back.

Darkness fell, and with it came the wind, and then the snow. Driven by these forces of nature, everyone gathered at the inn. Great dry logs crackled in the fireplace and cauldrons of stew began to appear as Randall and the others took stock of the damage inflicted by the pig men. The news wasn't good.

Ariel and Mearith sat with a few others facing the huge room and near the fire. They were enjoying the rest, the stew, and the warmth.

Randall sank heavily onto the bench as he joined them, his back to the heat. "Ariel, it looks bad. We've lost two Orcs, a Dwarf, and two humans as fighters. We've also lost six children and four women who tried to defend them."

"Why bring this to me?"

"Because you're the queen. I'm just an old soldier, Ariel. I can teach people to fight and organize them a bit, but you're a natural leader."

"I'm a former slave and a fugitive; I'm no queen."

Randall chuckled and shook his head. "When you arrived, Mearith threw herself into the battle, did she not? She's a natural warrior and there's none better. You, however, saw what was needed, organized the people, inspired them to get it done, and then fought to defend them while they did it. You are indeed a queen. Will you not help us?"

"Please, Lady," came several voices.

"You're all in cahoots with Mearith, aren't you? You're going to make me be a queen whether I want to be or not, aren't you?"

"Was that a yes?" grinned Randall.

"The plan was for us to stay the winter here," sighed Ariel, "so I'll be your queen for that long if it truly is your wish." To her great surprise there was a rousing cheer from the room.

Egma joined them then. "I have a matter to put before the queen," she said, trying to kneel.

Ariel leaped to her feet and caught the old Orc by the elbow, Keeping her on her feet. "Hear me well, people. There will be no kneeling to me. I take no joy in that; it turns my stomach. I'm no slave master, and you are all free folk. Stand and speak to my face as free men and women."

"Now that's a queen I can serve," came a voice from the room. Several others agreed.

"Sit with us, Egma. Tell me what you need." She seated the old woman then returned to her place beside Mearith. Mearith beamed at her in delight.

"Lady, I need more blue/green moss for my healing potions."

"Oh no," exclaimed Mearith, as she sat back from the old Orc. "Oh no you don't, Egma. Use something else, king's foil perhaps."

"Not strong enough, Mearith. You know that. No, if some of these folks are going to survive, I need the cave moss."

"Send someone else. Send the Dwarf."

"It's snowing outside, drifting too high. He'll be useless until it melts in Spring."

Mearith winked at Ariel then slowly pitched forward onto the table, lightly tapping her forehead on the heavy wood. "I don't want to go into the cave. I hate the cave. Send an Orc."

"They'd just get lost. You have to go." Ariel was laughing now. It was clear this was a game between old friends.

With a regal air and a wave of her hand, Ariel joined the game. "I'll go, good healer, and my devoted guardian, Mearith, will show me the way. I, Queen Ariel, have spoken." There was a great roar of laughter from the room at that.

Mearith sat up and gazed lovingly at Ariel. "You enjoyed that far too much."

"I confess, it's true, I did. When do we leave?"

"As soon as the storm settles, my delight. Egma wouldn't ask this if there were another way."

"I thought as much. Randall, what else do we most need?"

"The healing is the most urgent. Thanks to your Elves, the barn, the animals, and the food storage next to it were saved, so we have plenty to last the winter. When the storm stops we can dig out and begin to repair the rest of the damage."

"My Elves? They're not my Elves, Randall. They're free citizens of Fugitive."

"We are indeed your Elves, Lady Ariel." Olan smiled shyly as he approached. "I've been asked to beg you to be our queen and to lead us. Lady, you bear the mark, you're the queen, queen of the High Born."

"The High Born are no more, Olan. They were defeated, destroyed, and enslaved long ago. Mearith is of the Borni, the defenders of the forest. We shall be the Bornani, the children of the forest.

"We'll embrace our true nature as Elves, and forsake all pretense to the high magic and the destruction it brought to our ancestors. We'll heed the song of the wind in the trees once again."

The room had gone quiet. Olan smiled and nodded his approval as did the rest of the Elves who were standing nearby. Suddenly a huge Orc began to pound his fist rhythmical on the table. He matched it with a deep voiced chant the other instantly took up. "Ariel, Ariel, Ariel..."

The storm abated in the night. As the sun began to rise Mearith and Ariel were in the barn, saddling their horses. Egma appeared with four sacks for the moss and a healing potion for each of them.

The snow wasn't deep and the horses seemed to take delight in the canter through the glittering landscape. They pushed, but not hard, and the day passed pleasantly. The sun was starting to sink behind the hills as they neared the mouth of the cavern. They found a small party of Orcs there.

Cavern

O f the four Orcs, three were dressed in leather armor, shivering in the cold. The fourth was wearing a long cloak of rough wool. He was huge even for an Orc, old, massively muscled, and scarred. "What are you doing here, Elf?" demanded a young warrior, as he brandished his axe at the two riders.

"Getting in out of the wind," replied Mearith, as she slid lightly to the ground and led her horse into the welcoming shelter of the cavern. Ariel followed, perplexed and wary. "Come inside, there's wood for a fire."

"I asked you a question, Elf," snarled the young Orc, advancing on the two women.

"Hold, Sark," chuckled the old Orc. "That one will dice you up for a meal and cook your gizzard on her fire. Look at her markings. It's my guess she's that mercenary we've heard about. Mearith." The younger Orc paled slightly and took a step back, wary now, but still ready for a fight.

"Are you Mearith?" asked the big Orc as he stepped closer.

Mearith stood up, smiling. Her small fire crackling to life as Ariel fed it twigs. "I am."

"Saggit." He extended his huge paw. Mearith grasped his wrist and he hers. "Well met, Mearith. Tell me, are you for hire?"

"We are. Come, sit by the fire, and warm yourselves."

Cautiously, the Orcs came. Ariel said nothing, but she was keenly aware of every move the Orcs made. She was also watching

Mearith carefully for clues as to what to do next, what was going to happen.

Saggit slowly lowered himself to the ground by the small blaze. "What's your price?"

"For?"

"A killing."

"That depends on who I have to kill."

"If my information is right, there's a guardian deeper in this cave. He'll have to be killed."

"Why?"

"He'll block us from that which we seek."

"And that is?"

The old Orc gazed into Mearith's eyes for a long moment then sighed. "We're Scratite Clan, defeated and scattered in the wars that broke the world. Still some of us remember the tales of kinship and clan.

"Long ago the home of the clan was centered around a stone that marked the place where the first Scratite built his house. I believe that stone to be hidden within this cavern, guarded by a monster.

"We seek the hearth stone of our people in hopes of finding all who remain and pulling them together again."

"You seek to reform your clan," smiled Ariel. "It's a noble pursuit."

The old Orc returned her smile and nodded. "So, what's your price, Mercenary?"

"Fifty gold."

"What? That's..."

The young Orc's outburst was stopped by a backhand blow from Saggit's huge paw that sent him sprawling. "That's a bit more than we've got," he chuckled. "How much service can I buy with seventeen gold, five silver, and a few coppers?"

"The guardian was once a leader of the Ogre warriors. His Geni master feared he might start a revolt, so he was taken prisoner. Tortured and tormented by their dark magics, he was reshaped into the creature that guards this cavern's depths.

"His task is to protect the artifacts and talismans stolen by the Geni so long ago. The cavern and its contents have long lain forgotten, as has he. If you kill him, a number of things will be accessible once again, many of them best left untouched."

"I care not for magics or power; I just want the hearth stone so I can reunite my clan."

"Twelve gold."

"What?"

"Twelve gold and I'll join your band while you're in the cave. I've slipped past the guardian several times before. With luck we can do so again."

"And thus leave the old magics still guarded," grinned Saggit. "Agreed. Dare I ask what you seek here?"

"Blue/green moss. The healer in a village close by needs that for potions. They fought a hard battle against the pig men recently."

The female snorted in derision at that. "I wish I had been there to help the villagers." The others grunted their agreement.

"Agreed then, Mearith," rumbled Saggit's deep voice. "Twelve gold." He pulled a small pouch from his belt, counted out a few coins then tied the strings to the bag and tossed it to Mearith. She caught it easily and dropped it into a pocket of her cloak. "The fire's driven the cold from my old bones. Shall we be about the search?"

Mearith rose with liquid grace, pointing deeper into the cavern. "There are two branches of the tunnel. The moss lies in one, your treasure in the other. He guards both, but may let us pass if I can sing him to sleep." She swept up a torch and lit it in the fire. "Come."

Holding their torches high, they followed her down the tunnel. The entrance was long lost to sight when they heard the scream of challenge. That sound could not have come from any natural throat. "Hello again, bold guardian," Mearith sang in a low soothing voice. "Remember me?"

The beast roared a challenge and charged into the light, stopping short of the torch Mearith held up. It was manlike, three times the size of an Orc, heavily muscled with long sharp claws at the ends of its powerful hands. Slobber ran down its fangs and dripped towards the floor. Beating its chest, it roared again.

Mearith continued to sing an Elvish lullaby in her hypnotic voice. Slowly the beast began to settle. Even the Orcs seemed to fall under the spell and get drowsy. There was magic afoot here, Ariel could feel it. Mearith's voice was soothing her too, but she could see past that. She shook off the spell and watched carefully. The beast was getting sleepy.

Suddenly the youngest Orc shook himself and raised his axe. "Waste of time," he bellowed as he charged, swinging that deadly axe at the creature's head. The beast leaped to its feet and lashed out with a mighty blow. The Orc was blasted into the side of the cavern, his bones shattered and his body burst open, green blood everywhere.

Mearith was already in motion, diving to the ground to avoid the creature's blow. She rolled past and came to her feet, slashing at the beast's hamstrings. With a roar of protest it began to topple to the side, catching Mearith a glancing blow that sent her sprawling. Ariel leaped inside its reach and drove her sword through its heart. She ducked away as it reached for her.

The Orcs moved in as Mearith returned to bury her blade in its throat. The two younger Orcs hacked the legs from under it and Saggit buried his axe in its skull. With a final gurgling groan of protest the mighty guardian gave up its tormented life and slid to the ground, dead.

Mearith pulled Ariel's sword from the body, wiped the blade on the animal's chest then passed it back before retrieving her own. "The deed is done," she said, turning to Saggit. "That which you seek lies further down that tunnel. Ariel and I will gather the healer's moss from this one. We leave you now to mourn your dead."

"Impetuous young fool," sighed the big Orc as he nodded his agreement. "Come, we'll let them lie here together, warriors both lost in battle." He swept up a fallen torch and headed down the tunnel without a backward glance.

Mearith led Ariel deeper into the cave, down sloping floors to a place where water dripped from the roof high overhead. The blue/green moss grew thick on the walls and they soon filled their bags. Upon their return to the mouth of the cave they could see the tracks of the Orcs leading away to the east.

"Do we sleep now in the shelter, or do we press on?"

There was a glint of mischief in Mearith's eye as she spoke, and Ariel saw it. Smiling, she slung her bags across her saddle and mounted. "We press on. The sky's clear, the moon full, and Egma awaits. We can rest back at Fugitive."

"Yes, my queen," laughed Mearith as she leaped to her saddle. "Where you lead, I will follow."

"Always another test with you," sighed Ariel. "All right, as you wish." The wind had died off and she could make out their own tracks in the moonlight. She whispered something to her horse then set out, Mearith following closely.

They rode in silence for a while then Ariel dropped back beside her companion. "Mearith, why did we take that job?"

"We had no choice, my delight," sighed Mearith. "We could have fought and killed the Orcs then faced the guardian. I thought it wiser to have the Orcs help us."

"I suspected as much, but why Twelve gold? They had seventeen, why not that number?"

"I asked for gold as we'll need all we can gather to make our long term goal a success. However, I wouldn't leave them destitute.

That would only drive them to theft or murder. They can survive the winter with what they have, and that'll give them time gather more resources."

"You're so wise, I learn much from you every day. Now there's one thing more I should like to learn from you this night."

"What's that, my love?"

"The rest of the way back to Fugitive. The wind's filled our tracks with snow and I can no longer see the path."

"By your command, my queen," grinned Mearith, as she urged her horse onward once again. The sun was just breaking over the horizon when they heard the shout of greeting from the village gate.

Elfhome

E gma appeared from the inn and Mearith dismounted to pass her the bags of the precious moss. Ariel handed over her bags then passed the reins to Olan. Almost asleep on her feet, she started for the inn door, then she heard Mearith scream. "Noooooooooooo!" Ariel spun around to see Mearith disappear into a flash of light.

Ariel was suddenly bereft, a deep pit of emptiness inside her. She let out a heartfelt wail as she sank to the ground, awash in grief and tears. Randall was at her side in a heartbeat, helping her to her feet.

"It was foul magic, Ariel. Think now, you know where she is. Which way do we go. We'll get her back, just show us the way."

"You don't understand," choked Ariel. "I don't know where she is. She's gone from inside me. I..." She began to sob and fell into his arms.

"Then she's no longer in this realm," he sighed. "We'll need a mage for this, and a strong one."

Ariel sighed and gently pushed herself out of his arms. "I am soulless at the loss of her and the ache inside me. I need food and I need to sleep for it's been days without rest. When I've rested we'll puzzle this out and find her, no matter what realm she's in.

Egma took her gently by the arm. "Come inside, my queen. You need rest."

Ariel allowed the old Orc to guide her inside to a seat by the fire. Food was instantly before her and she nibbled at it but had no appetite. "It has to have been Dorgon," she mused.

"Has he that much power?" asked Egma as she passed a drink to Ariel.

"I doubt it. He'll have a mage with him. I'll capture that mage and force him to return Mearith to me."

Olan returned then from seeing to the comfort of the horses. "Rest first, my queen. When you awaken we'll be ready to travel." Ariel gave him a questioning look so he went on. "You're the Queen of Elves, we're yours to command. We'll accompany you."

"As will I," growled the Dwarf, patting his battleaxe.

"Me too," grunted a big Orc. The rest of the room joined in.

"People," sighed Ariel, "you cannot abandon your homes so recently fought for. I will..." Suddenly her heart sang with a wild joy and she leaped to her feet. "She's back!" She shouted as she raced outside to throw herself into Mearith's arms.

A FROWNING ELF, DRESSED in rich robes paced impatiently as two mages worked at a portal. "We have her, Sire."

Suddenly Mearith appeared through the portal, screaming her protest. Quick as a flash her blades leaped to her hands and then to the mages' throats. "Open that portal," she snarled. "Open it or I'll gut the lot of you right now. Do it!"

"Settle down, Mearith," sighed the robed man. "You wouldn't come home so I brought you here. We're in crisis and you're needed to..."

"Shut up, Evanseth or you'll be the first I gut. Get that portal open."

"Yes, Lady Mearith," choked out one of the mages. "At once, Lady."

"Begin then." Mearith slid her blades back into her belt and stepped towards her brother.

"Relax, angry woman," he grinned. "You're not going to kill me. We both know that."

"Is that so? Why shouldn't I?"

"Because then you'd have to come home and be the queen all the time."

"You damned fool, Evanseth, you're killing me, and you've torn the heart from another."

He lost his smile as he gazed closer at his elder sister. She was indeed in deep distress. Before he could speak one of the mages called out. "The portal is ready, Lady Mearith."

"Hold it open, I'll be right back. I just hope too much time hasn't passed there." She was still muttering as she stepped through the light and landed in the yard by the inn door, back in Fugitive. Her heart nearly burst with joy as Ariel's nearness filled her senses. A moment later Ariel came flying into her arms.

"Mearith..."

"Hush now, my delight. All is well. We're together again, all is well."

"What happened? Did you kill the mage?"

"I threatened to. Come with me now, there's someone I want you to meet. Randall, we'll be back in a day or two." He nodded as she led Ariel into the light.

Ariel clung tightly to Mearith's hand as they stepped through the portal. They emerged into a large room containing a long table of exotic woods, several gracefully designed chairs, beautiful tapestries adorning the walls, plush furs scattered about the floor, and a roaring fire in the hearth. There were also Elves, a king and two mages, plus a royal guard.

"Evanseth, I bring you a new sister," announced Mearith, drawing Ariel towards the king.

The king took one look at Ariel and went pale. "By all the gods, Mearith, what madness is this? What have you done? What price did you pay, will we all pay, for this."

Ariel's exhausted brain was trying to understand what was happening. Slowly, it began to make sense. Her resemblance to Mearith's first lover must be a lot stronger than she'd imagined. The king and both mages were slowly, fearfully backing away from her.

Mearith was grinning with delight now, for she understood the confusion as well. "Relax people, this isn't Elaith returned from the dead, this woman is Ariel, my bonded companion. She's the last descendant of the High Elf royal line. Show them the mark, my love."

Shyly Ariel pulled the collar of her tunic aside to show her birth mark. To her great surprise they all bowed deeply, including the king. He was startled at what happened next. Ariel reached towards him then started to collapse. "Damn that misbegotten Orc anyway," she sighed as she melted towards the floor.

Mearith caught her up in strong arms. "The healer must have given her a sleeping potion after I disappeared."

A tall Elf guard stepped forward. "Let me carry her, my Lady."

"To my rooms. Do you know the way?"

"I do." Gently he took Ariel in his arms and headed for the door.

Mearith followed close behind. "Evanseth, we'll talk as soon as Ariel is rested." With that she disappeared through the door.

Evanseth sank back into a chair. "And with that the king is dismissed."

"My lord, do you think Lady Mearith has returned to reclaim the throne?"

"No, I could never get that lucky. No, we dragged her back against her will, and she'll make me pay for it before all is done. I only hope she can help us find a solution before she goes running off to find another battle to fight."

"My Lord, did she say the woman is her bonded companion?"

"She did."

"But..."

"Yes, Mearith and Elaith were bonded by the Spiritpull ages ago. The Pull only happens once in a lifetime, but I'm sure Mearith has found a way around that rule as well." At that he seemed to get lost gazing out the window.

The two mages rose and quietly left the room, taking the rest of the guards with them, and leaving the king to his own thoughts.

ARIEL AWAKENED SLOWLY to find herself in a large bed covered in luxurious furs and soft blankets. She stretched then sat up to see what the splashing water was all about. Across the huge room was a pool of water, steam rising slowly from it and Mearith splashing lazily about. "Come in, the water's warm."

"What are you doing in there? Oh, how did I get dressed in this wonderful gown?"

"I'm enjoying a bath, and I put you in the sleeping gown. You were out cold. Egma must have given you a sleeping potion. Come on in here with me."

Ariel stripped off the gown and stepped into the warm water. With a deep sigh of delight, she sank into the slippery warmth and Mearith's arms. "When you vanished yesterday I felt as though I'd been emptied inside."

"As did I, my sweet."

"Mearith, was that what it was like for you when Elaith was killed?"

"It was."

"Did it ease with time?"

"Not until the day I saw you for the first time. I learned to live with it until it became a part of me, unnoticed for the most part, but always there. Ariel, I'm so sorry my demented brother did this to you."

Ariel sighed groaned with delight as Mearith began to wash her hair. Not since the death of her mother had she felt so pampered. "I thought it was Dorgon who had snatched you away. I was planning his slow painful death when you returned."

"Save those plans, my delight. We may yet need them. However, before we can deal with that we have my brother to deal with."

"Why did he capture you?"

"Because he knew I wouldn't come voluntarily."

Ariel gave a short giggle. "He couldn't have known about us, or he wouldn't have risked your wrath."

"That's the truth of the matter. Come, love, let's crawl out of this delicious bath and see if we can find some food before he comes looking for us again. Kings can be so impatient."

As they climbed out of the bath there was a woman laying soft towels and fresh clothing out for them. Mearith thanked her then began to dry off Ariel's hair. "That was so wonderfully done, my heart," smiled Ariel.

"What was?"

"The way you thanked her and treated her as an equal. Any of my people would sell their soul to be treated so."

"Amath is not a slave, my delight. She serves because it brings her joy to do so. She's been with my family as long as I can remember, and that's a very long time. Come, let's get dressed and seek out food before Evanseth finds us and drags us off to some room full of solemn and troubled faces that expect us to magically fix whatever crisis has befallen them now."

Ariel giggled as Mearith rolled her eyes to the heavens. Slipping the flowing dress over her head Ariel gasped with delight as it settled on her body and hugged her curves. She stepped into the soft boots, swept the wrap of fine linen about her shoulders then followed Mearith out of the room.

The next room was merely a passageway to another. Mearith stopped beside a pedestal with a decoratively carved box upon it. Ariel was inexplicably drawn to it. Slowly, carefully, Mearith opened it.

Inside was a chain of fine gold and from it hung a single jewel, a dazzling blue diamond. There was a ring also, a gold ring with a seal carved upon it. As she lifted them from the box, the diamond began to glow as though alive. "So, you are who I thought you were after all."

"That is so exquisite," sighed Ariel, as her hand unconsciously reached for it.

Without a word Mearith turned and hung the chain around Ariel's neck. Ariel gasped as the stone touched her skin and a voice whispered in her mind. "At last you've been found, and we're as one again."

Ariel felt a surge of strength and confidence sweep through her, filling and heightening her senses. Mearith slid the ring onto her finger and with it Ariel felt a new wave of determination.

"Mearith, what have you done to me?"

"I have returned what was rightfully yours, my delight. Remember the guardian of the cavern? Recall that I said he guarded many things? These were part of that treasure trove."

"What are they? How did you...?"

"I sang the guardian to sleep several times and explored his treasure. These I recognized as the jewels of the High Born Queen. Long ago, the greatest of the High Born monarchs created this stone and ring so she could pass her power on to her daughter. They became the symbols of the High Born ruler over time. They will grant you strength, but don't let them rule you."

Ariel nodded slowly as she gazed at her reflection in the mirror. "So you brought them out, hoping to find someone of the royal line still alive."

"Yes."

"Did you know you would bond with this heir?"

"No, that was the truly delightful surprise, a gift to me so golden I cannot express my joy in it."

"As you have said before, my love, there is a greater power at work here than we can understand. Already these jewels feel like a part of me."

"They are, my delight, they truly are. Now, let's get to the kitchens and hide from Evanseth for a while yet."

Mearith led Ariel through the tangled hallways and to the kitchens. Smells of food filled the air and caused Ariel's stomach to growl in anticipation. However, Mearith's plan to avoid her brother was not to be. He was there waiting for them. "About time you got here," he grinned.

There was a huge platter of food on the table before him. As they joined him, Mearith dragged the platter over to herself and Ariel. "All right, you tracked me down. Pleased with yourself?"

"Immensely. I see you've retrieved your jewels, Lady Ariel. I felt the surge of power as you put them on. May I see?" Shyly, Ariel let the wrap slide from her shoulders to expose the glittering stone. He smiled and nodded. "Yes, they belong to you. There's no doubt.

"Mearith, you said you two are a bonded couple. How can you...?"

"It's the Pull, Evan. I felt the Pull and was drawn to Ariel even as I was to Elaith so long ago. Believe me, I was as startled and dubious are you are now, but it's true."

"I believe you, sis, for I can see it in your eyes, and Ariel's. Truly this is a time of miracles. I won't ask you to stay longer than this day, for I know what you have vowed to do. Believe me, I wish you well on that quest, for you're my only hope, Ariel."

"Hope? For what?" asked Ariel.

"To be rid of the crown," he replied. "If you can free your people, we can blend both our people back together as they once were, and then you can be queen of the lot."

Ariel smiled warmly at him. She liked him and could see Mearith actually doted on him. "Why don't you want to be king?"

Evanseth gazed at her sadly. "The answer to that will come to you many times in the future, Lady Ariel. Eat hearty, Ladies. I'll have supplies and traveling clothes sent to your rooms. As soon as the meeting with the Lords of Doom is over you can return to your life of luxury on the road." He stood and walked away.

"The Lords of Doom?"

"The King's advisers," sighed Mearith. "If there's no crisis at hand, they'll surely invent one. Sadly, no one will listen to me. They hide here in this realm where it's safe, but that safety comes at a cost. The Borni have forgotten who they truly are. This is not the forest of their birth, not the forest that nurtured them and they it. They need to return home to find their vitality again."

"You could order them to do it," grinned Ariel.

"Yes, but then I'd be queen and I'd never get Evan to wear the crown again. I'd be stuck with it forever. No, I have a much better plan."

"Oh? Care to share?"

"Yes. We free your people, reunite all Elves, then stick Evan with the crown while we run off to play in the forest."

Ariel laughed with delight. "I like that plan, but we mustn't tell the king."

"Oh lord no, it's treason to plot against the king."

THE HUGE ROOM WAS OPEN and airy, the warm breeze gently wafting through the windows carried the scent of unknown flowers. The king was relaxing by a window as several older Elves sat around a large round table. Everyone stood up then knelt as Mearith led Ariel into the chamber. The jewel at Ariel's throat began to glow softly.

"About time you showed up," grinned Evanseth. "Have you two finished plotting against me yet?"

"Why, dear brother, have you been spying on us?"

"No need, Mearith, I know you too well. So, can we get to the business now?"

Mearith signaled everyone to stand, then guided Ariel into a plush chair. She sat close beside her and indicated everyone should sit. She introduced Ariel to everyone at the table then smiled at her brother. "All right, Evanseth, what is so urgent that you ripped me out of my world?"

He sighed as he eased himself into a chair facing her. "You've been gone far too long, and we need your thoughts. This is a somewhat delicate matter, but of the utmost importance. We need your insights and guidance." Evanseth paused and Mearith gave him a questioning look, urging him to speak further.

"We're dying, Mearith, as a people. Unless something happens to change the march of fate, our doom is sealed."

"Please get to the point before I pass into my dotage."

"There are no children, Mear. Not a single one. No child has been born to the Elves since the breaking of the world."

"You're quite wrong about that," grinned Mearith, as she relaxed back in her chair. "Thousands have been born. Let me explain. At the breaking of the world the High Born fell, as you already know. What you don't know is how they survived after we left that realm.

"Defeated by the Geni, they were stripped of power and left to die on the battlefield. Many did. I've been there and read the signs which are still visible.

"However, the humans and Orcs managed to cart away a great many of them and put them in slave chains. They're fed something called oshar which dulls their senses and shortens their lives greatly. However, they've born many children, and their numbers have grown to nearly equal our own once again.

"Working as a mercenary, I've searched far and wide for, and finally located, the last of the High Born royal line. To make matters even more interesting, I've succumbed to the Spiritpull for a second time. Ariel and I have bonded, both compelled by the Pull.

"It's my belief that only in the realm that gave birth to us can we bring children back into the world. It's something to think about, is it not?"

An older woman sat up straight at that. "It was the Pull? You are certain?"

"Of that there is no doubt." Mearith smiled as she gently squeezed Ariel's hand.

The voices came from all around the table at that. "And she is of the royal line? You are convinced of this? There can be no doubt?"

Ariel snorted in disgust. "Why have you brought me here, Mearith? To be judged worthy or not by this rabble of cowering doddering fools who fled the battlefield and left my own people to be enslaved?

"Take me back at once. I'd far rather sleep among the Orcs in a shabby inn than among such as these who hide in a forgotten realm, safe from harm, but stagnant and sterile." She rose from her chair and began pacing about the room, her jaw set hard.

Mearith stared at Ariel, her mouth hanging open. Suddenly a grin of delight spread across her exquisite features. The older female adviser chuckled and relaxed back in her chair. "There now, do you still doubt, my friends? You've all heard that voice before, have you not?"

"Indeed we have," sighed one of the men. "Forgive us, Queen Ariel. We feared a hoax, but it's clear you are indeed who you say you are. There can be no doubt."

"I don't understand," said Ariel, as she resumed her seat beside Mearith. "And I don't understand why I spoke the way I did. I beg forgiveness for my rudeness."

"It was the voice of the stone," smiled the old woman. "Allow me to explain, Lady Ariel. Long ago a great queen of the High Born created that stone and ring. She used them to help focus her power, but they also absorbed much of her energy and took on her personality as well. After her untimely demise her daughter inherited the jewels. They drove her mad and to her death. The next to inherit managed to impose her will upon them and they served her well."

"It is always a test with you, Mearith," sighed Ariel, as she took off the jewels and dropped them on the table.

"My love, you accuse me unjustly. I brought the jewels out of the cavern, saving them for the heir if I could find her. I felt no magic in them and feared they would be no more than a symbol since the power had left them."

"Lady Mearith could not have known, Lady Ariel," smiled the old woman. "The jewels lie ever dormant until the blood of the maker awakens them. See how dull the stone has become since you removed it? Watch as I pick it up. See, it will not respond to me, and I'm well versed in magic. It will respond to no other than the true heir, ever. The last queen to wear them often amused herself by having great mages try to activate the stone and ring. All failed."

Ariel sighed as she gazed that the jeweled stone. She picked it up and it flared to life in her hand. She felt the restlessness and impatience rise up in her again. Once again she dropped it on the table. "Forgive me, my heart. Please put these away where they can do no harm."

"Don't be too hasty, Ariel," said Evanseth. "The jewels of the queen can be great assets to you in your quest to free your people."

"I haven't the strength nor the power to wield them, Sire. They'll drive me to madness."

He smiled as he replied. "They can be overcome with force of will. I seem to recall your predecessor talking to them as though they were alive, as indeed they are. They are children, Ariel, children of your blood. If you guide them, control them, they will take on your personality and release that of the past."

"I will own no slave, not even the spirit of this stone."

"Then make friends with it," sighed the old woman. "Lady, if your heart is set on this dangerous quest, you'll need all the help you can get. The stone will protect you."

"And the ring?"

"It will guide your hand when it holds a blade."

The old woman smiled again as Ariel tentatively reached for the jewels. She held them for a moment then spoke directly to them. "In the city of Magdan there is a well that's said to have no bottom. Work with me and I will cherish you forever, try to take me over again and I'll place you in a box carved of stone, and drop it into that well. There, over time, you will pass from all knowledge of Elfkind. Are we agreed?"

The stone pulsed dully for a moment then brightened as she replaced the chain around her neck and slipped the ring on her finger. The old woman leaned on the table and spoke softly. "Lady Ariel, you may wear the face of one of our own, but you are of the High Born and have the strength of your ancestor, she who first made the jewel. Never doubt that. The jewels will serve you well."

"I do hope so. Lady Mearith, my love, you must watch me carefully and if I start to fall under the jewel's spell you must take them from me. Promise me now. I'll have your word on this."

Grinning, Mearith leaned closer. "I swear I will always watch you carefully, dear heart."

"Stop it. You know my meaning. Promise me now."

"All right. I promise I'll watch carefully and won't let the spirit of the jewel take you over."

"Thank you. And thank you all for your patience with me. I didn't mean to offend."

"You gave no offense, Ariel," said the king. "You did, however, confirm your identity beyond all doubt for us. The jewel took you by surprise. I'm certain it won't happen again.

"Now, back to the original business. Perhaps it's time to send another small expedition back to the home world."

Mearith gave him a puzzled look. "What's wrong with the one that is already there?"

"You really need to stay in closer touch, dear sister. They were driven back over two years ago."

"Driven back?"

"They were overrun by some sort of shambling swamp monster. Those who survived returned here."

"How many were lost?"

"Three."

"Three lost so a hundred fled? Have my people fallen so far? Has the courage of the Borni failed completely?"

"My dear sister, if you want to lead the Borni back to the home world and battle the monsters, I'll happily hand over the crown to you."

Mearith gave him a stern look, but another spoke up. She recognized him as the Elf who had been second in command of the expedition.

"Lady, you were there many times. You know the site was chosen because of its remote nature and of the difficulty of entry to the camp. What we didn't know was the danger lay beneath us.

"It was a week of heavy rains. The river overflowed, the swamps swelled, and something came from within them. Tall they were, and impervious to arrows and spears. Swords were useful, but barely. The commander ordered the retreat, then he and two others fought to give us time to use the portal."

"What sort of monster were they?"

"Unknown, Lady. We've never seen their like before. We believe they're the result of misused magic from long ago."

"Yes," sighed Mearith. "The Geni did do some terrible experiments. We didn't find out until it was too late.

"All right, brother mine, I propose that Ariel and I establish a safer landing site. It may take a couple of years, so don't get impatient and yank us out of there without warning."

"Agreed. Next time I'll send a messenger. You've not slain a messenger yet."

"Nor will I ever."

The older adviser leaned forward once more. "Lady Ariel, will you share with us what you know of the home world since we left?"

"Mearith can give you a better understanding than I can. I was born a slave to a slave. My mother had succumbed to the compulsion, the Spiritpull, as you call it. Her master was about to have her killed when Master Blake intervened. He bought her, paying far too high a price. He doted on her for many years until the day he slew her before my eyes. On that day I felt this mark burn itself into my shoulder.

"Unlike other slave children who grow up in drudgery, I was raised and educated in relative comfort. I was rarely beaten, yet I was made to understand I was slave. I did as I was bid and was prepared for whatever fate Master Blake had in store for me. He taught me the use of the blade, and in the dark of night, Mother would come to me to teach me the forbidden language.

"Overlord Ocra tried to buy me many times, but Master refused saying he wished to breed me himself. Once the mark was on me, things changed. They argued bitterly about this many times. In the end, Master granted me freedom to prevent Ocra from claiming me. In retaliation Ocra put me in the City Watch where he could keep an eye on me. That's where Mearith found me."

"I get the impression the granting of freedom is unusual."

"It is quite rare, and useless in any event."

"Oh?"

"The masters control the oshar. It's all the Elves eat, for without it we fall into madness and die. A freed slave is still a slave."

"What is this oshar?"

"It is a lie," sighed Ariel. "Mearith showed me the truth of the matter. The oshar that we all believe keeps us alive, is really a poison that robs us of our faculties. Sadly, convincing my people that it's safe to live without it will be the hardest part of the quest to set the Bornani free."

"The Bornani? The Children of the Forest?"

"That is who they shall become," said Ariel. "The High Born fell in the battle that broke the world. They are no more."

"You will truly return your people to the forest as of old?"

"I will, good people, or I'll perish in the attempt. Mearith, my heart, will you tell these folk what you've learned of my world? Your knowledge is so much more extensive than my own."

Mearith smiled and patted her hand, then turned to the others gathered round the table. "As you know, at the end, we tried to settle our differences with the High Born and to bring them with us to safety. They refused and fought the Geni. We had not the power to survive that battle, so we left.

"The High Born were defeated and cast down to be carted off as slaves to the humans and Orcs as well as the Geni.

"The great cities of the High Born were destroyed and broken, as was the world in general. Now there are places of twisted magics gone awry that should be avoided. Strange things live there, things created by the Geni to fight the Elves, things evolved from broken and twisted spells, and worse.

"New lands live where oceans lapped before, young mountains reach skyward and old ones lie as low islands or completely beneath the surface of the waters. Bits and pieces of the work of the High Born remain, as do some of our own works, but only enough to bring sadness to the heart.

"Much is left to be discovered, much is left for Ariel to learn before we begin the quest. We will send messages when we have prepared a place for your return."

Evanseth sighed and rose to his feet. He paced about the room for a moment then stopped to gaze out the window.

"Lady Ariel, come gaze out into the world with me." Puzzled, she rose and went to him. "See all those people out there going about their daily business? They're most of what's left of the mighty Borni. We haven't lost our courage, my new sister, but I won't risk the last of my people on a whim or a chance.

"However, you do bring great hope to us. Don't wait too long to signal our return."

"My lord King, that which you show me here also brings great hope to me. To see so many Elves unchained, unfettered, thrills my heart."

Evanseth stepped back from her. "My lord King? Forget it, My Queen. I know what you're planning and I won't be caught in your trap."

"Sire? Trap? I know not of what you speak." Even as Ariel denied it, the twinkle in her eye gave her away. Everyone around the table began to chuckle.

"Oh yes you do, Queen Ariel of the Bornani. You plan to have me help you rescue your people then you'll abandon them to me leaving me to be king over the lot, to try to meld the two peoples together while you and my scheming sister run off to play in the forest. I won't have it. Besides, plotting against the king is a serious offense."

Everyone was laughing, and Ariel glowed in the acceptance of these people of legend. They would help her, and she began to have hope of succeeding in her quest. She smiled with delight as Evanseth put his arm about her shoulders and led her back to her seat beside Mearith.

As Ariel sat and reached for Mearith's hand, Evanseth sank back into his own seat. "All right, Mear, what do you need?"

"For now, nothing, for the winter's settled on the village. It's in a remote place, protected by the deep forest on one side and the swamps on another. The open fields provide plenty of farmland, but too many of the people were lost when the pig men attacked."

"Pig men?"

"Yes, evolved from wild boars and magic gone wild."

"Again I ask, what do you need?"

"When the snows melt again, send a score of rangers to make the forests safe around the village. Free up all the villagers to produce food and clothing for, when the summer is high, Ariel and I will begin to send freed Bornani slaves to you there."

"Have you a plan to free the slaves, Lady?" asked the older female adviser.

"The same way you eat a giant elk."

"One bite at a time," grinned Evanseth. "That might work for a while at first, but then it'll get more complicated as the owners begin to understand what is happening."

"I know, dear brother. That's also a task for the twenty you send to us. They must take the new refugees and turn them into fighters."

He slowly nodded his agreement. "So, we have a plan of action and a possibility of solving both our problems. It's well done. When do you wish to return?"

"Now, as soon as possible," declared Ariel.

"The portals work oddly with time, my love. I was here for only moments, but you say I was gone much longer. If we stay a few weeks the winter could be gone before we return."

"Tease me if you must," smiled Ariel, as she patted Mearith's hand, "but those people, those wonderful misfits, begged me to be their queen, and I agreed. I can't abandon them, and you know it. My lord King, I begin to see why you resist the crown. It binds you with bonds far stronger than slave chains."

"It does, Ariel. It grieves me to see so young and beautiful an Elf saddled with the weight of it. Surely your lady companion, who is far older and more worldly wise, will take on the responsibility for you."

"Alas, my lord, I did try, but she refused."

"That's enough, both of you," laughed Mearith, as she first poked Ariel in the ribs then Evanseth. They flinched away then laughed with her.

"Very well then," grinned the king. "Give me a list of what you need, and I'll have it waiting for you. Meet us in the portal room in a turn of the glass."

At that the meeting broke up. Mearith swiftly scribbled a few notes then slipped the list to the king. "Come, Ariel, I have one more gift for you before we go."

She led Ariel back to the bed chamber where they'd spent the night. New and much finer traveling clothes were laid out on the bed for them. Ariel smiled with delight as she dressed in the new leggings and tunic.

As Ariel turned to show Mearith her delight she saw her unfolding a large leather pouch on the bed. She gasped as she saw what was inside.

"Ariel, my beloved, this bow and blade once belonged to she whose face you wear, and she had no equal in their use. Both are imbued with the magic of the forest and our people. Will you accept them as a sign of our love, let them help the jewel and ring keep you safe?"

"Oh Mearith, I can't..."

"I knew her as no other, my love. She would want this."

"Then I accept, for you and for she whom you loved so deeply. I will treasure them." She accepted the sword from Mearith's hand and felt a life force within it awaken. As the ring touched the hilt there was a sudden tingle run up her arm, a wild surge of joy.

"Easy my protectors. There are no enemies here. Be at peace." She slid the sword back into the soft leather scabbard Mearith passed to her then fastened the belt at her waist.

The bow came to her hand next and she gazed in wonder at the finely crafted weapon. It too seemed to spring back to life as it touched the ring. Ariel reverently bent the bow and slipped the string into the notch. The wood fit naturally to her hand; she pulled back the string easily then slowly relaxed it.

"The magic of the bow is that no other can bend it, not even I."

"Seriously?"

"I have tried many times to string that bow," smiled Mearith. "It's the same with the sword. Only you can wield it."

"How did you know it would respond to me?"

"Because I cast the spells myself long ago. That blade and bow will joyfully serve the one I love dearly and no other. They have lain dull and dormant since the breaking of the world. I gazed upon them again last night as you slept, and they shone with luster and life once more. They'd sensed your presence and were calling to you."

"I did feel something, but I thought it only a dream. My love, this is an incredible gift, but I have nothing to give to you in return."

Mearith smiled wickedly and pulled Ariel tightly to her. "I'm sure you can think of something."

They returned to the meeting room to find Evanseth and the two mages waiting. "We've adjusted the time line as best we can, Lady Mearith. I beg you to hurry as we can't hold it steady for long."

"I'm not going to bump into myself going the other way, am I?"

"I sincerely hope not, Lady Ariel," chuckled the mage, "but I make no promises."

Smiling, Evanseth stepped up to Ariel. "Here's a small gift for you, my new sister. It's a calling stone. Just hold it in your hand and call to me; I'll hear you. I've given Mearith several, but she keeps losing them."

Ariel's grin matched his own as she accepted the velvet pouch from his hand. "I'll guard it carefully. My Lord King, thank you for your great kindness to me. I have no way to thank you properly."

"Oh my dear, you've brought more excitement than we've had in ages, and there's a promise of more to come."

"Be careful what you wish for, little brother," laughed Mearith. "Come, Ariel, before the portal collapses."

A Winter of Learning

They stepped from the portal and into the Yuletide celebrations. There was a rousing cheer to welcome them back and Ariel smiled with delight. After having seen the ease and comfort of the king's court, she knew here was where she belonged. The level of comfort had reminded her too much of how the Geni lived at the expense of the Elves.

"Lady Ariel, welcome home," smiled Olan. "We feared you might miss the celebration. Can you tell us where you were?"

Ariel sighed and sat at the long table. The room had gone quiet. "I will explain, and then I'll beg your help. We were in the palace of the Borni king, Evanseth, Mearith's brother. There I was welcomed and presented with mighty gifts.

"I was also received and accepted as the true heir to the royal line of the High Born. As I was introduced to the King, I fell to the floor in a swoon at his feet." Here, she shook a finger at old Egma.

The old Orc chuckled. "Ah yes, the sleeping potion I gave you worked, did it?"

"It did. I realized what you'd done and cursed your name as I fell to the floor. I awakened to be accepted as, and treated like, royalty of old. I will confess, it was a heady experience, and I can see how easy it would be to want it to continue.

"That's the trap I won't fall into. My people are to be the Bornani, and we'll embrace the old ways from a time when the Borni and Bornani were one people." There came a soft round of approval, bringing a smile to her face and to Mearith's.

Suddenly Ariel's hand began to twitch and reach for her sword. The glow of her jewel could be seen from under her tunic. "Mearith, what's happening?"

"You tell me."

"You're grinning at me, but you too have reached for a weapon. I have a strong sense of approaching danger. Is that correct?"

"It is. That jewel senses it and so do I. What should we do, my queen?"

Ariel didn't hesitate. "You're the warrior, Mearith. You direct us."

"Direct, not advise?"

"There's no time for that. Direct us."

Mearith grinned with delight. "Come with me, Ariel. Let's go see what's triggered your guardians." She headed for the door.

As Ariel rose to follow Mearith she signaled the Elves to join her. Mearith quirked an eyebrow at that. "If Elves are to live in the forest we must learn how to discover and face danger," said Ariel, as she caught up the magic bow Mearith had given her. "Teach us." Mearith nodded and slipped through the door.

Snow was falling heavily outside. Mearith stopped to listen then trotted off towards the edge of the village. Ariel had heard it too, the faint sounds of horse harness as the beasts slogged through the drifts. Beyond the village they saw the outline of the beasts and crouched low in the snow. A moment later they heard the voices.

"I don't care how much Dorgon is paying us, it's not worth searching the entire countryside in this."

"Stop your damn whining, we're close. Look at the horses, they can smell the stables. Remember, kill the rest, but Ariel must be taken alive. If we fail in that Dorgon himself will flay the hide off us in the town square."

Ariel whispered to Olan who silently slipped away and raced back to the village inn. Mearith cupped her hands and whispered softly to Ariel who nodded and nocked an arrow. As the last horseman passed her position she drew and released smoothly. The man grunted then fell sideways from his horse. Mearith was instantly in the saddle that had been vacated. Ariel dropped another.

In all she brought down five men before she was discovered. As the riders began to shout, Mearith charged into them. At Mearith's charge, several Orcs rose from the snows and attacked. They were joined by Ariel and the Elves.

As the battle was joined, Randall led the humans into the fray. The surprise had been with the villagers. For a time, Ariel and a huge Orc stood back to back against the foe. Suddenly it seemed to be over as the men tried to flee.

"Orcs and Elves, find them! Kill them all!" shouted Ariel. "Find them, leave none alive. Randall, have your men gather the horses, get them into the stables. Mearith."

"Here, my queen."

"Find me a live one to question if you can."

Mearith nodded and vanished into the gloom. A few moments later she returned, dragging a wounded man with her. She dropped him at Ariel's feet. Ariel recognized him. "So, Kizen, you're a long way from Magdan. How came you here and why?"

The man caught his breath then spoke slowly. "The mercenary called you the queen, Ariel."

"And so I am, answer the question."

"Lord Dorgon has men searching the countryside from here to the seas and back again. Most are hired mercenaries. Three hundred pieces of gold are offered for the death of the mercenary Elf, and twice that for your return alive. One man of the watch is sent out with each group to make certain you survive." He coughed and gasped for breath.

"How did you find this village?"

"An old woman at an inn west of here spoke of men living in the mountains beyond the swamps. We lost a tenth part of our number to that damned swamp and the cold. Every inch of Eastshire has been searched. This had to be the place." He coughed again, blood mixed with spittle falling onto his chest. "Don't leave me to freeze like this, Ariel. Finish me clean."

She nodded then her sword leaped to her hand, and she drove it through his heart. The others began to return to her. "Are they all dead?"

"Twenty-two men dead, my queen," replied Olan. "Twenty-two horses taken to the stables."

"Then let's get in out of this storm. We'll leave them for the wolves." She led the way back to the inn.

Inside the fire was roaring and the smell of cooking stew filled the air. They stomped the snow from their boots and shook it from their cloaks and hair then gathered near the fire. "Randall."

"Yes, Lady Ariel?"

"How many did we lose?"

"None, my queen. We have a few scratches and a bit of frostbite, but no more."

"That is welcome news. What troubles you, Dirk?"

"Was it necessary to kill them all, Ariel? Kizen stood the watch with you many times."

Suddenly a blade appeared at his throat, two more at his heart and an Orc fist bunched in his tunic. "That's Lady Ariel to you, human," said Olan. "Put some respect in your voice when you speak to her, or we'll do it for you."

Dirk swallowed hard and stepped back. "I meant no offense."

"None was taken. Easy, my friends, easy. Dirk meant no harm and fought beside us this day. Randall, would you care to enlighten him?"

"The lady acted correctly, boy. First off, we don't have the resources to feed a bunch of prisoners, nor do we have a dungeon to keep them in. She couldn't let them go to report back and lead more men here either. No, better they disappear in the swamps never to be heard from again. This is war, not the town watch."

"We heard the men talking as they approached, Dirk," said Ariel. "They meant to kill everyone except me. The reward for me can only be collected if I'm alive. They chose the risk and lost the gamble.

"Know this, I'm queen here by the choice all of you made. This is now my home, and I'll defend it to the best of my ability. When the snows leave the lands I will leave to seek out and set free as many Elf slaves as I can. In my place, Fugitive will be defended by a score of Borni warriors who will arrive in spring.

"This will be the place the freed Elves will come to begin their new lives. I'll brook no harm to the town of Fugitive, or her people."

There was a rumble of appreciation through the assembled people. Olan spoke up softly. "My Queen, we'll be hard pressed to feed all those horses through the winter."

Ariel shivered then nodded as the heat from the fire began to penetrate her chilled body. "Understood, friend Olan. I'd love to keep them if we can manage it. We can sell some of them to fund our adventures, and others could be used by the folk here. We did lose a few to the pig men, did we not?"

"We did, Lady," said Randall. "We'll do what we can. Perhaps, if the snows aren't too deep, we can graze them in the fields once in a while. Now, what do you want to do about posting a watch?"

Ariel laughed and squeezed his arm. "I think I want to ask your advice about this, Randall. You have a far greater experience than I in these matters. Mearith, my love, what do you say?"

"I say we get back to the celebrating we were doing before we had unwelcome guests. A watchman could see little in this storm and would probably freeze to death."

"I agree with Mearith," said Randall. "It's now dark and snowing heavily, there'll be no further threat this night, I'll wager."

"So be it then. Let's celebrate both the day and the victory."

Later that night, as Mearith cuddled Ariel close, she felt the tremble as Ariel wept. "Oh my love, what troubles you?"

"I slew a friend this day. I commanded the death of many more as well. Mearith, what have I become? I don't even know if it was me or the jewels that gave the order."

"Be at peace, my heart, and hear me. You did your friend a kindness for I saw the blow that felled him. The Orc's war hammer struck him fair in the body, shattering his ribs and puncturing his lungs. He couldn't have survived, Ariel, and he knew it. You did him a kindness.

"What you're becoming is the Queen, my delight. You made the correct decision, and you made it when it was most needed. Never hesitate in battle, and you didn't. I'm so very proud of you.

"The jewels didn't make the decision, my sweet. They may have helped you, but, had they made the decision the death dealt would have been of a more magical nature."

"Are you so sure?"

"I am. Snuggle down here now and rest. Tomorrow will be a most difficult day."

"Yes, love. Wait. What? What do you mean, a most difficult day?"

"You've declared that we'll begin the quest to free the slaves when the snows leave the lands. I'd hoped to have another year to prepare you, but ..."

"Should we wait? Mearith, can we not start in the spring?"

"We can, but the training will be difficult."

Ariel propped herself up on one elbow. "Tell me."

"Each day we must practice with weapons. Each day we must practice stealth. From time to time, we must spend several days in the forest, eating what we can find, sheltering where we can best find shelter.

"Beyond that, as queen, you have responsibilities to these people, and they'll need to see your presence in the village. They'll need to see you taking an interest here as well."

"So, it'll be a busy winter?"

"Indeed so, my delight. In a very short time you'll have to become a ranger of the forests. If we had an army as in days of old we could build a castle ..."

"No, Mearith, no. That's how my people fell." She pulled the jewel from her tunic and spoke to it. "Do you hear? That's how our people fell. We forgot who we were and depended on the magic.

"I need you to help me. Can you do this? Help me to become one with the forest, learn the old magics of the forest, and regain the true power our people once enjoyed?"

The stone pulsed dully for a moment then flared up brightly. Ariel felt a surge of power run through her. "Yes, you're of the earth even as I'm of the forest. You and I, great jewel, we will return to what we once were." The jewel throbbed like a heartbeat and she tucked it back inside her tunic.

"Mearith."

"Mmm?"

"Olan and the others, should you be teaching them as well?"

"Yes and no. You and I, my delight, will work together. Evanseth will send a score of his best, it'll be their task to train the others. Evan knows this, and he well knows what they'll be expected to do. They'll prepare our people, have no fear."

"Prepare?"

"What we plan to do will bring war to us, Ariel. Have no doubt about that. Our people must learn to be warriors as well as runners of the forest."

"Yes, you're right. So much to learn." Ariel sighed and closed her eyes. "So little time. I wonder ..." Her breathing deepened and she didn't finish the thought.

Next morning Ariel awakened alone. She startled upright then relaxed, Mearith was nearby. She arose and slipped outside to the outhouse to relieve herself then swiftly washed her face and hands in the fresh snow.

As she re-entered the inn Ariel heard the voices of the gathered people and she smiled. It brought a warmth and comfort to her mind that she had not known before in her short life. She stepped into the common room to be wrapped in the scent of cooking food.

A place was made for her at the table beside Mearith and a bowl of the previous night's stew appeared before her. She tasted the stew then moaned with delight. "So, everybody seems to be in a jolly mood today. What news is there?"

Mearith gave her a warm smile that made her heart sing. "The good folk of Fugitive have been busy, my delight. They've found and looted the bodies of our fallen enemies."

"Oh?"

"Yes. Much of what was gathered has been put into common stores for the use of all, the coin is in that sack, and we now await your decision on the final matter."

"Final matter?"

Mearith was grinning again, and Ariel chuckled to see it. How she had come to cherish Mearith's sense of fun. "Yes, my heart. A weapon of great value was found and it's up to the queen to decide its fate."

Ariel dipped her bread in the last of the stew then chewed thoughtfully. "Show me this weapon."

"It lies there, my Queen," said Olan, pointing to a huge battle axe that leaned against the stone of the fireplace.

Ariel rose and went to inspect it. She grunted as she picked it up. "It's got a nice weight to it." This brought a round of laughter from the people and a smile to her face. She set it down again. "What's its value?"

"That axe will draw two hundred sixty gold or more at auction, Lady," rumbled the deep voice of a huge Orc who sat near the fire. "It was once wielded by Thyrgrim the Mighty, Chieftain of the Scratite clan, in the last great battle at the breaking of the world."

"How do you know this?"

"The runes etched on the blade are Scratite runes, Lady. I'm Scratite, the last of my clan."

"You're not. Mearith, you didn't tell him?"

"I didn't know or I surely would have."

"Tell him what?" rumbled the deep voice.

"When Mearith and I went for the healing moss we encountered a small group of Orcs. They were led by an Orc named Saggit."

"Saggit? He yet lives?"

"He does, my friend. Do you know him?"

"Saggit's my older brother, and a fierce warrior. Which way did he go?"

"He went south," said Mearith, "but the snows are too deep to track him now."

The big Orc sank slowly back onto the bench, nodding his head as he absorbed this information. Ariel gazed at the huge man for a moment then spoke. "Forgive me, my friend, but it occurs that I don't know your name, even though we've fought side by side."

"I am Drakkat of Scratite Clan, Queen Ariel, at your service."

"Then let us speak of that service, friend Drakkat. Even as the ring I wear is an heirloom of power from my people, so is this axe an heirloom of power for you. The axe is yours."

The big Orc was somewhat taken aback. "My queen, the value of that axe would go a long way to aiding your quest. Are you certain?"

Ariel smiled and laid her hand lightly on his shoulder. "That axe has far more value to me in the hands of an ally who can wield it, than it has on the auction block. Take up the blade of your clan, Drakkat, wield it well in the defense of Fugitive and her people."

He wrapped one huge hand around the haft of the axe and swept it easily into the air, then laid it across his knee as he knelt before Ariel. "By my honor and the honor of my clan I pledge to wield this axe in the service of Queen Ariel."

"Accepted with gratitude," smiled Ariel, as she raised him to his feet. "You should also know your brother retrieved the Scratite hearthstone from that cave."

"The hearthstone?"

"He's trying to gather the remains of the clan and find them a home. I think there could be room for a small clan of Orcs in this valley. What say you, Randall?"

"Oh, aye, Lady, there's room enough for certain. We could help them get settled."

"Then so be it. Drakkat, I'll keep an eye out for your brother in my travels. If I meet him I'll tell him where to find you." The huge Orc gazed at her with pure devotion in his eyes, but didn't speak. Ariel patted his arm then turned back to her place beside Mearith. "So, what other wonders did you find?"

Mearith smiled her delight and Ariel could see by the approval in those green eyes that Mearith agreed with what she had done. "The axe truly was the prize, my delight. Of the rest there were a few good swords and daggers, a number of cloaks, a few coins, but little more. So, now that you've given away the family fortune, are you ready to begin your training?"

Ariel's shoulders slumped. "You're going to make me sleep out in the snows tonight, aren't you?" Mearith merely smiled wickedly. "Fine then. If I must, then I guess I must." She winked at Randall then followed Mearith out the door.

The training was hard, harder than anything Ariel could have imagined, and it went on all through the winter. Sometimes they stayed in the village and practiced with weapons, other times they stayed in the forest.

Ariel swiftly became a warrior to be reckoned with and more. She learned where and how to find food, water, and shelter where none were apparent. She learned to listen to the wind and water, the song of birds, and the calls of animals. The language of the forest, Mearith called it.

Ariel learned that the trees could talk to each other through the root systems, and she learned to hear them. Once they took the Dwarf with them and he taught her to speak to stone.

Ariel was enthralled with all of it, and learned quickly. Once the jewel fully understood it was forest magic she wanted, it tapped deeply into that magic. With the aid of the jewel, she learned and absorbed at an astounding rate.

Spring arrived and with it a host of new life and new lessons. Ariel now felt the surge of new life in the forest as a rising energy and delight in her own body. Mearith was thrilled as they sped through the forest at a dead run yet leaving no trace of their passage nor making a sound.

On days like this it was almost like having Elaith back, for Ariel had truly become one with the forest. They burst silently from the trees to hear the sounds of battle from Fugitive.

They arrived to see Dirk circling Drakkat and trying to avoid that massive axe. A sudden flat handed blow from a huge hand sent Dirk sprawling. Drakkat laughed and helped him up. "You're watching the axe and nothing else," grumbled the Orc. "We go again."

"Ho, friends, what news?"

"Lady Ariel, it's good to see you again," replied Darkkat, as he saluted her. "The queen! The queen has returned."

The entire village came rushing to greet them, and Ariel basked in the warmth of the camaraderie as they entered the inn. "Randall, what news?"

"Not a lot new, Ariel, and nothing bad. The snows have gone and the air grows warmer. My old bones are grateful for that. All the horses survived and are now on the fields grazing. We've managed to avoid disease and starvation. All in all I call it a good winter."

"No more unwelcome visitors?"

"None, and we have kept watch. We've also been training. Every villager is now battle ready."

"All except Dirk," chuckled Drakkat. There was a round of laughter at Dirk's expense. He said nothing, but his very silence caught Mearith's attention.

"So, Queen Ariel, you've spent much of the winter in the forest. How was it?" asked Olan.

"Educational," Ariel replied with a smile, pushing aside her empty bowl. "I've learned where to find food, such as some of it was, as well as shelter from the snows and winds. I've eaten more beetles than I care to admit, this stew was ambrosia to my poor taste buds.

"I also learned how to disguise a trail in the snow and to read a trail even though the snows had covered it. Mostly I learned that I still have much to learn."

"Will you teach us what you've learned?"

"Olan, my friend, I'm still a child learning. Soon the Borni will return. When they come I'll ask them to teach you all they can. I've come to rely on you, my practical friend. I would ask you to learn what you can, and yet be here to welcome those we set free, to help them adjust."

"Is that because I was once a slave too, my queen?"

"Yes, it is. They'll see you, all of you, as their own, ones like themselves. They'll listen to you, look to you for comfort and leadership. Will you do this for me? You and the others here in Fugitive?"

"Of course, my Queen. It'll be an honor."

Randall smiled and nodded his approval. "Are you planning to begin the quest soon?"

Ariel sighed and sat back. She smiled her thanks as the cook set another bowl of stew before her. She tasted it, moaned with delight, then nodded. "Yes, I want to begin soon, but I want to confer with you, all of you first."

They waited patiently while she ate. Ariel finished the bowl, then set it aside, again smiling her thanks to the cook. "There is so much I don't know, and I do need to know. Here lies Magdan." She set the salt bowl near one end of the table.

"And the sea is to the east," she poured a fine trail of salt from the city marker to the edge of the table. "To the northwest lies Kress, here." Another bowl to mark the town, followed by a trail of salt to mark the road between them.

"This much I know, although I have never been there. What more is there? What other places are there where my people are to be found?"

"They are many, Lady Ariel," said Randall. "Here, between the two towns, lie several villages, all containing slaves. And here to the sea as well. This way lies vast forest lands, and beyond Kress lies a larger city called Shotar. It's the main stronghold of the Geni, and the villages are numerous along the highway that connects them."

"This way lies the mountains," said Mearith, as she laid out a cloth to represent the terrain. "And here, in the mountains, lies the ruins of Elanda, the greatest city of the High Born. This area here, between Elanda and Shotar is an area where the magics wrought havoc, the results of which can still be found in abundance."

Ariel sighed and rested her chin in her hands. "You knew all of this, didn't you, my love?"

"Yes."

"But you didn't speak of it. Why?"

"As you've said, my delight, one bite at a time to eat the beast. First you needed to become completely at home with the forest. This you have done. Now it's time to go exploring, to learn the lands."

"This is why you wanted to wait another year before we began, isn't it?"

"It is, my heart."

"Then I will heed your advice. We'll spend the year as wandering mercenaries while I learn the pathways of the forests and fields. We'll then return to Fugitive at the falling of the leaves. At this time next year we'll begin in earnest to set free the Bornani. Will this be acceptable to you, my lady of the forest?"

"It is wisdom, my Queen," smiled Mearith. "We'll seek out each town and village, explore the forests that surround them, so we know what to do when the time comes. Of course, should the opportunity present itself, we could pick up a few traveling companions from time to time."

Ariel laughed with delight. "So, it's to be a season of training? Very well then, so be it. Randall, what can we do to increase our supplies before winter next? We will have a score of Borni warriors to feed by then."

"The Borni can supply themselves, Lady Ariel," came a voice from the doorway. A tall Elf had just stepped through a flash of light. He stepped forward then knelt. "I'm Arlon, Lady Ariel. I've come to learn what you would have of us, and to see for myself the truth of the tale."

Ariel arched an eyebrow at him. "The truth of the tale?"

"Forgive me, Lady, when told the tale I did not believe, but there you sit, wearing my sister's face, her magic bow strung and slung across your back, yet wearing the jewel of the High Born royal monarch. I am yours to command, Lady Ariel."

"Mearith?"

"Yes, Arlon is Elaith's brother. Arlon, old friend, this woman is not Elaith, she is Ariel. Someone very different."

"I understand, Lady Mearith. I do, but I had to see with my own eyes. Lady Ariel, I know you're not my sister. You're the queen of the High Born and I swear to hold you in the regard you deserve. I'll take no liberties, nor will I hold any expectations."

"Rise, Arlon, and sit with us. Hear me well, the High Born are no more. They were destroyed long ago. My people are the remnants of those lost so far in the past. I intend to set them free and return them to the forests from which they sprang, their natural home.

"They'll be called the Bornani. I need two things from you, Arlon. First, know that I consider this village my home, and her inhabitants my people. I need you to keep them safe for me."

"That I'll do and gladly, Lady Ariel. What is the other thing?"

"This Elf is Olan, my comrade-in-arms, a friend, and an escaped slave as well. Teach him the ways of the forest, he and his companions. When my people begin to return they'll need to learn these things, and they will all need your help.

"Now, this man is Randall, headman for the village and my adviser. This Orc is Drakkat, Chieftain of the Scratite Clan, and a trusted ally."

The tall Elf with the warrior's facial tattoos smiled. "I'm honored to meet you, all of you. Lady Ariel, I swear I'll do all I can to meet your needs as you have instructed. When will you need us?"

"I hoped to leave on the morrow."

"Then I shall send for the others. Good people, once the royal ladies have departed I'd like to meet with you all to confer on how best to meet your needs.

"I'm also to inform you that the Borni intend to return to this realm, all of us. We'll need a safe place to land and the king hopes that this place will serve that purpose for us as well. Is this acceptable to you?"

It was.

On The Road Again

They'd been on the road for a full cycle of the moon. Ariel sighed with delight as she leaned on the pommel of the saddle, gazing out at the heaving ocean. "Quite a sight, isn't it?" said Mearith.

"It's magnificent, yet terrifying. You've seen it before, haven't you?"

"Many times, my delight. Many times. So, what do you think?"

"Its song is soothing, seductive, and yet dangerous. It's beautiful, and yet I sense no love of Elves in it. I prefer the forests we enjoyed on the way here much better. Let's be about the business then head back into the wilds."

"So be it." Mearith smiled with delight.

"You're having fun at my expense again."

"I'm truly enjoying you, my heart. The first time I saw that endless expanse of living water I spoke those same words. Come, the village is near."

They rode slowly down the long slope to the village below. From the top of the hill they'd been able to see the spires of the city in the distance. Those disappeared from view as the riders reached the low lands of the fishing village.

Everyone stopped to stare as the two hooded riders approached the inn then dismounted. As they stepped inside they were confronted by a huge man. "Who are you? What do you want here?"

"Rest and ale," replied Mearith, keeping her hood pulled forward, "nothing more."

The man peered closer and sneered. "I don't trust you. What would two rangers of the forest be doing at the shores of the sea?"

"Our business is our own. We seek only a short time of rest and ale to quench our thirst."

"You lie, I think you're here to rob me. Get out before I start breaking your bones." Several of the other men rose and drew swords.

"You're a bunch of complete fools," rumbled a deep voice from across the huge room. An old Orc shifted on the bench as he spoke. "That one is the assassin, Mearith the Merciless. She'll gut the lot of you in a heartbeat and drink your ale for nothing while sitting on your corpse.

"Put aside your blades and live another day. Her coin is as good as any other." The men began to back away nervously.

Mearith tossed a silver coin on the table. "Bring ale and food."

The big man snatched up the coin and turned away. "Wench, serve the guests, you lazy Elvish slut." A moment later a young Elf appeared with the food and ale. The signs of abuse were easy to read on her face.

Mearith gripped Ariel's arm tightly. She spun another coin to the girl who caught it deftly. "Girl, I seek someone."

"Who?"

"An old Orc named Saggit." Mearith hadn't softened her voice, so all in the room heard her words.

"It's a bad day to be you, Orc," laughed the big man. "The assassin has come for you."

The huge Orc rose and approached the table. "I have no fear of death, but I'm curious, warrior. Who would pay you enough to hunt me?"

"I did," said a soft voice from across the table, the assassin's companion. "Sit with us and share the ale. When we've finished we will return to the fields to finish our business."

"You'd invite a man to break bread, then kill him?"

"Sit down. No one said anything about killing you."

Tentatively, the huge Orc eased himself onto the bench. He knew full well what these two were capable of. He well remembered the battle of the cavern.

As he sat Ariel leaned across the table and spoke softly. "Drakkat sent us."

Saggit's eyes opened wide and his mouth opened, but he didn't speak. Instead he reached for a loaf of bread and tore it in half.

They ate in silence, but when they finished Ariel spoke, still keeping her hood well over her face. "Innkeeper."

The big man approached. "What do you want?"

"To buy your slave."

"What??? What the hell for?"

She replied in a voice so cold he took a step back from her. "I want to watch what happens when she no longer has the oshar to eat."

The slave girl whimpered and the man laughed cruelly. "Three gold coins."

"Two."

"Three or be on your way."

"Two. Any village girl will sell for less at auction. Two or I'll spill your guts on the ground."

"Agreed," he replied sourly. "What makes that one so special."

"That's my business and none of yours." She tossed him the coins. "Orc, bring the wench." She tossed a gold coin to Saggit then turned and walked out the door. The girl tried to back away, but the huge Orc took her by the arm and led her outside.

Ariel and Mearith were already mounted and walking the horses out of the village. The girl followed, weeping, but no longer struggling. The size of the Orc beside her made her resigned to her fate.

The sun was setting behind the hill as they finally reached the top and the welcoming forest beyond. Once out of sight of the village the two riders dismounted and swept back their hoods. "You're both Elves," gasped the girl, then she covered her mouth with her hand.

Ariel smiled warmly. "Yes, we're Elves, my sister. Be at peace, you will not be harmed."

The poor frightened girl didn't understand a word she had said so Ariel repeated it in the common tongue. "I don't understand."

"Come here and I'll get that accursed collar off you," said Ariel. "Mearith will soon have a fire going. We'll eat some decent food, and then there'll be a telling of tales."

"Will one be the tale of Drakkat?" asked Saggit.

"It will," grinned Mearith. She put strips of meat on long sticks then passed them around. As they cooked the meat she spoke again. "The snows were deep when the riders came to our home. We heard them coming and slipped out to meet them. A score of men rode towards our village, talking of the killings they would do and the rewards they would enjoy." Saggit snorted at that and grinned.

Mearith matched his grin. "We rose from the snows and fought them. In the end they were all food for the ravens, and we had gained twenty new horses as well as a pile of booty.

"Now, here's the interesting part. My traveling companion, my bonded companion, is Ariel, hereditary queen of the High Born Elves." The girl sucked in her breath and Saggit sat up straighter. "Ariel's been acknowledged queen of the village as well, a village of vagabonds, and fugitives, Humans, Elves, Dwarves, and Orcs.

"One of those Orcs is a savage warrior named Drakkat. He and Ariel stood back to back in battle. They're friends and comrades-in-arms." She stopped to take a bite of the meat and chew. No one spoke, they just waited for her to continue.

"Once that battle was over and the booty gathered, a great battle axe with Orcish Runes on the blade was found. It was the prize of the lot, valued at three hundred gold at auction. It was the Axe of Thyrgrim the Mighty, Chieftain of the Scratite Clan who wielded it at the breaking of the world." This time it was Saggit who sucked in his breath.

Mearith nodded and smiled. "What became of the axe?" asked Saggit.

"Well, as queen, it was Ariel's decision, and we did need the money, however that's not what happened. Queen Ariel gave the axe to her friend, Drakkat and declared him chieftain of the Scratite Clan. As Chieftain, Drakkat swore himself and his clan to the service of Queen Ariel."

"By all the gods," breathed Saggit. "Drakkat yet lives, and he has the axe?"

"He does," said Ariel, smiling. "When he spoke of the axe and its meaning to him I knew he had to have it. He was also excited to learn that you survive and that you have the hearthstone. I promised to keep an eye out for you on my travels.

"Saggit, I'll tell you how to find Drakkat. Will you do a favor for me in return."

"Name it, Queen of the Elves."

"This young woman is one of mine, Saggit. There are more free Elves in the village of Fugitive. That's where you will find your brother. Will you escort her there for me, see that she arrives unharmed?"

"I swear it by any oath you require."

"On your honor and the honor of the Scratite clan."

The big Orc grinned. "You do know something of Orcs. Yes, Queen Ariel, Companion of Mearith, I swear on my honor and the honor of my clan to see this young Elf safely to the village of Fugitive."

Ariel offered her hand and gripped his massive wrist in the warrior's grip. "Accepted and agreed. Saggit, did you ever find more of your clan? Do you still have the hearth stone?"

"I do and I did, Lady. They await my return in a village eight days journey from here."

"Then we shall make that journey together." Ariel smiled and turned her full attention to the Elf woman. "And now the tale for you, my sister."

The girl's eyed widened as Ariel passed her another strip of the delicious meat. "This tale began in the city of Magdan. I was held slave there even as you were here. Do you know the tale of how the Elves became slaves?"

The girl nodded so Ariel went on. "One night I met an assassin who took me away from the city and taught me how to be a true Elf again. She then told me of my heritage. I was declared queen first by Mearith Waleen of the Borni, sister to Evanseth, King of the Borni. I was presented to him, and he introduced me to his people who confirmed my identity.

"It's my intention to release all Elves from the chains of slavery. You're among the first."

The girl lowered her gaze and spoke. "How can I survive without the oshar?"

"The oshar is a lie, my sister. It doesn't keep you alive, it's a poison that keeps you asleep and shortens your life. I've experienced the awakening myself, it's a magical experience.

"I spoke the truth to the innkeeper in the village, I do want to see you find the wonders of life as the oshar's poison leaves your body."

The girl sat gazing up at Ariel in wonder. "Lady, are you going to bring back the great magics, the ones that destroyed our people?"

"No, never that, for you're right about that being the downfall of our people. No, we'll return to the forest which is the natural home of all Elves. We shall be called the Bornani, the Children of the Forest.

"Saggit will take you to the Borni who will teach you the ways of forest. So, now, what's your name, my new sister? Who is the newest member of the Bornani?"

"I have no name, Lady. First I was child, then I was girl, and then I was sold to be wench."

"Mearith, my love, would you devise a name worthy of the Bornani for our new sister?"

"Arlaith was always a favorite of mine." Mearith smiled as she focused on the girl. "Would that suit?"

The girl simply nodded, tears running down her face. Ariel smiled with delight. "Done then. Arlaith, you snuggle down with Mearith and get some sleep. I'll take first watch then wake Saggit."

"I get the dawn watch then," said Mearith, as she spread her cloak over the girl and settled down beside her.

Over the next few days they traveled slowly back towards where Saggit had left his people. Ariel and Mearith took huge delight in Arlaith's awakening to her true Elvish nature.

Even old Saggit often grinned at her childlike delight in the simplest of things. Once he'd gathered his folk and explained the reason for the journey and the nature of their task, Mearith and Ariel left them.

Mearith had already told the old Orc how to find the village and what to expect along the way. Ariel gave him twenty gold to help with the journey, then they parted.

They sat on the horses, watching the dozen Orcs and one Elf march away. "Will she be safe with them, do you think?"

"I do, my delight," replied Mearith. "So, where to now?"

"Let's swing north then around towards the mountains. I'd like to see them before the leaves begin to fall. We should also keep an eye out for brigands along the road."

"Oh?"

"Yes, we're running low on money. We need to rob a few robbers to replenish our purse." Mearith's rich laugh of delight floated through the trees at that.

A Troubled Love

They traveled for many days, always leaving the road to take to the forest at the first sign of traffic. It always amazed Ariel that Mearith could find hidden pathways that a warhorse could manage.

She'd also bonded completely with her new horse, a powerful dapple gray trained for war. Mearith had chosen the horse for her from those they'd captured at the battle of Fugitive. Drakkat had his axe, but Ariel had Grimm, as she'd named him.

The big horse paced easily along the forest trail, but suddenly his head came up and his ears tipped forward. He took a few dancing steps, but Ariel's gentle touch on the reins stopped him. Mearith's horse had heard the sounds of flight and pursuit as well.

"Shall we see what's amiss, my delight?"

Ariel grinned. "Perhaps an opportunity to fatten our purse? Let's see." She touched her heels to the flank of the beast, and with a scream of challenge the mighty horse leaped forward.

Rounding a bend in the trail she saw a wounded human turn to defend the Elf woman who stood beside him, helping him to stand. There were five riders closing fast on the wounded man.

As Ariel bore down on them, Mearith's black charger sped past. She swept three riders from the saddle, but two got past her. Ariel's horse slammed into one, sending it crashing to the ground atop its rider. Her bow took the last man from the saddle.

Mearith dispatched the fallen attackers, while Ariel leaped easily to the ground facing the human and Elf, a blade in her hand. "Drop your sword and no harm will come to you." He didn't move. She leaped at him, and with a lightning fast move of her wrist sent his blade flying from his hand.

"Thank you, now release your slave to me and be on your way."

To Ariel's great surprise, the woman stepped in front of the man protectively. "No, I won't leave him."

"You're no longer slave, my sister. You're free. I'll send you to a place of safety where you'll be welcomed. No slaves are kept there. I won't harm this man, I promise."

"I won't leave him. If you're going to kill us then do it or go away so I can tend his wounds."

Perplexed, Ariel turned to Mearith who was grinning at her. "You're having too much fun at my expense again. Help me here."

"Yes, my queen." Still smiling, Mearith stepped closer to the woman. "Good sister, this woman is Queen Ariel of the Bornani. She has vowed to free all the Elves from slavery. We'll see you to a place of safety. Please understand, you're no longer a slave."

The woman slowly lowered her eyes. "Please, if you truly are friends, please help me bind his wounds. I can't leave him, he's my bonded companion."

"Dammit, there's no time for this. Mearith, help him if you can." Ariel spun around and began to loot the corpses. She took only the money and a couple of daggers.

Catching the reins of two horses she returned to find Mearith helping the Elf woman to bandage the human. "Can you ride?"

"I think so," he replied. She nodded and whistled softly. Grimm came to her instantly and she leaped to the saddle.

Mearith helped the man onto a horse then tossed the Elf up behind him. "Hold him, don't let him fall." She leaped to the saddle then grinned at Ariel. "Where now, my queen?"

"Off the path, find us a campsite."

Once again Ariel was amazed as Mearith found a side trail that the horses could manage. They soon were at a small clearing beside a gurgling stream. "I'll set the camp, my heart. You confuse the trail, make certain none can follow."

"There is only one to follow," sighed the human, as Ariel eased him to the ground. "Once he sees the corpses of his companions he'll make haste to get far away from here." It was too late, Mearith had already vanished into the forest.

Ariel made the man comfortable then threw her cloak over him for warmth. "Tend him," she said as she set about starting a fire. Once she had the fire going she turned her attention to the horses, stripping off the saddles and rubbing them down while crooning softly to them.

She finished with the horses and had food cooking when Mearith returned leading another horse. Ariel looked up and smiled. "Another donation?"

"Yes, once our young champion recovers from his wounds he'll need a horse."

Ariel chuckled and waited until Mearith had rubbed down the horse, then she again addressed the two people in the common language. "All right, it's time for the telling of tales. Woman, explain what you meant when you said this human is your bonded companion."

"I'm not a slave," the woman began defiantly. "Marc freed me and bonded with me last winter."

"Unusual, but possible I suppose," said Ariel, smiling reassuringly. "Tell me the tale of it, my sister. How did this come to pass, and why were armed men pursuing you?"

The woman sighed and gazed lovingly at the man who was now asleep. "Five years ago, Marc bought me from a neighboring farm. My owner wanted to breed me to one of Marc's father's slaves. Marc said I was too young for breeding and so he bought me.

"In spite of his father's insistence, he continued to refuse to breed me. Instead, he freed me and bonded with me. In a rage, his father sold me and so we fled from the farm. We traveled for days until we found some likely land then we began to set up a small farm of our own.

"Two nights past, the nearest farm was attacked by the Rovers, a band of cutthroats that haunt this area. We watched helplessly as they slew and burned. Marc feared they might come to our farm too, so we slipped away, but they caught up with us in the night.

"Marc fought them in the darkness and slew three before we escaped. They overtook us again just as you arrived. The rest you know."

"He said there was one more."

"Yes, the leader, a big man with a scar on his face. He is said to be a vicious man."

"He's now a dead man," said Mearith. "He wasn't much of a fighter, but he did have a fat purse." She tossed a heavy bag of coins to Ariel.

Ariel grinned and dropped it beside her saddle then turned her attention back to the Elf woman. "So, this man is your bonded companion, and you wish to stay with him."

"I do."

"Why?"

"Why? He is gentle and kind to me. He would allow no other to touch me, and was gentle with me when he did, and then he asked my permission first. He has loved me and protected me against all others. Is that not enough?"

"Is it?"

"I love him. My heart aches for him. I want to be with him every moment of my life. He makes me smile, laugh, and holds me gently when I cry. What more could I want?"

"A place of safety," came a groan from beside her. "Meg, these folk say they can take you to a place of safety. Go with them, my love, be safe, live a long and happy life."

"How could I possibly be happy without you, my man. I won't leave you."

"Woman, you say you're a queen. For whatever reason you want her safe and so do I. Take my Meg with you."

"I won't go without you, Marc."

"Meg, be reasonable."

"No. You promised me a small farm with lots of children, now live up to that promise."

"Meg, you've seen how that dream worked out."

"Stop, both of you," sighed Ariel. "Mearith, my heart, your thoughts?"

"Oh, I think Fugitive could use both of them. Meg has some skill as a healer and Egma is getting old, she could use a helper. Farmers with fighting skills would be welcome."

"I do agree, but there is a problem."

"How to get them there," said Mearith, a smile playing at her lips.

"Yes, there is that," said Ariel, her smile matching Mearith's. "Good people, there's a village, a place where you'll be safer than anywhere else you might find on your own. We can take you there if you wish, or we can leave you to your own devises. The choice is yours."

"We'll go with you," grunted the man, as he struggled to sit up.

Meg helped him and held him gently. "Marc?"

"Meg, you saw what they did. If we travel with them we have a much greater chance of survival. Our love is forbidden, girl, we will always be hunted, a target for fools. If there truly is a place where we'll be left in peace I want to be there."

"As you wish, my husband. I do agree, it would be sweet to live openly as a bonded pair."

"And that you will be allowed to do in Fugitive. As queen of Fugitive I swear it."

"There is one small problem," said Mearith. She wasn't smiling now, but facing Meg sternly. "You've been told several times that Ariel is your natural queen, and she is also Queen of Fugitive by common consent. You, young miss, have yet to show proper respect, both for the woman who saved your life, and for your queen.

"I've stayed my hand so far, but should you show disrespect to Lady Ariel again, I will no longer."

"Mearith, dear heart..."

"No, my delight, my Queen, they'll treat you with the respect you deserve, or they will never see the lands of Fugitive."

"Easy, my heart, easy. She's a former slave, she doesn't know how. She means no disrespect. She just doesn't know how. It's all right."

"It's not, my Lady Queen. It is not. These two will acknowledge you as their monarch and instantly obey you in all things, or they will awaken alone on the morrow."

"So, you wish us to volunteer for another form of slavery?"

"You have chosen then," said Mearith, her voice so cold it made them shiver. "We'll share food and fire with you this night and at the break of day we go our separate ways."

"Wait, please. Meg, by all the gods, are you so determined to see us to our death? Since we bonded every hand has been turned against us. These folks saved our lives, and they offer a place of safety where we can live in peace as a bonded pair. Meg, they truly mean us no harm, they could find stronger servants anywhere."

"Less unruly ones as well," said Mearith. "I truly mean you folks no harm, and I would see you to a place of safety, but once there, a show of disrespect for Ariel would get you killed in a heartbeat. Her people are completely devoted to her, and for good reason. She's completely devoted to them."

Ariel sighed and sank to the ground beside Meg. "She's right, I fear. I tend to be a bit impulsive, and too trusting of all Elves. I guess it's because I want to see them all free of chains and happy.

"However, I won't force anyone to accept me or my rule. You're free to choose your own fate. You may go where you will. If you choose to come with me you must accept my rule. Mearith spoke the truth, the others wouldn't tolerate me being spoken to as you've done.

"Tell me, how did a former slave get so defiant?"

Marc chuckled and gently squeezed Meg's shoulders. "That's my fault, I suppose. I didn't beat her often enough. She's completely out of control now."

Meg lightly slapped his shoulder then kissed his cheek. "Perhaps he's right at that, he's far too good to me."

Ariel noticed Mearith saddling the horses. She nodded and rose to her feet. "I wish you well then, stay here a few days to let those wounds heal. Safe travels." With that she swept up her weapons and strode away. Leaping to the saddle, she followed Mearith into the forest and was lost from sight.

"By all the gods, Meg, there went our best hope for survival. I've told you many times that sharp tongue and attitude would be the death of us both."

"You set me free, do you now want us both enslave ourselves?"

"That's not what they asked of us, girl, and well you know it."

"Sorry you freed me?"

"Woman, I bought you, kept you safe from the breeding pens, fed you, loved you, wed you, fought for you, and was ready to die for you. I love you madly, but you sure don't make it easy.

"Girl, they weren't trying to enslave you, but they couldn't have you showing disrespect either. Their lives, and the lives of their people, depend on that obedience and respect being instant. They're building something, Meg, something special for all the slaves and downtrodden.

"That's why Mearith couldn't have us with them with that attitude of yours. It could eat away at their dream like a cancer. No

Meg, I do love you, and I love your fierceness, but this time it was misplaced."

Meg sighed and looked away, not meeting his eyes. "Do you want me to leave."

"Not yet, I still need you to nurse me back to health."

"What??? Oh, you beast, you...you...human." He was grinning at her and she laughed in spite of herself. "That's going to cost you."

Next morning Marc awakened to find Meg cooking food on a small fire. Perplexed, he looked all around, then back at the cloak that covered him. He got to his feet easier than he expected then went into the trees to relieve himself. When he returned she had the food ready. "How are you feeling?"

"Better than I had a right to expect," he replied. "Meg, do you notice anything odd?"

"Like what?"

"They left us the food, two horses with saddles, Queen Ariel's cloak, and that bag of coin."

"By all the gods," she breathed. "They left us the means to start up a new life and the means to travel while we seek a safe haven. Oh Marc, I was so wrong to suspect them. I was just so afraid. That's the root of my defiance, fear. In all my life you're the only one I've been able to trust. All others lied."

"I know, my sweet, I know."

He held her close as she wept bitter tears. "Marc, I've destroyed you. You should go see if you can find them, follow them to that safe place. Leave me here."

He chuckled softly and cuddled her closer. "Why in the world would I want to leave you here?"

"That was the last of the oshar, Marc. In a day or two the madness will begin to take me. It'll drive me insane and you'll have to kill me."

"I'll do no such thing, my girl. Fine, if you must go mad, then we'll go mad together. I'll never leave you."

They stayed at the camp another day until Marc felt fit to travel. All in all they were in good shape. They had horses and money. Their prospects were greater than they had ever been.

Marc led the horses back to the main trail then they mounted and started out. The trail soon led them to the main roadway, but it was still early and there was no one in sight. They moved out onto the road, but in less than a mile they heard the hoof beats behind them.

Looking over his shoulder Marc saw six riders bearing down on them. They kicked the horses into a gallop, but were soon overtaken. These men were all in uniform. "Dismount," bellowed one rider, "dismount or die in the saddle." Carefully, they dismounted.

The riders surrounded them, swords drawn. "Well, looks like we've caught ourselves a couple of brigands, men."

"We're not robbers, we just travelers," said Marc, fighting to keep his voice even and hoping Meg would keep her mouth shut. "We ran because we thought you were brigands."

"So you say, but that's an awfully fat purse for a poor traveler, a fine cloak as well. No, you're thieves. We'll just relieve you of that purse then we'll hang you from a likely tree."

He'd barely finished speaking when they heard the soft thud and a man fell from his horse with an arrow in his chest. Another thud and another man fell, then the war horse screamed.

The beast burst from the trees at full charge, slamming into two of the standing horses, flinging them to the ground atop their riders. The beast reared and lashed out with its hooves, causing the final two riders to back their plunging horses away.

All to no avail as another war horse slammed into them knocking them down. The rider was on the ground in a heartbeat, her sword flashing. The lone survivor trembled as he looked up at the cloaked rider on the plunging gray. "Who are you?"

"My question exactly," replied the rider. "Who are you?"

"We're the king's men. We patrol this highway."

"And which king would that be?"

"King Kratac of Shotar, king of the Geni and all the world."

The cloaked figure laughed. It was a woman. She swept back her hood and he gasped. An Elf. "When next you see your king of all the world, tell him Queen Ariel of the Bornani sends her greetings."

She turned her horse back to Marc and Meg. "I can't leave you two alone for a moment and you get into trouble. Mount up, she's waiting." They could see Mearith on her black stallion at the edge of the trees. They climbed onto their horses and rode quickly to join her.

"Now, king's man, know this, you may keep your roads, but the forest is mine. Trespass at your own peril." With that she wheeled the horse and followed the others into the forest to be lost from sight.

A short ways into the trees Ariel found them on the hidden trail. "Mearith, what am I going to do with these two?"

"Please," said Meg, her eyes downcast, "help us. Accept us. Lady, I'm so sorry to be so mistrustful and disrespectful. Please accept us and be our queen. I'll do whatever you want. I just don't know proper manners, and I..."

"Should stop talking now, Meggie," said Marc, as he dismounted and knelt before the still mounted Ariel. "Lady Ariel, you truly are the queen of the forests. I pledge my life and loyalty to you, my bad mannered companion as well. Lady, we're yours to command."

Ariel was grinning now. "I don't know. Mearith, what do you think, can you teach Meg some manners before we get back to Fugitive?"

"It'll surely be a difficult task," grinned Mearith, "but I'll give it a try."

"Accepted then. Arise, Marc of Fugitive, oathbound to the queen. Mount up, we have far to go yet this day."

"Lady, thank you for coming back for us," said Meg as they set out along the path.

"I don't abandon my people, Meg, and you are one of my people, even if you don't want to be."

"Please forgive me, Lady Ariel, but I do want to be. It was only my fear talking before. In all my life Marc was the only one who came back for me until now."

Ariel smiled and patted her shoulder then dropped back to keep an eye on the back trail.

A Bigger Burden

They crossed the highway and an expanse of open fields in the night. By dawn they were back in the forest. After a short rest they continued on until nightfall. The next dawn found Meg weeping quietly in Marc's arms.

"It's the madness, Lady Ariel," said Marc, as he saw Ariel's look of concern. He was shocked as a bright smile came to Ariel's face.

She sat beside them and took Meg's hand in her own. "Tell me, Meg. Tell me what you're experiencing."

"It's the voices, Lady."

"The voices?"

"Yes," Meg sniffed and went on. "It sounds like the wind is talking to me. The madness has begun."

"What did it say?"

"What??? What does it matter what it said? Why are you laughing at me?"

"I'm not laughing at you, Meg. I'm enjoying your awakening, even as Mearith enjoyed my own. Tell me what the wind said, and I'll tell you a great and terrible secret."

Puzzled, Meg gazed at her for a moment. "It said, welcome home, daughter of the forest, woman of the Bornani."

Ariel's smile broadened. "Meg, the oshar is a lie. It doesn't keep you alive, it poisons you and shortens your life. You're now awakening to your true senses as an Elf. All Elves can hear the voices of the forest. Brother wind was the first to welcome me, too.

"Over the next few days more of your Elvish senses will awaken. Your vision will clear, your sense of smell, taste, and intuition will all sharpen, and you'll feel more alive than ever before because that's what you will be, truly alive at last."

"Lady, can this be true?"

"Yes, Meg, it's true. I swear it."

Marc was grinning as he cuddled Meg close. "I was wondering how you and Lady Mearith managed it. Now it all makes sense."

"Oh?"

"Your fighting and woodcraft skills, you're far too strong and fast, and you find pathways invisible to all others."

"Much of this can be learned, Marc," said Mearith. "I'll teach you what I can."

They went slowly for several days while Ariel helped Meg adjust to her new senses and abilities, and Mearith taught Marc woodcraft. She also helped him improve his fighting skills.

One morning they sat on their horses beneath the trees and gazing out at the roadway. There was a group of travelers making their way along, albeit quite slowly. Mearith saw the snarl cross Ariel's face as it became clear that half the party were slaves tied together.

Ariel took the bow from her shoulder and reached for an arrow, but Marc's voice stopped her. "My Queen, let me. I'm human and, traveling alone, I'll arouse no suspicions or fears in them. Allow me to go see what they're about." Ariel nodded so he set out into the light rain.

One of the armed men sounded the alarm as he caught sight of Marc approaching. Marc called out to them, spreading his hands wide to show he wasn't holding a weapon and that he meant no harm.

Marc spoke with the men at length then turned his horse away and trotted off along the road. Once out of sight of the men he turned into the forest and returned to Ariel. "What did you learn, Marc?"

"Much, Lady, and none of it will please you. Those men are hired sell swords, working for the man driving the wagon. He's a slave merchant. Each year at this time there's a big slave auction in the city of Shotar.

"That's where he's going with his prize slaves, to sell them at auction. He owes a great debt of gold to Lord Dorgon of Magdan. Even though it'll impoverish him, he hopes to clear the debt and rebuild his business."

"At this pace he won't reach Shotar for several days," mused Mearith. "I assume he's not destined to arrive."

"No, that he will not do, at least, not with his stock in trade," said Ariel, her voice cold as a winter's wind. "Tell me, my heart, what's the best way for us to proceed? Do we wait for darkness?"

Mearith shook her head. "No, my delight. In less than a turning of the glass they will reach that bend in the road. We will take them there.

"Marc, did you see bows or spears?"

"None, Lady. I saw swords in sheaths and whips in hands. They believe they've reached the safe part of the roadway now, and are more concerned about keeping the slaves under control. There are eight men-at-arms and the merchant. Fourteen slaves in all."

"We go. Once we reach the place of ambush, Meg must remain in the trees. We three will attack." So saying, she turned her horse and trotted off down the trail with the others close behind.

Hidden within the trees they waited, listening to the men draw nearer. "With what you're paying me, merchant, I might just buy that one there with the golden hair myself." This brought a great round of laughter from the others.

"You'll need thrice times that for one of these," replied the merchant. "These are the finest I've ever bred, all young and fertile. If the gods favor me I'll make enough to pay off Lord Dorgon and still remain in business."

The guardsman began to respond, but an arrow pierced his heart and he fell sideways off his horse. Another man fell to an arrow, then a warhorse screamed and charged from the trees, slamming into them.

They had all been bunched up and thus were knocked flying. A second charger trampled over them then the three fighters were on the ground with swords drawn. The fight was swift and merciless, and soon over. The merchant sat trembling on his wagon, a sword at his throat. It was the man who'd spoken with them earlier.

"Shall I kill him?"

"No," replied the woman with the tattooed face as she leaped easily to the saddle and approached. "We'll let Dorgon have him. You can carry a message for me, Merchant. When next you see Dorgon, Tell him Mearith the Mercenary is not happy she was paid with tainted coin. Tell him there'll be a day of reckoning for that piece of treachery."

"Is there anything of value in the wagon?" asked Ariel, as she cut the ropes that bound the Elves together.

"Nothing, my queen. Just the merchant's fat purse and a large supply of oshar."

"Bring the purse. Come, my people, to the forest."

The slaves just stood staring, unsure and frightened. Ariel smiled and pointed to the trees. "Go. Someone will meet you there, and I'll soon join you. First I must speak with your former master."

"Lady, the oshar ..."

"Go, I'll deal with that. Go." Unsure, they started toward the trees. Marc joined them and led the way.

As they vanished into the forest, Ariel turned back to the merchant. "Tell me of this slave auction. Does it happen each year? Are there others?"

Trembling, he leaned away from her. "Yes, the big auction is every year, once in the spring and again at the falling of the leaves. There are always smaller auctions."

"I knew of the smaller ones. Are there more large ones?"

Again he shrank from her. "Yes. Lord Dorgon hopes to hold a large auction next year at this time. He hopes to draw from all the people who would rather not travel all the way to Shotar."

She nodded her head then leaped to the saddle. Without another word the two Elvish warriors rode off into the forest. Fearfully the merchant whipped up his horses and sped off down the highway toward the city.

Back in the trees Meg was tending to the minor injuries the Elves had incurred on the journey. "All are here? Can they travel?"

"Yes, my Queen," replied Meg. "They're all young and strong. They can travel, but ..."

"I know, Meg, I know. They need clothing and horses, weapons as well. Mearith, my heart, I think we should turn our steps homeward."

"Agreed, my delight. We must go slow, but for now we should hurry. That one will come looking for his slaves, and the king's men will be with him. We must be far away from this place as quickly as possible."

"Find the path for us while I speak to these people." Mearith nodded then dropped to the ground and set out. Marc took a stance where he could see the back trail. He had his sword in his hand.

Meg spoke softly. "I've told them who you are, Lady Ariel. I don't think they believe me."

Ariel chuckled and faced the confused and frightened Elves. "My name is Ariel and I'm the hereditary queen of the High Born Elves. You are descendants of those people as I am. Do you understand?"

"Yes, Lady," replied a young male. "We've all heard the tales. We know why we're slaves. It's to prevent us from destroying ourselves and the whole world too. It's too dangerous for us to be free."

"Yes, that's what I was told as well." She took the reins of her horse and began walking. "Come with me, now. We'll follow Mearith and I'll tell you many things. They'll be hard for you to believe, but they're all true.

"I too was raised slave, in the town of Magdan, as were you."

There was a sudden gasp behind her. She heard a woman's voice speak in hushed tones. "She's that hunted runaway. She's that Ariel. She's been without the oshar for over a year, she's completely mad."

"Yes, I'm that Ariel, a former slave, freed and promoted to the Watch. No, I'm not mad, I'm a true Elf as you will be very soon. As I was saying, I too was raised slave in Magdan. Lady Mearith of the Borni took me from that accursed place and set me free.

"The oshar isn't a food, my people, it's a poison. It robs you of your true senses and shortens your lifespan."

"Shortens our lifespan?" asked a voice.

"Truly, it does. Mearith has never tasted the oshar, yet she has lived a long, long time. She was there, and fought in the great war that broke the world, the war when the High Born fell.

"I've learned much since leaving Magdan, and I'll share this knowledge with you all."

"Where are you taking us?"

"To a place of safety," replied Ariel. "It's my home now. There you will learn what it truly is to be an Elf, and then you'll decide what to do with the rest of your long lives."

"We must decide?"

Ariel turned and smiled warmly at the girl. "Yes, little sister, you will decide, even as I did. There are no masters where we're going. You'll decide things for yourselves."

"What if we don't want to go with you?"

"Then I'll leave you here in the forest. I've done so before with stubborn Elves."

At that both Marc and Meg burst out laughing. "That was me," said Meg. "I was so afraid, and stubborn, Queen Ariel left us there in the forest."

"What happened?" asked another girl.

"We got lost. Then, when we found our way to the high road, we were captured by the king's men. They were going to hang Marc and sell me."

"So what happened?"

"Queen Ariel and Lady Mearith came charging out of the trees and saved us. Our Lady Queen does not abandon her people. Please, don't be afraid, we'll all help you and no one will ever beat you again."

"But the oshar ..."

"Lady Ariel told you the truth of it. I myself have recently experienced the awakening. Oh my brothers and sisters, it's such a magical experience."

"Are you sure you're not just crazy?" asked another youth, a grin on his face.

Meg laughed with delight. "Well, if I am, I'm truly enjoying it."

At that point Mearith returned. She looked worried. "I've found a path into the mountains. Hurry now, we must move quickly. Already there are king's men on our trail."

"Lead them, Marc and I will protect the back trail."

"Ariel ..."

"Lead them, my heart," she said, as she passed the reins of her horse to Meg. "We'll take no chances, but we'll delay them if necessary. Quickly now."

Mearith was unhappy about it, but she obeyed. "Quickly now, good people. The way is rough, but you can manage it. Once we've all gained the higher ground above the trees the men will not be able to follow. Come, unless you prefer the lash of the slave masters." With that she trotted away, leading her horse. The former slaves followed.

Ariel and Marc gave them a good lead then turned to follow. They could hear the complaining voices of the men tracking them. "Come, let's lead them astray," grinned Ariel. She waited until one of the men spotted her then she ran down the wrong path, Marc right at her side.

Cursing and shouting the men gave chase.

Steadily working her way back towards the high road, Ariel continued to let them see her. Twice she was nearly struck with arrows, but she fled on.

Darkness was falling as they neared the road again. With a look of pure mischief, Ariel took Marc's hand and pulled him off the trail they were on. Silently they watched as the tired cursing men went past them, staying on the path until they sighted the road again.

Marc marveled at the woodcraft of the Elf Queen as she led him back up the hills toward the place where they'd parted from the rest of their people. Finally, as the moon rose high, they stopped to rest. The next day they found their people in a pitched battle with a giant.

The dawn saw them back on Mearith's trail. It climbed from the trees up onto a rocky incline and from there to a high meadow. The day was growing late, and Marc was tiring when Ariel held up her hand for silence. He could hear the shouts as well. Ariel broke into a run.

She rounded a bend in the trail to find a swampy area where Mearith and a band of Dwarves battled a gigantic creature that seemed to be made of sludge and plant matter. The axes of the Dwarves and Mearith's sword were having little effect.

Ariel felt the jewel around her neck begin to burn and glow. "All right, my friend, help us here."

She pulled out the jewel and aimed it at the monster. A shining beam of light burst from the stone and struck the giant. It howled in pain and turned to face her. Ariel gasped but held the jewel steady as the monster advanced on her, roaring in pain as it came.

The beam of light from the jewel did not falter, and the giant toppled to the ground, dead, right at Ariel's feet. With wide eyes she swallowed hard and gazed at the rotting corpse as it decomposed before her eyes. The jewel faded back to a stone as the beam of light died. She tucked it back in her tunic with a soft, "Thank you, my friend."

They were all staring at her, wide-eyed. One of the Dwarves approached and spoke. "That was well done, Mage. We owe you a great debt. What'll you have of us?"

"This woman is no mere mage, good Dwarf," said Mearith as she approached. "She is Lady Ariel, Queen of the Bornani Elves."

"The Bornani? Never heard of them. You're of the Borni or I'll miss my guess, but ..."

"We were once called the High Born," said Ariel.

"Ohhh, now, those people I have heard of, but we thought all were broken and enslaved."

"Most are, good sir," replied Ariel. "We're trying to change that. These few you see here are being taken to a place of safety where they can be reawakened to their true nature."

"A place of safety? In this world? Good luck finding that. Closest I've heard about is a village called Fugitive, lost in the mists."

"And that's where we're going," said Mearith.

"Do you know the way?" he asked. "We've been seeking that place ourselves ever since those swamp monsters rose from the ground and destroyed our home. We few are all that escaped."

"We'll take you there, good Dwarf," grinned Mearith.

He was instantly on the alert. "At what cost?"

"The woman before you, she who saved your lives, is also Queen in Fugitive. Accept Ariel as your queen, no more is required."

"No more, she says," grumbled one of the females, "as though that wasn't enough."

"Easy, lass," said the older fellow. "Elves and Dwarves have ever been strong allies. Our chances for survival will be a lot better with these tall folk than on our own. Besides, even if we could find Fugitive by ourselves, we'd be faced with the same problem."

He turned back to Ariel. "Lady Ariel, I, Gormin, Chieftain of this small clan, pledge our loyalty to you and beg your protection. Will you accept us?"

Ariel smiled and placed her hand on his shoulder. "I do accept you, Gormin. You'll be welcomed in Fugitive. Mearith, my heart, the day grows late, but I doubt this is a safe campsite. Should we retreat to yonder meadow for the night?"

"We should push on, my delight. Beyond this swamp lies a trail down into the forest and a fine campsite that's known to me."

"Then lead on, for I would leave this swamp as quickly as possible. Gormin, are there more of your people nearby?"

"Three more lassies and six elders, Lady. They're part of the clan, and you did accept us."

"You tricked me. Worse yet, Mearith knew, didn't she?"

"She did, for we were all together when we met. We were speaking of sharing a camp when the giant arose from the swamp. Mearith's an amazing fighter, for we managed to hold that thing off without losing a soul until you arrived."

"That she is, my friend, that she is. She's also my bonded companion and my teacher. I believe she's just taught me to be extremely careful when bargaining with a Dwarf." His great bellowing laughter brought a smile to every face.

They gathered the Dwarves and followed Mearith. Her chosen camp was farther away than expected. It was nearly dark when they arrived.

The Dwarves got a fire going while Mearith slipped off into the trees. She was soon back with a deer carcass across her shoulders. Everyone relaxed back while the Dwarven women saw to the cooking and Ariel tended to the horses. As the meal was finishing up a young female Elf shyly approached Ariel and Mearith.

"Lady Ariel?"

"Yes?"

"Lady, what is to become of us?"

Ariel smiled at the earnest young woman. "What's your name?"

Embarrassed, she looked away. "I have none, Lady."

"That won't do. You all need to choose names for yourselves. Now, I've told you that you're free to choose your own path in life. However, I do want to keep you with me until you are ready to choose that life path. Do you have any idea what path you might choose?"

"None, Lady."

"What tasks did you enjoy? What's looked appealing to you in the past? Surely you had dreams of what life could hold."

"We're breeders, Lady. Our purpose is to bear healthy children until we're too old to do so. We have no other purpose than that."

"Have you no training for other tasks, even basic simple tasks of life?" asked Mearith.

"No, Lady. As children we played, but at twelve years we began our training for breeding."

Grinning wickedly, Mearith turned to Ariel. "I think I need to see to my horse." She arose swiftly and strode away, leaving a wide eyed and sputtering Ariel behind with the girl. With a sigh Ariel turned back to the hopeful looking youngster.

"Bring the others to me." The girl leaped to her feet and hurried back to the rest of her companions. Bemused and fearful, they followed her back to Ariel. She patted the ground and indicated they should sit.

"So, now it's time to begin your new lives. Let's start with this. First, each of you must choose a new name, a name that speaks to you of who and what you want to become. Think hard on this now, choose carefully."

As she finished speaking Ariel noticed the girl who at first approached her. She was smiling. Ariel returned her smile. "So, you have chosen?"

"I have, Lady. May I be called Beren? It's a name from the past."

Ariel smiled. "Yes, I remember the tale of Beren the magic healer. Beren it is."

"Lady, I think I'd like to learn to be a healer too."

"Excellent choice, Beren. Meg has healing knowledge and I hope she'll assist the healer at home. Egma is old now, and with all the new people I'm bringing in she will need the help. Shall I ask Meg to teach you while we journey?"

"Oh, Lady, would you?"

Ariel smiled and raised her arm to catch Meg's attention. She hurried over and knelt. "Yes, my Queen?"

"Meg, this one is Beren. She wants to learn healing skills. Will you teach her the things you know?"

"Of course, Lady Ariel, it'll be a pleasure. Come, Beren. I've gathered a few herbs on our journey, I'll show them to you and explain their use."

Ariel turned back to the others. "There's no hurry. Take your time before deciding." She left them there and sought out Mearith.

"You've had your fun, my heart, but soon they'll face the awakening. As well, they've learned no useful skills at all."

"No useful skills?" Mearith had a wicked grin and Ariel laughed.

"Stop it. You know what I mean. Mearith, we have to teach them how to survive."

"You're right, my delight. We can't wait to reach the Borni, we must begin. Tell me, are you completely certain you've thrown off our pursuit?"

"As certain as can be. We let them see us then led them through the forest and back to the main road where we abandoned them. They were tired and angry as they passed our hiding place. I truly doubt they took up the trail again."

"That is indeed good news, as I believe we'll have our hands full with the newly released in the coming days."

She was looking past Ariel's shoulder. Ariel turned to find the young Elves behind her. They knelt as one. "Lady Ariel," said the nearest. "We have chosen."

"Oh?"

"Not yet names, Lady, but we've chosen a path in life."

"Indeed? Please do tell us, what catches your interest?"

"You do, my Lady Queen, you and the Lady Mearith. Ladies, you've said you wish to free all the Elves. You'll need help to accomplish this. We want to help you. Teach us wood craft and fighting skills. Ladies, you've granted us freedom, let us help you bring that to others."

Both ladies were somewhat taken aback. "Are you certain?" asked Ariel.

"We are, Lady."

"May I ask what brought you to this decision?"

"Lady, my mother was killed for breeding without the master's permission. All of us have similar stories of cruelty against the Elves. We were told we deserve no better because we broke the world. Lady, none of us was alive when the world was broken.

"You told us that the oshar is a lie, and Meg says so as well. If that's a lie, then perhaps the rest of what we've been told is also a lie. Please, accept us and teach us how to help you."

"You would be the queen's warriors, the runners of the forest?"

"Yes, Lady."

"All of you want this?"

"Yes, Lady Ariel," they replied in unison.

"Very well then, I accept you. Mearith will begin your education in the morning." With a regal toss of her head she strode away, but soon turned to see Mearith gazing at her, wide eyed. With a mischievous grin, Ariel turned away again.

Shortly Mearith joined her under the cloak by the fire. "You're naughty."

"Me? You didn't tell me about the Dwarves."

Mearith chuckled at that. "Fair enough. Ariel, my delight, these young ones have chosen a hard and dangerous life."

"I know," sighed Ariel, as she snuggled down on Mearith's shoulder. "We'll teach them what we can, then the Borni can teach them more. I couldn't refuse them, you know that."

"I know. They're just beginning to taste freedom, and now they're starting to resent the lives they were forced to live, the lies they were told. They'll grow angry, and we'll have to help them move past that into dedication to a cause, not seeking revenge."

"And there's no one better to teach them than you, my heart."

"Go to sleep, Lady Mischief. Tomorrow we must begin to train our children."

A Learning Experience

Next morning they were awakened with a start. Mearith was shouting and banging on a cooking pot. "Up! Up you get! The days is half gone and you're still asleep. The king's men will have you at this rate while you're still in your beds. Up!" All the young Elves scrambled to their feet to find the sun not yet risen. The sky was just growing light.

Ariel groaned as she crawled from under her cloak and stretched. She smiled at the confused youngsters. "Lesson one. Always sleep light in the forest, especially with Lady Mearith around." She grinned and went to relieve herself.

"Lesson two," grinned Mearith, "food. Come, we'll see what we can find that you can eat."

Old Gormin chuckled as he returned from his watch post. "Personally, I'll feast on some of last night's meat." The Dwarves built up the fire and began to prepare food while Mearith led her charges into the trees.

Beren had looked to Ariel for guidance. Ariel smiled and pointed at Meg. Beren sighed her relief and moved closer to Meg. The queen went to the Dwarves and looked hopeful. Smiling with delight, they fed her.

After her meal Ariel and Marc saddled up and checked the back trail. They didn't return until nearly dark. They were in a hurry. "Up! Up and moving. Mearith, find us a defensive position. They're nearly here."

"This way," shouted Mearith, as the folk swiftly broke camp. A short distance away they found the steep trail climbing into the boulders. Up the trail they found a fairly flat area defended by tumbled stone. It was a scramble for the horses, but they made it.

"Ariel, who comes?"

"Pig men, dozens of them."

"Squealers?" asked Gormin. "Well then, let them come."

He got his wish as a horde of the small savage men appeared on their trail. Ariel's bow began to drop them, but they were far too many. As they swarmed up the steep path a boulder half the size of a man rose into the air then dropped onto them, crushing a few, bowling over several more and scattering the rest.

"Ha!" shouted Gormin. "Come on, Squealers, come to me. I'm hungry for pork!" He hurled another boulder at them.

The young Elves began to throw stones at them as well, but one of the Dwarves stopped them. "No, no, lad, not that one, this one here."

"Why?" asked the Elf. "What's the difference?"

"This one will shatter," grinned the Dwarf. "See that bunch there, behind that tree? You can't hit them from here, but you can hit the stone beside the tree. Watch now."

He turned and hurled the stone. It struck the boulder beside the tree and shattered on impact, sending shrapnel in all directions. He was rewarded with a few squeals of pain. "Ha. Now then, Lads, see the lines and layers in the stone? That's what you want to look for in this. If they were out in the open then a solid stone would be better."

The youngsters nodded and began hurling stones. A few were successful and they grinned with delight at every squeal.

Ariel continued to pick off the unwary few who showed themselves. A few spears flew up the hill at her, but she easily dodged them. The Elves gathered them up and threw them back. Suddenly

Ariel threw up her hand to stop the stones and spears. She'd heard Mearith battle song.

While the young Elves and Dwarves had held the attackers' attention, Mearith, Marc, and Gormin had slipped around and approached from behind. The battle was sudden and deadly.

As soon as they engaged the enemy, Ariel drew her sword and raced down the hill to join the fight, her young Elves right on her heels. As the queen waded in with flashing sword, the youngsters attacked with clubs, stones, and bare hands. The pig men broke and fled.

Ariel grinned and leaned on Gormin's shoulder while Mearith directed the Elves in looting the corpses and dispatching the wounded. They'd taken wounds themselves, and as soon as they were finished, Ariel directed them to Meg and Beren for bandaging.

"Well, my delight, what do you think of our fierce warriors?" asked Mearith.

"They have no lack of courage," replied Ariel. "However, I think they might have done better if you'd fed them more than beetles for breakfast."

"Lady Ariel," grinned one young fellow, "Lady Mearith says you've survived on beetles many times. How do you manage the taste?"

Ariel grinned. "There's a hardened gum that clings to the bark of the spruce tree. It has a sweet taste. I always keep a few knobs in my pocket for chewing after a meal of beetles. It crumbles at first, but keep chewing. It will soften. Chew, but don't swallow."

"That's good information, my Queen, and I will remember." He nodded and returned his attention to Meg who was bandaging up his arm.

"We need weapons for them, my heart."

"Agreed," said Mearith. "I'll distribute what we have."

"We have some to spare as well," said Gormin. "You'll have to teach them how to use them."

"We will," said Mearith. She stepped towards the youngsters. "I'm quite pleased with you all, my young fiercelings. Sadly, we have much daylight left and I would be well away from here before nightfall. Thus is the way of life in the forest. Come, we must hurry."

"The pig men are of the higher reaches," said Ariel. "We'll descend into the lowlands. On the morrow I'll ask you to hold the camp, Gormin. Mearith, Marc, and I have another errand."

The old Dwarf raised an eyebrow at her. "Oh?"

"We need cloaks, weapons, and horses. We'll buy what we can."

"And take the rest from whatever brigands we can find," said Mearith.

Just then there was a gasp from one of the youngsters. "What is it?" asked Ariel.

"The madness, Lady. I hear a voice on the wind."

Grinning with delight Ariel knelt beside him. "It isn't madness, your senses are awakening. All true Elves hear the song of the forest. What does Brother Wind say?"

"It said, welcome home, Bornani. Go below, snows will soon come here."

"Yes, you have heard truly."

"Ariel, perhaps you should stay with them for a few days while Marc and I go forage for supplies." Reluctantly, Ariel agreed.

Darkness had fallen when Mearith finally chose a campsite. Everyone was exhausted, so they ate whatever was available cold and settled down to rest. The youngsters awakened to heavy frost and three great cloaks covering their huddled forms.

Ariel was hunkered beside a small fire. She smiled as she heard them stirring. "Stay under the cloaks until we get the fire built up." The Dwarves quickly pitched in, and the fire rose up to warm the area. Food was soon cooking.

"Where is Lady Mearith?"

"She's gone for supplies. Yesterday you learned some of what can be eaten in the forest, and much more. You also learned that danger ever lurks in the forest. You fought well, and I'm proud of you. However, for today and tomorrow we will remain here."

"Lady?"

"It's the awakening. Do you not feel it? Hear it in the trees? This is where we'll concentrate today, and perhaps tomorrow, for we each awaken at our own pace. This day will bring many wonders to you."

Another gasp caught her attention. The young Elf who seemed to be the natural leader of the group had a bemused look on his face. Ariel quirked an eyebrow at him and he smiled. "The wind, it gave me a name. Tanis."

"That's a fine name," smiled Ariel. "It means strong."

"Lady, may I ask, what is that language is you speak to Lady Mearith?"

"It is the elder Elvish speech, the natural language of our people."

"The forbidden language," he nodded. "It's said it's the language of the evil magic that broke the world. Another lie?"

"Another lie, Tanis. The world was broken when our forbearers strove against the Geni who were invading our lands and enslaving our people. The Geni deceived and betrayed the Borni, then defeated the High Born in a battle of magic, for they called upon obscene powers. The world was broken, and we fell into slavery."

"Are we going to regain our power, Lady?"

"Yes and no, my friends. Yes, we will regain our rightful place and power, but not the place and powers held by the High Born. Once, long ago, the Borni and the High Born Elves were a single people, a people of the forest.

"In time the High Born became enamored of the high magic and separated themselves from the Borni and the forests. That, not the magic, was our true undoing."

"Is the magic our people used truly evil?"

"Lady Mearith says no, and she was there. She says magic is just another tool, like an axe or a hammer. It can be used to build or destroy."

They seemed to mull that over for a while then Tanis spoke again. "Lady, when you said we'd regain our place and power, what did you mean?"

She smiled at them as she spoke. "We were once of the forest, a part of it, at one with it and our fellow Elves, the Borni. We knew forest magic then, and lived incredibly long lives. That was in a time before the humans, Orcs, Geni, Ogres, and the rest came here.

"That's the place and the power I want us to regain. I want us to become one with the forest that gave us life as a species, to relearn her ways, her magic, and to reunite with the Borni. We will no longer be the slaves of the invaders, and we will never again be the High Born, we'll be the Bornani, the Children of the Forest."

Even as Ariel spoke the breeze began to dance in the treetops, birds sang in the branches, and the skies brightened. All the young ones smiled. "Lady, will you teach us the true language of our people?"

"I'd love to, shall we begin?"

"Wait for us," said one of the Dwarf women. "If we're to live among the Elves we might as well learn to talk to them." Ariel smiled with delight and welcomed them.

For the rest of the day and the next they worked on language and the newly awakened senses of the Elves. On the third day Ariel began basic weapons training with them and on the fourth they moved out. Mearith had not yet returned.

By the eighth day Ariel was getting concerned, there was no sign of Mearith and the air was growing colder. They'd moved slowly, but steadily deeper into the forest, ever heading in the direction of Fugitive, but Mearith grew no closer even though Ariel could feel her following. And then it hit her, she suddenly understood what had happened to Mearith.

Ariel was rubbing Grimm down with sweet grass and smiling as Tanis approached. They all wore weapons now; some Ariel had given them and some from the Dwarves. Gormin was with Tanis. "My Lady Ariel, I grow concerned about Lady Mearith. Should she not have returned by now?"

"Yes, my young friend, indeed Mearith should have rejoined us by now, but she won't, will she Gormin?"

"Lady?"

"Don't play coy with me, sir Dwarf. Mearith told you she'd be gone a long time and asked you to watch over us, didn't she?"

He grinned broadly. "Aye, that she did."

"Thought so. Tanis, Mearith and I are bonded companions. We were drawn together by the compulsion. No matter where she goes, no matter what she does, I can feel her here, inside me. For the past number of days she has paced along behind us, yet drawing no closer."

"Why would she do that, Lady?"

"To test me. Tanis, when I was awakened from the oshar I vowed to free all my people from slavery. Mearith vowed to help me, to teach me. Everything with her is a lesson, a test.

"Right now she's testing my ability to lead you, teach you, help you survive in the forest. She's testing my ability to inspire you, and testing my determination to continue in the face of the reality. It's one thing to make a vow in the arms of your lover when you're alone, and yet quite another to keep that vow in the face of adversity."

"What should we do? Lady, we'll try harder to ..."

"No, Tanis, no, this is my test to pass," said Ariel, a bright smile playing at her lips. "Do? We are the Bornani, are we not? You have all completed the awakening. Now we will pick up the pace and run through our beloved forest."

They moved out and ran, the trail was wide, and the horses were carrying all the camp supplies. The Dwarves were short legged, but seemed to have endless endurance. Three days later, Ariel awakened to see Mearith poking at the small fire and Meg curled up contentedly in Marc's arms.

Mearith grinned at Ariel, but she turned away, "I'm not talking to you. Everything with you is a test, a challenge."

"That is ever the way of life, my delight. Yes, I test you, and each time you rise to the challenge and exceed my expectations, my hopes. I'm so very proud of you."

Ariel laughed and rose to come to her. "You are no such thing; you're mean to me. That's what you are."

"If I kiss you will I be forgiven?"

"A single kiss? I doubt it. Three might work."

Mearith chuckled softly. "Three? Well then, I'd better get started."

They slowed the pace again. Now they had horses and better weapons, cloaks and proper boots, leggings, and tunics of wool. Every day now began with weapons training, wood craft and horsemanship while they marched, and ended with language practice.

Winter was fast approaching. A cold wind drew down off the mountains the day a strange Elf stepped out of the trees into their trail. Tanis stepped into his path with drawn sword, but the man just laughed merrily.

Ariel pushed Tanis' arm down then knelt before the stranger, "My Lord King."

A King Has Come

"**S**top it, Ariel. You're not getting away with this. Stand up and embrace me properly." With a merry laugh she rose and hugged him.

She stepped back and Mearith took her place in the man's arms. "Evan, what in the nine hells are you doing here alone?"

"Who says I'm alone?" He raised his arms, and with a sound like wind sighing through trees they came. Hundreds of them, all Borni warriors. The king pointed to Mearith's back trail and the wave of warriors swept past the weary travelers.

"Evan, why are you here?"

"Aren't you going to introduce me to your traveling companions?"

"All right, little brother, have your fun." Mearith turned to her party. "Hear me, friends and fellow travelers, this man is my brother, Evanseth, King of the Borni and all Elves."

"Oh no you don't. You and Ariel aren't saddling me with that title. I'm king of the Borni. Ariel is Queen of the Bornani, my compatriot, my ally, and fellow monarch. There will be no escape from your fate, Lady Ariel." He was grinning merrily and they all relaxed. Mearith introduced each in turn.

Four of the newly freed Elves still had not chosen names. When Ariel explained it to Evanseth, he nodded and approached them. They all knelt. "My Lord King."

"Rise, Bornani. So, you await your names, do you? Shall I give them to you?" They suddenly looked bemused. "Mearith says you have sworn to aid Ariel in her quest, If you're to be the queen's guard, you must have names, names that carry power, names to live up to in the days to come."

He was still smiling and they shyly nodded. He reached for the tallest. "You're an earnest looking fellow, I think Korath would suit you. It means wisdom in the Elder Tongue." The youth smiled his thanks.

He stepped to the next, a girl. He had a twinkle in his eye and so did she. "I name you Ollanth, child of joy." She beamed her delight.

The next was also a woman. He gazed into her liquid eyes for a long moment then spoke. "Belia, it was my Grandmother's name. She was a wise and strong woman. I charge you to bring honor to that name."

The girl swallowed hard. "Sire." He patted her arm and stepped past her to the last, a male. "Dorath. Young sir, that was my father's name. Wear it with pride, bring it honor."

He slapped the youth on the shoulder then turned to Mearith and Ariel. "Evan, why have you truly come? What's happened?"

"What's happened? You know full well what's happened, you and that scheming companion of yours. You come waltzing into the chamber of audiences, blabber on about all the beautiful and fertile young Elves being held captive in this realm, and you ask why I'm here?

"You were no sooner gone back through the portal when the word got out. Soon there was a steady stream of petitioners wanting to return to this realm of mortal danger. I was quite content to remain safely in my royal chambers, but I'd have faced a revolution. I had to come.

"Mear, you've reawakened the Borni from their slumber. The people have remembered who they are, and they're anxious to return to take up the task of defending the forests once again. I've come to see for myself what we're up against. It's a lucky thing I did."

Evanseth sighed deeply as a sudden light of understanding reached Mearith's eyes. "When?"

"As soon as I stepped through the damned portal. There was such a fuss, and I was intrigued, so I decided to have a look for myself. That was my undoing. Mear, what's this going to cost me?"

The merriment in her eyes brought a smile to his face again. Ariel looked puzzled, but Mearith made eye contact and gave a slight nod at the girl he had named Belia. Ariel's eyes widened as she noted the girl moving closer, her eyes fixed on the king. A wicked grin reached her lips and Evanseth groaned.

Ariel turned that grin on him. "Sire?"

Evanseth sank to one knee before her. "Lady Ariel, Queen of the Bornani, I come to beg a mighty boon of you."

Ariel's grin widened. "Rise, Evanseth, King of the Borni, my friend and ally. Ever you've been kind and generous to me. Ask your boon. If it's within my power to grant, you shall have your heart's desire."

"You're as bad as she is," he said as he rose, smiling in spite of himself. "Lady Ariel, I have, for the second time in my life, felt the Spiritpull, the call of Elvish love to another, a compulsion that cannot be ignored. There is a woman in your personal guard I would have as my bonded companion. I beg you to release her to me."

"What is her name?"

"She is called Belia." There was a gasp from behind him. He turned and took the girl's hand. "Come, my pet. If she won't release you we'll run off together anyway." Blushing furiously, she allowed him to raise her up and pull her close to his side.

Ariel was still grinning. "Belia, you've heard this man's plea. I must ask a great sacrifice of you, for the Bornani desperately need a tight alliance with the Borni. Will you do this for the good of all?"

A look of pure mischief crossed the girl's face as she cuddled closer to Evanseth. "If I must, Lady Ariel, I will do this for the good of the people."

Evanseth groaned and rolled his eyes as his arm encircled her waist and pulled her tighter to him. "By all the gods, I'm truly doomed, for now there are three of you to torment me."

"I didn't ..."

"Hush now, Lady Belia, I'm teasing, and so are they. Ariel wouldn't have agreed to this if you appeared to resist."

"Nor would he have asked it," said Mearith. "That's why he took so long to choose the name and why he chose that one. Come embrace me now, my new sister."

The girl seemed overwhelmed as first Mearith hugged her then so did Ariel. At that point the warriors returned. A tall man knelt before Evanseth. "All is well, My Lord, there are no enemies to be found and this new forest is welcoming. Did you find that which you sought?"

"I did, and I'll present Belia to the Borni as soon as we reach Sanctuary. Ariel, the Borni will return to the forests with the coming of spring. How many do you need for the winter?"

"As many as the Village can support, Sire. I need to ..."

"I've already fully supplied the village and more. That damned Orc is a demanding swine, but he's fierce and completely devoted to you. I've supplied his clan and their homes as well. Would twenty be enough? The rest of us are but a call away."

"I'm in your debt, Sire."

"No, Ariel, you brought Belia out of slavery and kept her safe for me to find. There's no debt here." Smiling, he turned to his gathered warriors. "Hear me, warriors of the Borni. This woman at my side is Belia of the Bornani who has agreed to be my companion and your queen. Welcome her."

The voices sounded as one as they all dropped to one knee. "Welcome, Lady Belia of the Bornani, Queen of the Borni."

Mearith stepped up to Belia and whispered to her. The girl nodded. "I promise, Lady." Mearith nodded then stepped back as Evanseth led his bride to an open spot between the trees. At his signal a light appeared and the Borni followed their king through it and disappeared.

Another Winter

They stood in silence as the portal faded with the last of the Borni passing through. After a long moment Ariel sighed and squared her shoulders. "Perhaps this is as good a place as any to camp for the night. Tomorrow we will arrive at Fugitive."

Camp was soon set up, the fire built up, and the horses rubbed down. Ariel smiled as she gazed at the extra supplies the Borni had left for them. Mearith sat beside her. "Where are your thoughts, my sweet?"

"With Evanseth and Belia. He's lived so long, and ever as a royal. She's known only slavery."

"Much like you and I."

"More so. You've lived as a warrior, a ranger of the forest, and a mercenary. I was raised in privilege by slave standards. Belia was raised as a breed slave and Evan has ever lived as a royal. The gap is greater for them."

"They'll be fine, my treasure. Tell me truly, what's robbing you of your joy?"

"It was the Borni," sighed Ariel. "I truly thought I had become one with the forest, that I was ready, that I could teach them, make them ready."

"But?"

"Hundreds of the Borni were here and I was unaware of them. The forest didn't tell me of them, and I sensed them not. I'm still a lost child compared to the Borni. If I can't sense the presence of so many how am I ever to keep safe those I bring out of the chains?"

Mearith put her arm around Ariel's shoulders and hugged her gently. "My delight, I knew nothing of their presence until Evan stepped into our path. If a Borni doesn't want you to know she's there, you won't know.

"This was Evan's little joke, you see. He knew by the Pull she was drawing closer. He would also have guessed she would be with us. He hid them to have his fun surprising us.

"Ariel, trust me, we're ready to begin the adventure, or we will be by the spring."

"Mearith, my heart, I do wish you'd stop keeping the bad things from me."

"Ariel?"

"I'm going to start a war, aren't I?"

"There was never any doubt about that, my delight. The humans, Orcs, and Geni see the Elves as property, nothing more. When we take them away we will be seen as the worst of thieves. People will be impoverished, angry, vengeful, and they'll want their property back.

"They'll make war on us if they can, they will set out bounties, hunters will arise seeking easy riches, every hand will be turned against us. The mages will be among them and great magics will be brought to bear against us, especially by the Geni."

"You knew all this in the beginning, didn't you?"

"I did, yes."

"Why didn't you tell me?"

"Why would I try to discourage you, my delight? No goal worth achieving comes easy. That jewel lay dormant for centuries waiting for you, your people have suffered intolerable abuse for generations, waiting for you, the forest itself has lain quiet, waiting for you."

"For me?"

"For the return of the queen, the one who would bring the Elves out of their chains and return them to the forest from whence they came, to reunite the Elves as one people, the people of the forest.

"We were born of this world untold ages ago to be Her guardians, to care for and nurture Her. The others came from other places. The Geni brought the Orcs and Ogres from a dark realm, but many of the Orcs changed once they lived in the light. The Ogres, not so much.

"The Dwarves came to the world as builders, the children of stone even as we are of the forest. We've always been allies in times of trouble. The humans came in massive metal ships of terrible power, but the ships left them here and did not return for them.

"Ariel, my heart, this world needs you if it's going to survive. The others will rip and tear at Her until nothing remains if we allow them free reign. The High Born failed to stop them, the Borni failed to stop them, our only hope lies in reuniting the Elves."

"So we must continue. You knew this as well, that's why you tried so hard to find the heir to the High Born."

"It was, yes."

Ariel snuggled down on Mearith's shoulder. "So, what are you not telling me?" she waited but got no reply. "My love, I must know. I can't do this in the dark of ignorance. You must tell me."

Mearith sighed deeply and relented. "When Evan returns in Spring he will make you Queen of all the Elves."

"Now wait ..."

"You must accept this, Ariel. I can't do this. I'm a warrior, not a monarch. Evan can't do this. He hasn't the vision for it, and he knows that as well. That's why he led the people to Sanctuary, to keep as many as possible alive until a true monarch returned.

"As time passed and no children were born to the Borni in Sanctuary, I knew it would be the heir of the High Born, if any had managed to survive. I was thrilled to learn they had, albeit in slave chains and under the curse, robbed of their senses and their lives shortened."

"Mearith, I can't ... I'm just an escaped slave ... I just ..."

"Yes?"

"I'm scared, terrified. I can't be queen of all the people. The Borni are so strong, wise, and powerful. I'm just ..."

"Lady Ariel, heir of the High Born, Queen of the Bornani. Ariel, my delight, think for a minute. You already had the desire and the vision when first we met. You already knew what had to be done. You already were thinking like a true queen, a queen with a vision."

"A queen with a vision of a free people, not of being a world savior."

"In this case they are one and the same, my delight. Think now of the magnitude of the task we've set for ourselves. Without the Borni we have no hope of any real success. You know this to be true."

"Will they truly accept me?"

"They will. Ariel, you heard Evan say how anxious they are to return. They know, and they're ready."

"And so you test me at every turn. You've been trying to prepare me for this all along, haven't you?"

"I have, yes."

"Then stop playing around and prepare me. The winter is little enough time."

Mearith's grin of approval made Ariel's heart soar. She wouldn't be on her own, Mearith would guide her, prepare her, and the Borni would fully support her. It would be another long winter of learning, but Ariel was suddenly looking forward to it.

Later, as Ariel took her turn at watch she spoke softly to the jewel that rested on her breast, it and the ring on her hand. "Listen carefully, my friends. We have a mighty task before us. The day may come when I'll need to call on you for all your power. Do not fail me." Both jewels glowed warmly for a moment and she smiled.

Next morning, when they set out, Ariel rode in the lead with Mearith at her side. Upon leaving the forest they saw the open fields and the newly erected huts of the Orc clan. Drakkat was the first to greet them.

Ariel leaped from her horse to grip his huge arm in the warrior's grip as she raised him to his feet. "Saggit found his way here all right?"

"He did, my Queen. The hearth stone lies within my hut as does the axe. Our fields are planted, our homes built, and our clan reunited."

"Then I'm well pleased, my friend."

They rode on to the village. Ariel was puzzled. She sensed Drakkat was holding something back. As they drew near she noted new buildings, repaired palisades, and a watcher in a new tower. Randall and Olan appeared and knelt. "Lady Ariel, you're a welcome sight indeed."

"Rise, my friends. Rise and embrace me. I've brought newcomers for you."

"So I see," grinned Randall, as he gently returned her hug.

"Ollan, this man is Tanis, captain of my guard. Take him and the rest to the Borni. Tanis, I'll be safe enough here, take the others, go with Ollan. Learn what the Borni can teach you."

She smiled as Ollan led them away. Mearith led the Dwarves to the smithy to introduce them to the smith who was the lone Dwarf in Fugitive. Ariel smiled as she watched them go, then turned back to Randall.

"Now, Randall, this man is Marc. He's a good fighter as well as a farmer. This is Meg, his bonded companion. Meg's a healer and this one is Beren, Meg's assistant. I thought Egma could use the help."

"Alas, Egma is beyond help now, Lady Ariel."

"No. What has happened?"

Randall sighed deeply. "What happens to us all with time. Egma has lived far longer than most Orcs, and her healing skills were mighty, but now her mind wanders along pathways long forgotten by most. She lives more in the past than the present."

"Meg, Beren, you are most welcome and badly needed."

"Take me to her," said Meg. "The wanderings of her mind may yet reveal much knowledge. She will need tending as well."

"She lives with Drakkat's folk now. Come, Marc, bring your women folk. There's an empty hut you can have and a field to tend."

As Randall led them away and Mearith returned, Ariel noticed how stiffly he moved. She also began to take a closer look at the village. There was a sense of unease, and she didn't like it. Everyone was heavily armed. "Mearith?"

"Yes, my delight, I feel it too. Something is amiss here. Olan returns, perhaps he can enlighten us."

The old Elf approached, a look of sadness on his face. Ariel beckoned him to her. "Olan, tell me, what has gone amiss here? Why is everyone so on edge? The fields have been harvested, the storehouses filled to bursting, and there was no need for Randall to journey to Magdan this year. The people should be celebrating."

He didn't speak, he just looked at the ground. It was the response of a slave who had the misfortune of delivering bad news to a master. Ariel recognized the posture.

Ariel took his arm and smiled. "Olan, you're a friend. More, you're my eyes and ears here in Fugitive. I can hear bad news without lashing out at an innocent. Please tell me what is amiss."

"I failed you, my Queen," he replied, sinking to one knee before her.

Ariel raised him up and linked her arm through his. "Come, old friend. Let's go into the inn and share a pint of ale. You can give me all the news."

Olan sat with downcast eyes; his hands cupped around the mug of ale. He still had not spoken. Ariel reached across the table to lightly grip his shoulder. "Olan, talk to me now. What happened?"

The old Elf sighed then brought his gaze up to hers. "It happened just before the Borni King appeared with his warriors. The Borni have been watching the forests, but we've been watching the road and fields. I was on watch at the great tree by the swamp road.

"Deep in the night Dirk put a knife into Randall's back and fled. He reached my post at the swamp and said he was there to relieve me. It was time for the change, and I thought nothing of it.

"I returned to find Randall lying in a pool of blood. I woke the others then went after Dirk, but he was long gone. Arlon sent two warriors after him, but I know not if they succeeded in capturing him or not. My Queen, I..."

"Hush now, old friend. The fault here lies with Dirk, not with you. Have you any idea why he did this?"

"None, my Queen."

"I do," said Randall as he joined them. "The young fool. I've seen this before, but didn't notice it in him at first. He doesn't like being close to the other races. He kept it well hidden, but I began to see it.

"He resented Drakkat's teasing as he tried to teach the boy better fighting skills. He let his disdain for Olan and the others show when he thought no one was looking, and he began to resent me as I started to rely more and more on Olan to help me. He felt he should be given more authority, after all, he had been a member of the City Watch."

"So, if we're lucky he returned to the south, and if not, he ran straight to Dorgon," sighed Ariel.

"Tell us the rest of it, Randall," said Mearith.

"The boy had eyes for Ariel," sighed Randall, "but you knew that already. I thought it would pass in time, as it so often does with the young.

"Anyway, as I began to trust him less and less he became more and more distant. I'd hoped to speak to you about it at your return, but it was too late."

"Dammit anyway," said Ariel, as she slammed her mug on the table. "I trusted that man. Mearith, what'll we do if they failed to catch him?"

"The options aren't good. We could abandon Fugitive, or we could fight. If Dirk went to Dorgon he'll likely send a hundred men. If we contact Evan we can easily have enough warriors to repel them."

"I know the Geni well enough to know they'd just amass an army and come at us again. I like Fugitive, it's my home. Evanseth wants to bring the Borni here as a landing site for a full return to Elendor."

A glance at Mearith told Ariel this was going to be another test. She sighed and pulled the jewel from her tunic. It throbbed with power in her hand. "Tell me, my friend, do you know of a way to protect Fugitive without getting everybody killed in the process?"

The jewel pulsed in her hand and her attention drifted away. As though in a dream, she saw the swamp with the magic road, then beyond it. She saw the forest move and shift until the road they had traveled with Randall was obliterated. Only vague forest paths remained between Fugitive and Magdan.

Ariel shook off the spell as the jewel stopped pulsing with light and returned to a soft glow. The others were watching her carefully, concerned. "My friend and protector has shown me another possibility.

"In the vision I saw the forest move, change, until not a single trace of the road remained between Magdan and the swamp. Mearith, is this possible? Is it the high magic or is this old forest magic?"

"It is possible, my delight. Yes, it's old forest magic."

"Could you do it?"

"No love, I'm a warrior, not a mage."

"Could those ladies of the Borni do it? The ones who made the portal we passed through?"

Mearith grinned with delight, making Ariel's heart sing. She'd gotten it right. Ariel pulled a small pouch from her pocket. A stone was dumped into her palm, and she called out. "My Lord Evanseth, are you there?"

"I am here, my Queen. What do you need?" Ariel explained the situation. "I'll prepare my people, Lady Ariel. If the traitor is caught I'll send only the magic workers. Should an armed force be sent against you, I'll send warriors to deal with them first before we disturb the trees."

Ariel thanked him then dropped the stone back into the small pouch. "Now, Mearith, my heart, tell me the price."

"The price?"

"The price for using this magic. I have seen the mages in the city and listened to them talk to their apprentices. One thing they all agree on is that there is a price to be paid for using magic.

"When I used the jewel to kill the swamp demon the stone lay cold and lifeless at my breast for days until I brought it into the sunlight and there it returned to life. I used it and for three days thereafter I was without its protection, a price paid for its use."

"When the mage comes ask her, my delight, for she will know far better than I. In times past such magics were often used to confound enemies. The price was always a promise to protect the forest, a price we happily paid. That was the old forest, but I see no reason why this new forest would be any different."

"So, the question then becomes, would Dorgon know this, and if so what would he do?"

"He will surely know," replied Mearith, "and then attack the forest with axe and fire to draw us out."

Ariel sighed and rested her head in her hands. "I don't want this to become a war of magics. We're no match for the Geni in such a battle. That's a mistake of the past that I don't want to repeat."

"What else can we do, Lady" asked Olan.

"I don't know, but we need to find a way. Olan, fetch Drakkat, Saggit, Arlon, and Gormin. We need to have a council of war. Gormin is the leader of the Dwarves who accompanied us at our return. I believe you'll find him at the forge."

"My Queen." With that he was up and gone.

Ariel arose and began to pace. "Mearith, will you not help me here?"

"With all my power, my delight. Tell me what you need."

"Do you see another way?"

"No. I would lead the people deep into the mountains and take my chances with the winter. Ariel, my way is the last resort. Consider all others first."

"Yes, before I risk my people with the mountain snows I will explore all other options first. No, there must be another way, and I'm determined to find it." She resumed her pacing.

Olan returned with the others and Ariel soon brought them up to speed. She gave them time to absorb the situation before asking their input. "Well, my friends, there it stands. I'm willing to hear any and all suggestions."

Arlon was staring at her open mouthed. "You aren't willing to defend the trees? Truly you are not my sister." Drakkat's axe and Mearith's sword appeared at his throat instantly.

"Let him go," said Ariel. She paced towards him, her eyes cold and the jewel at her breast pulsing. There was a sneer on her lips as she spoke. "You'd have me defend the trees at the forest's edge where the woodcutters harvest winter's fuel as well as building timber?

"You'd have me commit the last of your people as well as my own to a position we could not defend, but would leave us exposed to the enemy?"

She leaned across the table to go nose to nose with him. "And what would you suggest I do when the Geni set fire to that forest, their armies waiting for us to act?

"Your king wants to return to this realm to save his people who are dying. Would you then have me sacrifice the last of the Borni to a lost cause?"

Ariel thrust herself away from him and resumed her pacing. "I need council here, Arlon, not childish censure."

"Forgive me, my Queen, for I spoke foolishly and out of turn. I forgot myself and spoke as though to my sister. There is more of her in you than you know for she would have responded as you did."

"Queen Ariel isn't your sister," said Drakkat, his voice cold and implacable. "Show her disrespect again and I'll have your head from your shoulders before she can stop me."

Arlon swallowed hard and moved back from the angry Orc. "Be at peace now," said Ariel as she lightly patted the big Orc's shoulder. "Let's get back to the issue at hand."

"We could get lucky," said Gorim. "The Elves might catch him."

"Feeling that lucky, are you?" asked Darkkat.

"No, not really. All right, if we can't move the forest, can we move the swamp?"

"What do you mean?" asked Mearith.

"I don't like swamps, they breed those monsters. Is there enough water flowing up stream to make a river where the swamp lies?"

"Probably," said Randall. "We only diverted enough to make the swamp because we still needed the road."

"For what reason?" asked Arlon.

"Trade. As a small village we had need of many things, food, tools, weapons, medicines, etc. After a few years we began to make goods of our own to sell and trade in the city. Each year different people went so we wouldn't be recognized from year to year."

"We no longer need the road," said Drakkat. "We can trade among ourselves and with the Dwarves or Elves. We can grow food and fodder as well as make leather and steel."

"Agreed, and there are other ways to reach the city now," said Ariel. "So, we don't need the road, but we come back to it. How do we move it without tying ourselves to a bargain we can't keep?"

"We could be getting ahead of ourselves here," grinned Saggit. "First, we need to know if the traitor was caught. Second, if he wasn't then we need to prepare for the attack. If he was, then we can deal with the road."

"He's right," sighed Ariel as she resumed her seat beside Mearith. "However, let's assume he got away and prepare. Mearith, my heart, the impending attack is the type of thing you're most experienced with. Will you advise me on this?"

"Yes, my delight. I suggest we gather our best fighters and start out to meet the Elves who pursued him. If he eluded them we call Evan for reinforcements, try to be well into the forest when they come.

We let them march a few days then we take them in the night, removing the bodies and all trace of them from the road. If they are ever found it should be deep in the forest, far from the path the traitor gave them."

Ariel nodded then turned her attention to Gormin. "You have an idea how to divert the waters?"

"I'm a Dwarf," he grunted. "Building is what we do best. I'll need to see the place, but a dam or two are easy enough to construct."

"So be it. Randall can show you the place. Decide what you'll need and prepare your plans. Arlon, gather your people. Drakkat, bring a few of your best and join us on the road?"

The big Orc grinned as he leaped to his feet. "How many do you need?"

"Enough for a personal guard. I won't risk my young Elves in a pitched battle with seasoned warriors just yet. Olan, find the youngsters and keep them here to defend Fugitive if necessary."

"My Queen." He was up and gone instantly.

"You have another issue, Arlon?"

"Lady Ariel, the Borni should be your guard, not the Orcs."

"Drakkat has defended my back successfully before, Arlon," replied Ariel. "He's earned the right and the trust. You haven't." His back stiffened at that. "Speak to me as your sister again and you never will have my confidence."

"My Lady..."

"It was not the concern you voiced," she said, "it was your tone that offended them, and me. Arlon, I've said before I need your instant and complete obedience. The way you spoke suggests you still think of me as a child, an untried and inexperienced leader. It tells me you would argue when I most need your support and compliance."

"Please don't send me away, Lady Ariel. I just ..."

Ariel went nose to nose with him again. She gazed deeply into his eyes for a long moment. "You blame yourself for her death."

His voice choked as he replied. "I was supposed to be with her that day. I was supposed to be with her on that patrol, but she sent me away to defend our mother's retreat to Sanctuary." He was trembling and trying to get control of his emotions.

"Whatever am I going to do with you? Mearith, my heart, help me here. What should I do with him?"

"What do you want to do with him, my delight?" Mearith was grinning.

"I trusted Dirk because he was a friend and he betrayed me. I don't like Arlon at all, so I think I can probably trust him."

"I do agree."

Arlon was stunned. He tried twice before he found his voice again. "My Lady?"

Ariel lightly gripped his shoulder for a moment. "The problem here is quite simple, my friend. In spite of your best efforts, you still see me as your sister returned. I'll keep you close to me for a few months until you get accustomed to the difference.

"Once the Borni return, we'll see where we stand. If you survive."

"Lady?"

"Drakkat will be watching," said Mearith, "and so will I."

Traitor

They set out at a canter, Ariel leading with her personal guard close behind and Mearith at her side. Arlon seemed somewhat uncomfortable riding among the Orcs. Mearith saw his discomfort and grinned. Darkness fell and they camped just off the road then set out again at first light.

Late in the day they met the two Borni returning with Dirk. His hands were bound, and he'd been in a fight. They threw him to the ground then knelt to Ariel. "Here is the traitor, Lady Ariel."

"Well done. Rise and tell me of his capture." She leaped from the saddle to speak directly to them.

"Lady, a horse was always kept at the watch station to provide a faster warning for the village. He took the horse but rode him into the ground. We found the poor beast in the road, dying. We gave it peace then we continued on.

"We finally caught up with the traitor. He was speaking to a talisman held in his hand, describing the way to Fugitive. We stopped him before he could complete the task, but I fear he conveyed enough. That was three days ago."

"Thank you, you have done well." She patted his shoulder then stepped past to face Dirk. "Why did you betray me, Dirk? We're friends."

"Tell that to Kizen, he was a friend."

"He gave up that designation when he set out to capture me and to kill Mearith. Tell me of this talisman you spoke to, what was it? Where did you get it? Who did you speak to?"

He just spat at the ground by her feet then looked away. Her blow sent him sprawling. "Arlon."

The Elf was beside her in an instant. "My Queen?"

"You heard my questions. Get the information from him, the rest of us will find a suitable campsite for the night."

"Yes, my Queen." He grabbed Dirk and hauled him to his feet. "Speak."

Dirk spat at him, but Arlon just laughed. A dagger leaped to his hand and pressed against the man's genitals. "Speak," he said again. He pressed hard with the blade and Dirk pulled away, his eyes wide with fear.

"That's what humans do to unruly slaves, isn't that right?" Arlon advanced on him. "They geld them, don't they?"

"Don't, please..."

"Answer Lady Ariel's questions. What was the talisman, where did you get it?"

"It was a fetish, Lord Dorgon gives them to all the men sent out on missions. It's so they can report back to him."

"Where did you get it?"

"From Kizen's body."

"And you spoke to the Geni?"

"Yes." Dirk hung his head, beaten.

Arlon turned to see Ariel still waiting. He turned back to the hapless man. "Why? Why did you betray those who had taken you in?"

"Took me in? They were planning to make me slave. Randall wouldn't trust me with any authority, the damned Orc enjoyed embarrassing me at every turn, and your arrogance was more than I could bear. Tell me, Elf, what possible reason could I have had to stay?"

"You were free to go at any time, Dirk," said Ariel. "No one would force you to stay. If all you wanted was to get away, there was no need for betrayal."

"Where would I go. Ariel? How would I live with no money and no prospects? No, I needed the bounty."

"You'd see us all killed for gold? I truly thought better of you, Dirk."

"Truly, Ariel? You never once showed it."

"Apparently, my instincts were wiser than I. Bring him, we'll geld him and send him back to the Geni." Dirk screamed a protest and leaped at her. He fell to the ground, Arlon's blade through his heart. Her face like stone, Ariel mounted Grimm and turned away.

Mearith soon found a suitable campsite, and everyone settled down. All were quiet and gave Ariel space to her own thoughts. Finally she spoke. "Mearith, my heart, how did it come to this? Dirk and I were friends in the Watch, and again at Fugitive. How did it come to this pass?"

Mearith sighed then spoke. "He was a man of small thoughts. At first he was a friend to you in the Watch. Once he was with us in Fugitive he was almost a pet at first as you helped nurse him back to health. He felt important, and important to you.

"However the small places where he felt important began to shrink. More people came, and they embraced you as queen. After the battle you heaped honor on Drakkat, but not him. His resentment grew.

"As it became clear Fugitive would soon become larger and his role there would grow smaller, he responded with betrayal, hoping for riches and accolades from the Geni. He was a man with a lot of potential, but he was in too much of a hurry. Randall could have taught him much, and with time, who knows."

Ariel nodded as she absorbed this. She looked to Drakkat and he nodded his agreement with Mearith's assessment.

"Arlon."

He was instantly at her side. "Yes my Queen?"

"I tested you this day and you proved your worth to me. You resented riding with the Orcs, yet you held your peace. Knowing Dirk was once a friend you found a way to make him talk without hurting him, yet when he came at me you acted."

"My Queen, I assumed you said what you did to provoke him to act."

"Yes, you were right. I couldn't bring myself to hang a friend, and your blade was faster. It was the only mercy I could spare him. Please resume your station as commander of the Borni."

"Thank you, my Queen." He turned to see Drakkat blocking his path. The big Orc grinned and offered his hand. Arlon sighed and, with a sheepish grin of his own, accepted the hand.

"So, Mearith, my heart, where are we now?"

"Facing a problem, my delight. Dorgon knows of Fugitive now, and of how to reach it. There is probably a fighting force already on the road."

"That's my thought as well. There has to be a way to fool them up without compromising everything. Is there anything you can think of to throw them off the scent?"

Mearith thought for a moment then grinned. "There is one possibility, but it could prove dangerous."

"Tell me."

"There's a certain mushroom that grows in this forest. It's a powerful intoxicant, causing visions and more. If we could manage to get some into the cooking pots of the soldiers, it could prove interesting."

"Indeed, but how does this help us?"

"Dorgon sends a communication fetish with the men he sends out, so Dirk informed us. Now, imagine if his men began to hallucinate and contacted him with description of what they are seeing."

Ariel chuckled. "That truly could be fun. So, can you find some of these mushrooms for us?"

"They're growing beside the tree you rest against, my delight."

Ariel turned and noticed a ring of spindly mushrooms. "Those?"

"Those, yes. That handful there would be more than enough. I'll need help to get them into the cooking pot, though."

"I can help with that," grinned Drakkat. "We enter their camp together just as they begin to settle down. You pretend to be my slave and I order you to help with the cooking."

Mearith laughed with delight. "I like it, Master Darkkat. I'll go gather a few herbs for the pot right now." She rose with liquid grace, chose a broad leaf from another plant, and used it to harvest the mushrooms. Grinning, she folded the package and stored it in her saddlebag.

The next morning they set out, two of the Borni ranging far ahead. The day was well along when they came hurrying back. "They're coming."

At that warning everyone faded off the road and hid in the trees. They watched as nearly eighty men rode past, all heavily armed. They had three Elvish slaves with them. Intent on the road ahead they were unaware of the shadows that followed silently through the trees.

Soon enough the leader called a halt. "We'll make camp here. This will be the last night we dare chance a fire. Get the fire started and some food on the go, I'm half starved."

The slaves had run alongside the pack horses. They swiftly pulled down a bundle of firewood and lit it. Shortly the cooking pot came out and water was put on to boil.

The men tethered the horses then gathered round the now roaring fire. Guards were posted and the remainder settled down to rest. All at once there was a commotion on the road. "Halt, who goes there, friend or foe?"

"That depends," came Drakkat's deep booming voice.

"What do you mean, it depends?"

"It depends on if you'll share the food or not." The guard began to bluster, but Drakkat nudged his horse forward, pushing the soldier aside. He suddenly faced a number of drawn swords, but ignored them. "Elf, get your useless hands out of your pockets and go assist the cook."

"Yes, Master." Mearith fought to hide her grin as she grabbed the two sacks from the saddle of Drakkat's horse.

"Hey there, what's in that sack?"

"Meat, mushrooms, my Lord."

"Get on with you," said Drakkat. "I said I'd share the food if they do. So, are you men headed for Magdan?"

"Magdan? You're going the wrong way, you foolish Orc."

The man who'd spoke suddenly gulped and leaped back as Drakkat's huge battle axe leaped to his hand. The party leader stepped between them. "All right, settle down, settle down. He's right, Orc, Magdan is back the way you came."

"Can't be," grunted Drakkat, as he slung the axe across his shoulder. "Nothing back there but that thrice damned swamp. Cursed thing is old mad magic, every time you manage to cross it, you're on the wrong side again. That fool we met said Magdan was this way."

"What fool would that be?"

"Some babbling human, going on about Elvish armies, towns lost in the mist, queens of old, couldn't make sense of any of it. So, you lot look like you're here with a purpose. Got any use for a mercenary?"

"You?"

"If you doubt my worth in battle, friend, I'd be happy to demonstrate for you." The axe had slipped to the ready position again.

"Relax, Orc. Relax. You can join us if you wish, take all the booty you can carry, kill as many as you like, just keep one Elf alive."

"Which one?"

"The one they call the queen."

"That again. You sure you haven't already been through the swamp of madness?"

While Darkkat kept the soldiers distracted, Mearith helped the Elves with the cooking. "Don't eat any of this," she whispered. "Don't even taste it." Their eyes widened as she pulled her hood back a bit to expose her tattoos. She winked then pulled the hood forward again.

Soon the men began to file past the fire, the cooks filling each bowl as it was presented. Mearith winked at Drakkat as she filled his bowl. As the others ate their fill, he carefully spilled his on the ground. A short while later the fun began.

Suddenly a man screamed in fear and lashed out at something in the air. He leaped to his feet and ran into the forest. Another began to sing a bawdy song and tried to kiss the man next to him. Another screamed, "Dragon!" and tried to hide beneath his saddle.

It got worse, much worse. Mearith chuckled with delight as Drakkat gave her the signal. The leader had pulled out his fetish and begun to babble at it. Drakkat grinned as he heard the Geni raging at the leader to make sense.

There was no sense to be had, just inane babbling about a naked Orc woman riding on a wild boar while feeding berries to a dragon. He reported the road dancing a jig and suddenly rising into the air to disappear into the stars.

Still grinning with delight, Drakkat rose and helped Mearith to lead the slaves back down the road and into the trees. It was near dawn when the men began to recover their wits, then they became sick.

It was the day after that they managed to get into the saddle again and turn back towards Magdan. Through it all Ariel and her party watched from the trees. When they were satisfied the men would not return, they turned back to Fugitive.

Laying Plans

A riel watched from hiding as the soldiers rode away. When they were well out of sight and hearing she returned to the road. "Arlon."

"My Lady?"

"Send someone for the horses, it's time to go home."

"My Queen." He bowed and turning, began to bark orders. Six Elves rose easily to their feet and disappeared into the forest. They were soon back with the horses.

"Mearith."

"Yes, my delight?"

"How many did we kill?"

"We killed seven and among themselves they killed another dozen more, several more are wounded. They will have a tale to tell when they return, and an angry Geni to face."

"How did you know of the mushrooms?"

"The great healers, spirit walkers, and mystics sometimes ingest a small portion of the mushroom. They believe it will carry them to the spirit realms where they can learn more healing, or obtain greater knowledge."

"You don't believe that?"

"I don't, no. Experience has taught me otherwise."

"Experience?"

"Yes, my delight, experience. Distraught and tormented at the loss of Elaith, Arlon and I both ingested a tiny portion of the mushroom potion. We found no spirits, no Elaith, only a madness we could not understand."

Ariel sighed. "I'm sorry I'm not her returned to you both. You have suffered so much."

"Ariel, my heart, my delight, listen to me carefully. You are more than she could have ever been. So much more you bring to me. Yes, I lost her, and mourned her for centuries, but were the option given I would not give you up, not even for Elaith returned."

With tears in her eyes Ariel raised her gaze to meet Mearith's. "Truly?"

"Truly, my delight," replied Mearith, as she gently took Ariel in her arms. "Never doubt that, my love." Gently she kissed the trembling girl.

Ariel hugged Mearith tightly. "Forgive me, my heart. Sometimes I don't feel like a queen, just a lost little girl."

"Hush, now, all is well. Here come the horses, it's time to put the queen's cloak back on."

With a sigh, Ariel released her hold on her lover and stepped back. "I begin to see why Evanseth wants to pass off the crown. It weighs heavy at times."

Mearith smiled and handed her up into the saddle then mounted and brought her horse alongside. "Eat this, it will help ease your mind."

"Mearith?"

"It's been far too long since you've eaten. The hunger brings a sadness with it. The rest of our party made a cold meal, but you spent your time making sure all was well with them, and the newly freed slaves. You took no time for yourself. Eat now, my delight, it will help you feel better."

Ariel chewed thoughtfully on the meat as they rode along. When she finished Mearith passed her a piece of bread. When that was finished Ariel was much revived. Mearith smiled with delight to see her renewed.

Randall was waiting for them at the edge of the swamp. "All went well, my Queen?"

"It did, old friend. Come, join us at the inn and we'll swap tales." Smiling, he turned his horse and joined them.

As they reached the inn Ariel called out. "Drakkat, Arlon, Randall, Saggit, join us for a council of war. Someone fetch Olan and Gormin as well."

As soon as all were gathered, and she had related the tale for the mushrooms, Ariel turned to Randall. "Now, Randall, what news?"

"Fugitive grows stronger my Queen, however, I don't. I find myself relying more and more on Olan to perform my tasks for me."

"Randall?"

"Fugitive grows, Lady Ariel, and you need a headman with more energy than I have to spare. I've already lived far longer than I had a right to expect. Olan has a talent for organizing and everyone knows and trusts him. I suggest you make him you new headman."

Ariel sat back, wide eyed. "You're serious?"

Randall shifted uncomfortably on the bench. "I am, my Queen."

"Very well then, I so declare it. Olan, will you take on this task for me?"

"I will, my Queen, until such time as you can find another."

"Olan?"

"My Queen, with your permission, I'll join your forces in the forest as you set free our people."

Ariel sat quietly for a moment. "Very well, someone fetch Marc for me."

"I'm here, Lady Ariel."

"Please join us. Marc, Randall wants to retire, and Olan wants to go to war. I need a headman for Fugitive, a man I can trust, will you do this for me?"

"Lady, I'd be honored. Will the people accept me?"

"It's my hope they will, and I'll speak to them all soon. Now, in the spring the Borni will return. Fugitive must be ready to welcome them. Randall, I now appoint you chief adviser to the new headman. Arlon, you have until spring to make certain Olan is ready for war.

"Now, Gormin, what of the dams and rivers?"

"The dams are nearly built already, Lady. Marc suggested we let them fill up, but not change the water's course as yet. I like his reasoning."

"Marc?"

"I thought we could leave them ready until needed. With the water being held back suddenly released, half an army would be swept away if they were already in the swamp."

Mearith nodded her approval and Ariel smiled brightly. "I like it. Olan, how are the members of my guard faring?"

"They are becoming fierce warriors, my Queen. They thirst for knowledge and constantly badger one and all for more wood craft and weapons training."

"Arlon, don't kill their spirit with over training, but make sure they're ready when the snows melt."

"Yes, my Queen."

"And now for the roadway." She pulled out the calling stone and called to Evanseth.

"I'm here, my Queen. What do you need?"

"We've dealt with the soldiers for now, but someone who could wield the old forest magic would be a great help."

"They'll be there within the hour, my Queen."

"Wonderful. Oh, Evanseth."

"Yes, my Queen?"

"You're not going to get away with it, you know."

His great bellowing laugh was heard by all. "It was worth a try." The stone went quiet and he was gone.

"Ariel?"

"Relax, my heart, I was only teasing him. Now for the rest of our defenses. The mountains guard our backs, and Drakkat holds the fields between here and the forest. So, let's now look forward to the future.

"They will raise armies against us, but I believe I have a way to keep them away from Fugitive. However, there's more I must learn. Mearith, my heart, tell me of the mountains."

"The mountains?"

"Yes. What of them? Are there tracks through them? What are the dangers there? What lies beyond? Does anyone live there and if so might they make allies or enemies?"

Mearith smiled her delight at Ariel. "The mountains are broad and much I have not yet explored. However, there are a few tracks through, depending on where you want to go. Far to the west they fall away into deep waters.

They are too high for much forest to grow, but some does in broad hidden valleys cut by swift moving rivers. I have found many wandering monsters as well as the pigmen there, and a few small villages of hardy Dwarves. Why do you ask?"

"Only a dream. I'd hoped to hear that vast forests lay beyond that could be reached, a place beyond the reach of the Geni."

"I do believe such a place might exist, but I've not yet traveled there since my return. You know of where I speak, Randall."

"Narthwood. The endless forests of the north, known as Narthwood, lie well to the north of Shotar, Lady Ariel. There are a few hardy rangers who venture there, and they speak of vast forests and broad rivers. They go there to hunt and trap animals, but even they don't venture far into the reaches of Narthwood."

"What are you thinking, Ariel?" asked Mearith.

"I was thinking of the peace and the homes of the place you call Sanctuary. We dare not make such homes anywhere near the Geni's reach. I wondered if there was such a place in this world for the Borni to retreat to. A place for the elders, young mothers with children, the mystics, scholars, etc.

"I want a place for them to be safe and that won't be possible here."

"You don't want them at Fugitive, Lady Ariel?" asked Marc.

"There's too many, Marc. Ah well, perhaps we can make Fugitive safe for all. We shall approach that task first of all."

Just then the door opened and two people entered, an older Elf and a younger Elf woman. They approached and knelt. "Lady Ariel, you sent for mages of the forest?"

"I did, yes. Come, sit with us. Introduce yourselves."

They sat. "I'm Orin and this is my niece, Trelanth. I've studied the ways of forest magic all my life and have taught my apprentice as much as I could. What would you have of us, Queen Ariel?"

"There's a roadway to this place. We have defenses, but the roadway is a weakness that the Geni have recently been made aware of. Now, the city is here," she said, placing the salt bowl at one end of the table, "and we are here." She set the ale tankard at the other end of the table.

"If possible I'd like for the roadway to peter out into a small swamp about here." Ariel had trailed salt to indicate the road. She broke it at the halfway mark with her finger. "Is this possible?"

"Easily," smiled Orin. "The process would take about two days. We'd need to be left in peace to work, but it's not a difficult spell. May I ask, why the swamp?"

"There's a wide swamp near here, and the Geni know about it now."

"Ah, so if the road ends at a swamp, but there is nothing on the other side, they'll believe they received false information."

"Exactly. Now, tell me the cost."

"The cost, Lady?"

"The use of magic comes at a cost. If the cost to you is too great we'll find another way."

"Lady Ariel, have no fear of the cost. We'll need to eat and rest a bit extra, and the forest will ask for protection, but that's a given for the Borni anyway. The forest knows the Borni. My Queen, there is no reason to fear on our account. We can do this for you easily enough."

"That is good news, Orin. When can you start?"

"Would right now be too soon?"

Ariel laughed with delight. "The day grows late, my eager friend. We will eat then rest and set out in the morning. Two days steady travel should put us where we want to be.

"Arlon and the Borni will stand guard for you, Drakkat and his Orcs will watch the road from behind, and I, with my young savages, will watch the road ahead. Arlon send the young guard to me then get some rest."

Mearith smiled at Ariel. "What else is going through your mind, my delight?"

"Well, here's what I want to do, if we can. I want to hit the slave auction at Magdan next year. I want to let them see us take the freed people into the forests here, at the south. While they seek us there I want us to swing around to the north and disappear into the northern forests.

"If all goes as planned there will be Borni there to meet us and to nurture the newly freed. We then return to Fugitive for the winter to lay more plans. This is my hope."

Mearith nodded. "Perhaps we should make Fugitive safe first."

"Getting ahead of myself again, was I?"

"Just a bit."

Ariel laughed then grabbed Mearith's hand, "Come, my heart, let's go rub down the horses."

They set out the next morning. Two days of steady travel brought them to the place Ariel wanted. A small stream crossed the road at a tight turn. Orin smiled as he looked it over. "An excellent choice of location, Lady Ariel."

"We camp for the night. Tomorrow we'll guard the road so you can work." They set up camp in a clearing a short distance from the road. They were just about to make a fire when Tanis came rushing into the clearing. "Riders."

"Where? How many?"

"At least twice our numbers, Lady Mearith. Lady, they have a mage with them."

"Human or Geni?" asked Orin.

"Human, sir."

"I'll deal with that one. Lady Ariel?"

Ariel had a hard look in her eye. "We tried to frighten them away, but no. This time they will not return. How long do we have?"

"Moments only, my Queen."

"Then come." With that Ariel swiftly saddled Grimm and mounted. A glance showed her the others readying bows. Only she and Mearith were mounted.

"Choose your targets carefully," said Mearith. She urged the big war horse into the trees. The Elves followed swiftly.

As they reached the road they heard the jingle of harness and the thunder of hooves. The riders splashed across the stream then a hail of arrows came from the trees. Half their number fell from the saddle.

In the confusion a stallion screamed a challenge then burst from the forest. Grimm slammed into the remaining riders knocking down several horses. He screamed again and reared up, lashing out with his hooves.

Even from the back of the plunging mount, Ariel brought down two more men with her bow. Mearith wove through the melee, cutting and slashing with her sword. Men fell and others fled before her, but they ran into Drakkat and his Orcs.

Suddenly a light flared and an Elf exploded in fire. The mage waved his hands and prepared to cast another bolt, but he was suddenly hurled face down in the stream. With a snarl of rage he spun and thrust out his hand.

Orin staggered back, but didn't fall. He grinned as he thrust out his own hand and closed it into a fist. The mage gagged then fought like a fish on the hook, but he could not draw breath. His struggles weakened and he slowly sank to the ground where his body withered and decayed into dust.

"As I thought," muttered Orin. A ball of light surrounded him and Trelanth. A sword bounced off it, but they ignored the weak blow.

There were a few cries for quarter, but none was given. Ariel was impressed with her young guards. They fought like demons, as did the Borni. Soon all were dead. Ariel stood watching as the Elves looted the bodies then stacked them out of sight in the trees.

In the midst of the carnage crouched two Elves, trembling with fear. "Tanis."

He was at her side in a heartbeat. "Yes, my Queen?"

"You and your companions did well. I won't leave you behind for another again."

"Thank you, my Queen." He was beaming with delight.

"Now, take those two there back to the campsite. Get those slave collars off them and give them some real food."

"With pleasure, my Lady." He whistled and his troops came to him. They gathered up the two frightened Elves and led them into the forest.

Orin approached Ariel. "Orin, what happened there? He seemed to dissolve; did you do that?"

"No, Lady. Humans are quite short lived. To gain true power takes a long time, ages of study and practice. That one had remained well beyond his years, kept alive by the magic. By closing off his breath it weakened him so time could reassert her authority. I didn't kill him, he perished because he could no longer control the spell that kept him alive."

His attention was drawn past her shoulder. "Lady Mearith returns."

Ariel nodded. "Arlon as well."

"None escaped to report back," said Mearith, as she lightly dismounted beside Ariel. "Arlon?"

"None escaped behind us, Lady Mearith. My men will search on the morrow in any case, just to be certain."

Ariel nodded her approval. "We will search ahead then," said Tanis, as he returned. "Lady Ariel, the others have set up the camp and have the fires going. The newly freed are still trying to understand that the collars are gone forever."

Smiling with delight, Ariel patted his shoulder. "Well done. Come, people, the Royal Guard has food on the fire. Let's be away from this place of blood and take our rest." She caught up the reins of her horse, linked her arm through Mearith's and started out. The others followed.

Two days later Ariel stood in the road smiling with delight. Mearith and Trelanth were with her. The road before her looked unused for many years, tall grasses growing up through aged wagon ruts. A short ways beyond it disappeared into a swamp. Beyond the swamp only dense forest greeted the eye.

"Trelanth, this is amazing, far more than I'd hoped. You did this?"

"Thank you, Lady Ariel. Yes, this is my work. I passed the test."

"The test?"

"Yes, to become a full mage in my own right. Lady Ariel, may I ask a boon of you?"

"Ask what you will, Trelanth. If it is within my power to grant you shall have it."

"Lady, my Lord Evanseth gave us to believe the Bornani are all quite young. The Borni can, and will, teach them woodcraft and fighting skills. As well, Lady Mearith is beside you and she has no equal in these things."

"But...?"

"Lady, it is my understanding there are no scholars or mages among you, and these skills take far longer to learn."

"That's true. First we must free the people, then teach them to survive in this world. Only then will we have the time to look to other things."

"Yes, Lady, and that's why I would ask to join the Bornani and serve you. The king believes you will have need of a mage in the coming days."

"Let me guess, you remained an apprentice far longer than there was need because the master was a close kinsman. In truth you've been a well accomplished mage for some time, yet refused to take the test."

Trelanth laughed with delight. "Yes, Lady, that is indeed the way of it."

"And so Evanseth sent you to me."

"Lady, I begged for the chance."

"Life was a bit boring on Sanctuary?" Trelanth blushed and lowered her gaze. "What think you, Mearith, my heart? Do you think we can keep things exciting enough for her?"

Mearith laughed with delight. "Indeed I do, my Queen."

"Granted then. Trelanth, welcome to the Bornani. I hereby appoint you the official court mage." The girl's eyes were alight with excitement. "Now, court mage, your queen is lost and alone in this magical forest. You must now lead her to safety."

Trelanth fairly giggled with delight. "Right this way, my Queen," she said as she turned and stepped to the swamp. There was a road just beneath the surface of the water. When they reached the other side she turned and spoke a single word. "Alereigh!"

Ariel watched as the road broke up and the tightly held stones washed away in the slow moving stream. Trelanth led the way into the trees. They soon reached a game trail that led them to the clearing where their camp was located. Everyone was waiting for their return.

Trelanth stepped up to her uncle and spoke softly. He smiled broadly then kissed her forehead. A wave of his hand and a light appeared. He stepped through and vanished.

"Mearith." said Ariel.

"Yes, my delight?"

"We appear to be lost in the forest. Would you find a path home for us?"

A round of laughter came as they all heard that. "It will be my great pleasure to do so, my Queen." She set out and the others followed.

"Arlon, ride with me?"

"A pleasure, my Queen." He nudge his horse ahead until he was beside her.

"We will have much of the winter to plot and plan, my friend, but I would like to discuss with you the training of the newly freed."

"Of course, Lady Ariel."

Mearith saw them in conversation and looked away grinning. Ariel was giving Arlon plenty of time to realize she wasn't Elaith. By the time they reached Fugitive again it was clear he'd lost the notion. Ariel was Ariel, Queen of the Bornani and no other.

All in all it took an extra day to make the journey back to Fugitive. When they arrived Ariel asked Drakkat if there was anything from the adventure he'd like.

"My Queen, we've gathered some gold and silver, cloaks, boots, and weapons ..."

"But?"

"Perhaps an extra horse or two?"

"Take them, my friend, and welcome. What more?"

The big Orc was grinning now. "Winter is nearly upon us, my Queen. I could see to your war horse for you, if you plan to stay in Fugitive."

Ariel laughed with delight. "Yes, he is a big strong lad, isn't he. Grimm, my brother, Drakkat has a mighty task for you. Perhaps you might like to join his herd for the winter. Go with Drakkat now, my darling boy, and I'll visit you often. I promise. Go and make mighty foals for Drakkat's herd."

She smiled and watched as the big Orc led the stallion away towards the fields. A snowflake touched her nose and melted. "Winter's here," she said, looking up at the gray sky.

A Season to Prepare

The next morning Mearith found Ariel in the watch tower, a soft snow falling to gently cover the ground. "Taking a turn at watch, my love?"

"I couldn't sleep. My mind is filled with plots, plans, deeds that must be done, hopes and dreams for our people."

"Tell me."

Ariel stepped into Mearith's arms and laid her head on her lover's shoulder. "I dream of a time when the Elves run free in the forests, unhampered by the oshar, unfettered by time, unafraid of the Geni or the rest. I dream of a time when all Elves are accepted as true and free folk as they are here in this village.

"Mearith, my heart, I ..."

"Have a task for an assassin?"

Ariel leaned back to gaze into her eyes. "How is it you always know what I'm thinking?"

"Your heart is hurting; this I can feel because of the Pull. Your beautiful eyes are sad as you look at me, therefore there is something you need, and it will put me in danger's path. I'm guessing you want me to kill Dorgon."

"Yes."

"He was already marked, my heart. He paid us with tainted coin. He will pay for that bit of treachery, if for no other reason. Have no fear for me, my delight. Dorgon will meet his doom at my hands."

"Does his magic not deter you? Is it no threat?"

"Be at peace, Ariel, my delight. These are not the Geni of old, and I've fought far stronger than Dorgon. I have defenses against Geni magic and Trelanth can help me strengthen that. All will be well, I promise."

Ariel turned in her arms and gazed out across the open fields between Fugitive and the Orc village. She could see smoke starting to rise from the morning fires. Grimm's great bugle floated on the air as the mighty beast pranced through the snow.

She turned to the inner village to see smoke rising from chimneys and the sounds of people greeting the morning and each other. "This is a good day, Ariel, my delight. This day we have no battles to fight, no one to rescue, and no great decisions to make. Here comes Tanis to stand the watch. Let's see what cook has going for breakfast."

Ariel was thoughtful as she finished her meal. "Tell me more of this Narthwood forest."

Mearith set aside her empty bowl and thought for a moment. "Narthwood means north forest in the old Dwarven language. That forest has survived since long before the breaking of the world. There are few who know much about it for the Elves rarely ventured there."

"Why?"

"The trees are smaller and the lands colder, winters are longer. The further north you go the longer they become."

"So, that forest is left to the beasts and a few hardy souls?"

"It is, yes. What are you thinking, my delight?"

Ariel sighed and rested her chin in her hands. "I'm thinking it might provide a place to hide, should all else fail."

"The forests to the south hold greater promise."

"No, my heart. To the south lies the homeland of the Geni. There the Geni rose to power over all races, Orcs, giants, Ogres and more. Their thirst for magic and power laid waste to the lands which now lie barren, unable to produce crops or forests."

"How do you know of this?"

"I was young when the travelers returned to Ocra at Magdan. They had been sent south by Ocra to enlist help against the king in Shotar. They met in secret at master's house. I hid within the walls to listen. They spoke of strange lands and fierce, but starving folk, destroyed lands, and foul magics gone amok.

Ocra couldn't expect to find any help there and he was angry. Worse, the travelers spoke of groups planning to march north to these fruitful lands as their ancestors had before the world was broken. The travelers didn't believe this would happen as those people were too few to be a threat."

Mearith nodded as she absorbed this new information. "So, the lands to the north are cold and inhospitable, to the south they are barren, and only here are the lands nurturing enough for our people. Where does that leave us?"

"It leaves us with much work to do and too little time to do it."

"Ariel?"

"The Borni wish to return, my heart, but they are too few to defeat the combined strength of Geni, Orc, and Human. This you have said before."

"That is the sad truth of it."

"Even when we free great numbers of the Bornani, they will need to be nurtured. They won't be able to fight any wars and I don't want then to have to."

Mearith nodded her agreement. "So, what's the answer?"

"Narthwood." Mearith quirked an eyebrow at her so she continued. "We need time, my heart. Time to grow stronger. We need a place for our people to rest and grow strong, for our numbers to increase, before we go to war with the Geni."

"You want to war with the Geni?"

"Mearith, my heart, how else can we free all the people? As we are we can raid, pillage, and strike from hiding to release a great many, but only by defeating the Geni can we free them all. I will leave none in chains, not a single one."

Mearith gave her that bright smile of approval. "Agreed, my delight. We shall leave none in chains. Yes, Narthwood seems to be a strong possibility. However, perhaps we might discover a hidden valley within the mountains that would serve better."

"Could such a place be defended if it were discovered? No. Those who came before me remained within the walls of their great cities and there they fell. No, I would take our people into the vast forests of the north.

"Should the Geni pursue us there we could lead them deep into the lands of ice and snow and abandon them there. The Geni are of the warm lands to the south. For much of the year they huddle by their fires, seeking warmth.

"No, we must become one with the lands of winter, for there lies salvation for all our people."

"What of Fugitive?"

"I would give it to our Human and Orc allies, a home away from home for us all and a refuge for our friends."

Mearith thought for a moment them smiled. "Perhaps there is another way." It was Ariel's turn to raise an eyebrow. "The mountains rise behind us, my delight. I know of a pathway all could travel. It leads to a broad valley where they could rest before moving on to the north.

"The way from there takes us well past Shotar. We could use Fugitive as a way station for the newly freed. We have set up defenses here. An army could be held off long enough for a retreat into the mountains, and from there to the north."

Ariel nodded. "So, you agree with my reasoning for wanting to claim the northern forests."

"From the first I believed it to be the only way."

"Too bad we couldn't escape to Sanctuary to pass the winters then return each spring."

"Is that what you want to do?"

"No, it isn't. That's the easy way, and, just like the magic, it can become a drug. Besides, Sanctuary doesn't nurture Elves. It lulls them into slow decay. No, we'll embrace the northern forest. It will be Trelanth's task to make that forest understand we come as friends."

Mearith chuckled at that. "So, which one of us has to tell Evan he must give up his warm bed and sleep in the deep snows of Narthwood. In that land there will be no trees large enough to create grand houses from."

Ariel looked thoughtful for a moment. "Surely there will be places within that forest where the trees grow taller, great caverns to shelter in, broad valleys away from the cold winds. How is it no one ever goes there? Tell me truly now, what has prevented people from entering that forest?"

"One of the lore speakers could tell you better, my delight. As I understand it, once, long ago, our kind did live there. However, the land turned colder, and we moved farther south rather than adapt to that land.

"Some remained behind, however. Here in the south we were changed over time. We grew taller, stronger, wiser. Those who remained behind did not evolve as we did, and, it is believed, they eventually died out. The forest of the north became a place no one entered.

"In time the Borni and the High Born separated and the rest you know."

"I wonder, could any of the ancient race have survived there? Could they be the evil spirits the hunters and trappers speak of?"

"Perhaps, but I doubt it."

"Hmm, so, once long ago, our kind were able to live there, to thrive there. Perhaps we can again. When the snows leave the lands I wish to see this forest for myself."

"Planning to take Evan with us?"

"Yes, Evan and many more. My heart, I can't just decide for everybody without giving them a chance to consult. Should we call him and ask for a consultation?"

Again she got the bright smile of approval. She pulled the small pouch from her pocket, held the stone in her hand and called. "My lord king, are you there?"

"I am here, my Queen. How may I serve, your majesty?"

Ariel sighed, then straightened her back. "I think we should confer."

"My palace or yours?"

"Yours."

His voice sobered instantly. "I'll call the council at once, Lady Ariel. A portal will appear in a moment."

Ariel stood and the portal appeared. Arlon stepped through the door as did Trelanth. Ariel beckoned them to accompany her as she took Mearith's hand and stepped through the portal. They landed in the royal meeting room.

Ariel stood gazing out the window at the comings and goings of the Elves. As she did, the king and his councilors assembled behind. None spoke, nor made a sound. Mearith lightly touched her arm to draw her attention.

Ariel turned and everybody dropped to one knee. "Hail Lady Ariel, Queen of all Elfkind."

"Rise, everyone. Evanseth, I've warned you about this..." Ariel's playful grin faded as he rose and she saw the look on his face. "Evan?"

"Ariel, let us put aside the game and speak truly. We all know that for your people to be freed and for my people to survive, you must command. Ariel, you're of the blood royal, and Mearith, who is the rightful monarch of the Borni already defers to you. You are the one true queen."

Ariel looked each Elf in the room in the eye and each nodded their agreement. "So be it; I accept you. Now, we must confer." She gestured at the long elegant table, but no one moved. With a merry twinkle in her eye, Mearith took her arm and seated her in the high seat then sat on her right. Only then did the others join them.

The gathered people gazed at her expectantly. Ariel sighed then felt the warmth of the jewel beneath her tunic as it glowed. She nodded then turned to Evanseth. "My lord king, I assume that each person you sent to me was the best you had."

"Yes, that's true, my Queen."

"Arlon."

"Lady?"

"I charge you to choose the warriors to assist me in freeing the slaves and defending the forests."

"My Queen, I'm honored. Am I to be supervised by the Orc?"

Ariel and Mearith laughed heartily at that. "I think Drakkat will be too busy elsewhere. I'm afraid you'll have to muddle through on your own."

Seeing the confused looks on the others, Arlon spoke of the joke. "I spoke out of turn. Lady Ariel so closely resembles my sister, I responded as I would have to Elaith. The queen then chose to ride to battle with a small band of Orcs as her personal guard. I rode with them under the command of the Orc chieftain. It was quite instructive."

The old Elf woman who'd befriended Ariel on her first visit smiled. "What did you learn, Arlon?"

"I learned that blasted Orc is an utter savage in battle, and he's completely devoted to the queen. I also learned Lady Ariel will not tolerate my loose tongue as Elaith was wont to do."

He stopped smiling then. "I learned that Lady Ariel is an able commander determined to keep every Elf alive if possible. She's as devoted to the Elves' well being as the Orc is to her. Forgive me, my King, but your decision to serve Lady Ariel is the right one if we are to survive as a people."

Evanseth nodded and smiled. "So, my Queen, you called for us. How can we serve?"

"Arlon will bring the warriors to me when it's time. You, my King, have a different task. This place, these homes, are magnificent. Nothing like any of this exists in my world that I am aware of. These places were built by the Elves, were they not?"

"They were my Queen."

"Then those builders, scholars, mages, and the rest will be your charge. You must find places where they can work and direct them as you see fit. You will also have to direct them in assisting the newly freed to assimilate into their new lives."

"With pleasure, my Queen."

"Now, for the rest. Mearith, my heart, can you give us the lay of the land on this table?"

Mearith patted her arm then rose and accepted the huge map Evanseth passed to her. She unfurled it face down then, taking up a charcoal stick, she began to sketch out a map of the new land masses of Elandor as she knew them.

"Here, to the south lie the ruined lands abandoned by the Geni at the time of the great war that broke the world," she said. "Here is the ocean, and ..." She continued as she sketched it out.

"So, here's the problem, as I see it," said Ariel. "We could hold the lands around Fugitive, but I fear we would always be at risk of attack there. Arlon? Your thoughts on this?"

"I agree, my Queen. I believe we could hold the lands easily enough, but there are issues as you say. We would always be open to attack, for the enemy would know where we are. Once we begin to free the slaves the masters will rise up against us.

"It was your original plan to keep the Elves mobile within the forest, was it not, Lady?"

"It was."

"I believe that is the wisest course of action. We warriors remain in this general area, mobile, active, and always probing them, freeing every Elf we find. However, as you have pointed out, the scholars, historians, healers, teachers, builders, and others need more permanent homes."

"How was it done before?" asked Ariel. "Before the coming of the Geni. I know the High Born lived in their great cities, but how did the Borni live?"

"We built small villages in the clearings of the great forest," replied the old councilor. "The home of the king and his court were of course larger, but for the most part we lived in small villages. The builders nurtured and grew the groves of oak in which we made our homes."

"Is it possible to return to this way of life?"

"It is," said Evanseth, "but that will take time to do."

"And you will need to be left in peace to do it," said Ariel. "I mean to see you have that peace. Evanseth, I need you to see this done. It will be my task to see you're left undisturbed to do it. Will you take this on for me?"

"Of course, and with a glad heart, Ariel. You're being awfully soft on me. What are you up to?"

Ariel's sweet laughter brought a smile of delight to every face. "Saw through me did you?"

"It was too easy. What have you done to me, sister Ariel?"

She sighed then leaned forward in her chair, reaching across the map Mearith had drawn. "The only place to do this where you will be unlikely to come under attack will be here." She tapped the map with her finger. "Narthwood Forest."

"Narthwood?" Evanseth sucked in his breath.

"What is known of that place?" asked Ariel.

"It's dead," said one of the elders.

"Dead?"

"The spirit of that forest hasn't responded to an Elf in living memory, Lady."

"Tell me what you know of that place."

"Long, long ago the Elves came from Narthwood. Some remained behind and failed, to be lost in time and memory. The Elves came to the younger forests and were welcomed by them. There we grew, evolved, and prospered. A few have returned to Narthwood from time to time, but the forest will not respond to them."

"I see. Bear with me a moment, if you will." Ariel pulled the jewel from her tunic and held it in her hand. "Speak to me of old stone and ancient forest." She closed her eyes and breathed deeply.

The stone began to glow softly in her hand. With closed eyes she saw vast reaches of forest. There was life there, birds, beasts, trees, rivers, and streams. She got the sense of a sleeping giant.

She saw an Elf and recognized the man who'd just spoken, although he was much younger in the vision. She saw him speak to the trees, but get no answer, and he sadly walked away. Long after he'd gone she saw a glimmer of warmth there and a sense of sadness as it faded. She opened her eyes.

"You left too soon."

"Lady?"

"When you tried to awaken the forest. You left too soon. Narthwood isn't dead, but sleeping, dreaming, waiting for the return to those who left it behind. There you must go, seek out the places of safety, build new homes, and awaken the forest once again.

"There you must take them, Evan, there to rebuild. Come to me in the Spring and we will go exploring together. The summer will be well along before the slave auction is to be held in Magdan. We will have time to go exploring."

Evanseth nodded and gazed at the map once again. He turned to one of the councilors. "Bring me everything you can find on Narthwood. Everything."

"At once, my Lord." He rose to his feet and faced Ariel. "With your permission, my Queen." She smiled and nodded. He sped away.

"My Queen," said Arlon, "if we're going to capture a city with a Geni in residence we could use a mage or two with us."

Ariel smiled. "Agreed. Trelanth, as the royal mage it falls to you to see what you can do about this."

"My lady, forgive me," said the girl, "but my uncle, Orin is the royal mage, all answer to him."

"Apparently, no longer," said Orin, as he stepped away from the wall where he'd been standing. "It is well past time I retired. Lady Ariel, you have chosen your mage wisely."

"Thank you, Orin, but I doubt Trelanth will let you retire yet. I'm sure most who study magic will be in Evanseth's party, and I'm quite certain he'll want you there. However, it's Trelanth who must decide who goes where in this."

"Queen Ariel is right, Uncle. The king will need you, and the others are accustomed to your direction. I'll gather a few who would prefer a bit more excitement and take them with me. It falls to you to direct the rest as they assist the king in acquiring new homes for us all."

The old Elf grinned and, bowing slightly, stepped back.

"So," said Ariel, "are we finished for today?"

"I believe we are, my delight," replied Mearith.

"We shall meet again, soon," said Ariel. "Now, before we return I would like to see Lady Belia."

"I'm here, Lady Ariel."

Ariel turned to see Belia smiling at her. With a smile of delight Ariel stood up and embraced the girl.

IN THE CITY OF MAGDAN the snows began to deepen. Standing far from the window, Dorgon the Geni huddled deeper into his cloak and stepped nearer the fire. Shivering in the cold air, he turned to glare at the mage in the room.

That ancient was still the strongest Geni mage Dorgon knew, but the old one was in failing health and his grasp on magic was slipping as was his mind. "Any sign?"

"None, my young friend. She has stepped onto a different realm, and I cannot find her, wait, she returns. Ah yes, I see her clearly now. So, my young beauty, what does your future hold?"

"That's not important right now. Tell me where she is. Speak! Where is she?" He stopped speaking as he saw the old one's eyes drift out of focus.

"She has returned to the forest, now the Queen of the Elves. She has called and they have heard her voice. When the snows leave the lands they will come, and she will lead them for she is now the queen of them all." The old one slumped forward and began to snore.

With a snort of disgust Dorgon left and returned to his own chambers. "If you want something done right, do it yourself," he muttered, as he sat to the table and began to focus his sight deep within the crystal that rested there.

Slowly the mist within the stone began to clear. The vision he wanted did not come, but another came unbidden. The face of the assassin appeared and gazed into his eyes. "You paid me with tainted coin, Geni. I'll come for you when the snows melt in Spring."

Dorgon shouted a denial and thrust the ball of crystal away. He cursed as he stomped about the room. He hadn't been able to see Ariel in the stone since the arrival of that damned mage, and apparently, the mage was always near. Not only had he failed to capture her, but now he could no longer locate her.

Queen of the Borni

T he winter wore on in plots and plans as well as training. Arlon was back on Sanctuary, training and drilling his troops. Evanseth worked with the artisans, mages and scholars, making plans, and deciding the best way to go about the return. Eventually they came to an agreement, and he journeyed to Fugitive to confer with Ariel.

As usual, they had gathered at the inn for the morning meal. Ariel and Mearith had just returned from weeks in the winter forest with her young guards. The former breed slaves were now completely at home in the forest, even in winter. They were taking the watch so Ariel's advisers could report.

Suddenly Trelanth stood up. "The King comes."

Even as she spoke a bright light appeared in the yard then the door opened and Evanseth entered. "My Queen."

"Rise and embrace me, my new brother." Ariel gave him a gentle hug, then passed him to Mearith. "So, what brings you to the royal palace this warm summer's day?"

Evanseth chuckled as he seated himself. "I'd forgotten how cold it can get here. We're all going to need toughening up; Narthwood will be even colder. Yes, yes, the reason for the visit.

"The people have proposed, and I do agree with them, that we should return in smaller groups rather than all at once."

"Oh?" asked Mearith. "What's the plan?"

"First the warriors, the fighters under Arlon's command return. Lady Ariel, you said you wanted to go with us to see Narthwood. We believe the fighters should make that first journey unencumbered by the rest. We'd like to leave the elders, artisans, scholars, and the like in Sanctuary until a site for the new home is chosen.

"Once we have a camp established the mages can create the portal and they can join us there, ready to begin work. In this way your forces can move faster and we won't lose anyone on the way."

"I like that plan," said Ariel. "Why did you come to me with it?"

"You're the queen, Lady Ariel. We need your approval before we can begin to implement the plan."

Ariel sighed and gripped his shoulder lightly. "Hear me well, my brother. I will not supervise every living Elf like a slave master. This is your task, and as the plan shows, you are more than capable of getting it done.

"Evan, you're still the king of the Borni, do this in the way that seems best to you, and I'll rejoice in that. I trust you to get it done. My Lord King, I'm not my ancestress. I have no need or desire for complete control. I just want my people freed and living happy lives. Help me make this happen."

Evanseth smiled and patted the hand on his shoulder. "So, not going to let me out of this king job, are you?"

Ariel laughed merrily. "Not a chance. Evan, this is a good plan, and it eases my mind somewhat. Mearith tells me the journey to Narthwood is long and fraught with dangers unknown. This will make the task easier for me."

"Forgive me, Ariel, but we could make the march on our own. You need not divert yourself from your main goal."

"It's not that I feel the great need to oversee the choosing of a new home for the Elves. It's about learning the land, the streams and forests, the dangers, and the joys for myself. With this knowledge I can better understand the journey and more safely lead the newly freed to Elfhome.

"Also, I want all my fighters to have experience with the pathways to Narthwood. If I should fall in battle it'll be up to them to escort the newly freed to safety. All must know the way, the joys, and dangers, for when we take that journey we'll have many newly freed slaves to nurture and protect. I, we, need to know the pathways."

Evanseth nodded then smiled and winked at Mearith. "You have chosen well, Mear. And, even if the Queen still wants me be king, at least she's making the job a lot easier."

Mearith smiled warmly at her brother. "Evan, you're coming with us on that trek, aren't you?"

"I am, and so is every mage I can find. I can feel what Trelanth has done here and that tells me there's at least one Geni hunting for you."

Trelanth smiled brightly at that. "Yes, my king, he hunts, but he grows frustrated. He has no real idea what's happened and he clings to an old plan that can never bear fruit."

"When first I found Ariel," said Mearith, "the Geni were already aware of who she was. Their plan was to have her lead the Elves in war on their behalf. They still think of her as a slave they can manipulate.

"Magdan was ruled by a Geni named Ocra. He was an able leader and could have been a problem, but fate smiled upon us. A lesser man with greater ambitions hired me to slay Ocra. This is what carried me to Magdan where I found Ariel.

"Once the new Geni, Dorgon, took command of the city, he learned I had robbed him of the prize that drew him in the first place. It's Dorgon who hunts us now and he's no match for Trelanth. When we free the slaves of Magdan, I'll kill Dorgon."

"Oh?"

"He paid me for the assassination with tainted coin. He's a treacherous scheming fool and I will make an end of him, but for now we want him where he is. As long as he rules in Magdan no more able man can gain control."

Evanseth sat up straighter. "You're going to take the city, aren't you?"

"We are," replied Ariel. "They're planning a huge slave auction in late summer. We'll take the city then and free those slaves. With luck we'll all be in Elfhome before the snow falls on Narthwood."

"Then it'll be my task to see there's an Elfhome for you to come to and that it's ready to receive refugees." With that Evanseth rose. "With your permission, my Queen, I shall return to Sanctuary and prepare."

Suddenly Ariel's eyes flew open. "By all the gods, Evan, I didn't think. You and Belia must be tormented. Go, return to her, and next time bring her with you."

"Thank you, my Queen." With that he turned and left the inn.

Magdan

Tereen hurried to the well, keeping her head down and trembling. The woman was terrified. She could feel the burning of the compulsion gnawing at her, pulling her towards the wall, calling her to race past the guards and flee into the forest.

Shuddering as she lowered the water pail into the depths, she allowed her eyes to wander about the square. It was full to bursting as were the slave pens. The auction would begin on the morrow. Even in the heat of the day Tereen shivered.

Master had said there were over a thousand slaves in the city now, but it wasn't to the pens she was drawn. It was the forest she was pulled toward. Her pail was full, but she let it fall back to splash into the water again as a wild thrill flared in her heart.

Her water pail forgotten, she watched agape as a huge Orc and three companions approached. "Give me water," demanded the Orc. Tereen shook off the spell of wild soaring joy and, lowering her gaze, pulled the pail from the depth and passed it to the Orc who drank deeply then passed it back. "Well, happy now, L'ark?"

"Beyond measure, Drakkat my friend." The speaker pushed back his hood slightly to expose his Elfin features to Tereen, then he pulled it forward again as he reached for her hand. "Come."

"I can't, I dare not. Master will flay me alive if I don't return to him and swiftly. I..."

"Will not return to him, my sweet," replied that hypnotic voice, "ever again."

"We're drawing attention," grumbled the Orc. "If I start a fight now the Queen will have my hide for a winter's blanket. Get her out of sight."

"With extreme pleasure," replied the voice. An arm was suddenly around her waist and a soaring joy in her heart. All thoughts and fear of an angry master vanished in that surge of delight. The Orc and a human began to argue loudly and, as eyes were drawn to them, Tereen was whisked away.

She sat tightly to his side as the afternoon faded into twilight. L'ark hugged her to him and whispered softly in her ear. She trembled with the excitement of his nearness and fear as she understood what was about to happen.

The Queen of the High Born had returned. With the falling of darkness she and her warriors would come. Even now those men and Orcs who followed her were in the city, quietly making their way to the gates, watch towers, and walls. Soon the Watch would fall and the Elves would swarm over the walls.

While one of her Elvish warriors gently held his new love, Ariel and Mearith were already inside the walls. The Queen gazed with mixed emotions at the makeshift room atop the roof that had once been hers. It was filled with a variety of things, now only a storage room as it had once been. She sighed and turned her attention back to Mearith.

"Memories?"

"Yes, my love, powerful memories. This is the place where I first heard your voice, touched your hand, and felt the power of the compulsion. You were here to assassinate the city overlord that night as well."

"And so I am again, yet there will be no prize half as great for me this night." Mearith smiled and kissed her cheek. "The streets are full. Let's wait a while until sleep claims a few of these folk." She settled down and Ariel sat beside her.

As the darkness grew deeper they became aware of the Watch disappearing from the walls. The natural fights and rowdiness of an event like this would keep the Watch busy on the ground. The few who manned the walls fell to Drakkat's Orcs and Marc's humans.

Ariel's nervousness caused her to shiver and Mearith pulled her closer. "Be at peace, my delight. Marc and Drakkat won't fail. Look, already the Borni scale the walls. The city will soon be ours."

"Mearith, my heart, I confess this place brings fear back to my mind. I can smell the oppression and the stink of the oshar. Oh gods, what if we fail? What if ...?"

"Hush now, my delight. Marc's already reported the numbers of the Watch and by now they are all defeated. They, and the men-at-arms will all be in the dungeons by now. It's the waiting that plays with your fears. Come, let's be about the business."

They rose easily and dropped from the roof to the alley below. A huge shadow was waiting for them. "Drakkat?"

"The Watch and men-at-arms are all in the dungeons. L'ark proved useless. I sent him and the woman to the slave pens to clear out those guards."

"Woman?"

The big Orc chuckled. "A woman came to the square to draw water. He was lost from there. Marc and I had to start a fight to distract the guards. Be at peace, all is in readiness, my Queen."

Ariel grinned her delight. "Excellent. Mearith and I have an errand. See to the securing of the city, Drakkat."

Mearith led the way and Ariel followed her closely. When they reached the great house now occupied by Lord Dorgon they found several dead guards and Marc. "The way is clear, my Queen," he grinned. "Shall I wait here to make certain your visit goes undisturbed?"

"Excellent idea," said Ariel, patting his arm as she passed.

They entered and slipped silently along a corridor. As they approached the private chambers of Lord Dorgon they could hear him inside.

"Come on, come on, where are you Elf, I know you're out there. Queen of the Elves, are you? You're nothing but a runaway slave, but you will be found. I'll have you in the collar yet and those damned Elves of yours will take the brunt of the attack. Come on, show yourself. Pah!" There was the sound of the crystal shattering as it was hurled against the wall.

"If you're trying to find someone it's more often useful to use your own eyes than a seeing crystal."

Dorgon spun around with a gasp. "You."

"Me," replied Ariel.

With a leap that was startling with its speed, Dorgon raced for another passageway. He didn't make it; Mearith's thrown dagger struck his hamstring and brought him down. Before he could turn to defend himself her sword pierced his body from behind. Gasping and reaching toward her he managed only one word. "Why?"

"You paid me with tainted coin. Treachery comes at a price." Even as she spoke his eyes clouded over and he fell dead at her feet. Mearith grabbed the Geni's hair, and with a single pass of her dagger removed his head.

"Come, my love," said Ariel. "The dawn comes swiftly, and we should be about the business."

Mearith nodded and followed her out. Outside they found Marc and his humans waiting. "It's done," said Ariel. "Loot the place, Marc. Take what you will, take all the slaves you can find to the auction square." He nodded then led his men inside.

Ariel and Mearith reached the auction square to find it already full of anxious buyers and sellers. Drakkat was waiting for them as well. "Drakkat, my friend, I can't thank you enough for what you've done, the risks you've taken."

He grinned with delight. "Most fun I've had since the battle of the snows."

"Have you gathered sufficient payment?"

"We have, my Queen. Our horses are already laden down with loot."

"Here comes Marc now. Marc, are you satisfied?"

"My Queen, I am that and more. We're weighed down with treasure."

"Go then, my true friends of Fugitive, we'll meet again one day. Go now, slip away while I hold the attention of all." The men and Orcs of Fugitive melted away from the square, but none paid them any attention. All eyes were on the hundreds of slaves being led from the pens.

When Drakkat and Marc reached the gates they found Elves standing as guards. They saluted and headed out on the road to the forest. They would be long gone from sight when Ariel led the slaves from the city.

Back at the auction square things were getting ready. The sun was now up, and the proceedings were about to get under way. The auctioneer grabbed an Elf by the arm and jerked him forward on the stage.

"All is in readiness, my Queen," whispered Arlon, as he appeared at Ariel's side. "The archers await your signal."

The excitement was clear in her eyes now; her dream was within her grasp. The jewel at her breast throbbed with power and the ring itched for a weapon. As the auctioneer called for the first bid Ariel stepped forward and blew a long blast on a horn.

At the sound of the horn there was a hail of arrows and all the guards as well as the auctioneer fell to the ground with an arrow to the heart. Confusion and fear registered on every face. The horn sounded again then suddenly Ariel was surrounded by armed guards, swords in hand.

Tanis grinned as she patted his shoulder then strode towards the raised platform with a frightened slave cowering on it. Ariel hopped onto the stage and blew the horn for silence.

"Attention, pay attention." The square fell silent. "This city is now under my command. Here is the former ruler of Magdan." Mearith held her grisly trophy high for all to see.

"Hear me well, the guards and Watchmen are all dead or in the dungeons. We now control the city. Bring forth all the slaves that are not already here. We will await them. Anyone attempting to leave this city or to hide a slave from us will be killed. Bring them all here at once."

The gathered people just stared her in stunned silence. "Arlon, unless these people get moving and obey me, begin killing them. Start with him." She pointed to a man and that man fell with an arrow through his body. The rest stampeded.

By late afternoon every slave in the city had been brought to Ariel at the auction square. When she was satisfied she blew the horn again for silence. "Hear me, people of Magdan. We are leaving now, make no attempt to hinder us and we will leave you alive and your homes intact.

"Try to stop us or interfere with us, and we'll slaughter you all then burn the city to the ground."

"Just who are you people?" demanded a man, a Geni, as he pushed forward. "The king will have your head for this."

Ariel looked down from the platform. She pulled the jewel from her tunic and held it high. Blazing with power the jewel cast a bright light over the whole square. When she spoke, her voice reverberated across the city.

"I am Ariel, Queen of the High Born Elves. I have returned for my people. Hear me, Geni, and fear. I want my people back, and I will have them. The forests are mine, enter them at your own peril. I leave your cities to you." She lowered the jewel, and it sent a blast of energy that knocked the Geni back several feet.

"Come, my people, we return to the forests." With that she descended the stairs and strode past the cowering Geni. The Elves gently herded the slaves along behind her. As Ariel reached the gates she found Tanis, holding the reins of her warhorse. She mounted, as did Mearith and the Queen's Guard. Slowly they led the parade of slaves from the city gates.

They headed south, but by nightfall they were still within sight of the city. Several riders had tried to leave Magdan, but were brought down by the Elvish archers.

Through the night men watched from the walls as the fires of the Elvish encampment glowed in the distance. Several more messengers tried to slip away in the night, but all were found and dispatched. By late afternoon the next day the army of Elves was seen disappearing into the forests to the south.

Near nightfall a lone rider sped through the gates. He raced away towards Shotar unhindered.

A Quest Ends, A Journey Begins

In a forest glade, well beyond sight of the city walls, dozens of small fires danced and crackled. Around those fires huddled many hundreds of Elves, slaves, all hungry and terrified. They had been given food, but it wasn't oshar.

The queen had been going among them, smiling, speaking to some in a soft voice. They saw her again as she approached. Those close enough heard her speak to the stone in her hand and it answered. They spoke in the forbidden language.

"Evanseth, my brother, are you there?"

"I'm here, my Queen. What do you need?"

"Do you still have people in Sanctuary?"

"Some few, yes. Why?"

"Evan, we succeeded beyond all expectation. We have close to a thousand new people with us. However, none of us had the foresight to know we would have elders, children, pregnant women, and infirm with us. You and I know well the journey before us will tax even the strong."

"Give me a day, my Queen. I'll send a few folk back to greet them and care for them until we're ready here to receive them. They'll be waiting for you when you arrive."

"My king, you're the best. Are you sure you don't want your job back?" His roar of laughter brought a smile to every face.

Ariel returned the stone to the soft bag she carried it in and dropped it back into her pocket. Smiling, she walked to the center of the encampment and pulled the jewel from her tunic. When she spoke all were able to hear her.

"My people, my friends, my name is Ariel. I am descended from the queen of the High Born Elves. That's who our ancestors were, the High Born. They weren't evil, as we've been taught, they were just people. The Geni invaded our lands and defeated them, forcing those who survived into slavery.

"People, everything we've been taught is lies, lies designed to control us, to keep us in slavery. That slavery has ended for you. The collars have been removed; you are now masters of your own fate.

"I will explain my plan for you, and you can decide if you want to join us or go your own way. I really want you to come with me. As you can all see, the Borni have returned to the forests. They have accepted me as their queen and, at great risk to themselves, they have helped me free you from your bondage.

"I've declared us, the descendants of the High Born, the Bornani. It means Children of the Forest. We will not return to the ways of the High Magic that brought about our downfall. Instead we will return to the forest from which we came so long ago. This I have done myself and this I want for you.

"Now we reach the time of decision. When we break camp in the morning I will ask you to accept me as your queen. If you don't wish to be ruled by me you will be allowed to go your own way."

She saw one man trying to be noticed and yet trying not to be noticed. "Many of you have questions and now is the time to ask them." She faced the man and smiled. "Tell me, what's on your mind?"

She was looking right at the man and he was clearly frightened. "Lady, this is the second day we've been without the oshar. Will we not all die of madness in the next few days anyway?"

Ariel smiled brightly. "No, my friend, my kinsman, you won't die, but you will awaken, awaken to what it truly means to be an Elf.

The oshar is the greatest of the lies we've been told. It doesn't keep us alive, it poisons us, dulls our senses and shortens our lives.

"As the oshar leaves your body, your Elvish senses will reawaken. It is a magical time, and we'll travel slowly at first to help you through it, help you enjoy it."

"Lady, you said we could go our own way," said another voice. "What does that mean?"

"If you choose not to become one of the Bornani you will go where you will, your fate will be of your own choosing. You can go back to your master if you wish, or strike out on your own. I truly hope you all choose to come with us. We will be able to help and protect you, take you to a place of safety."

"Why did you bring me, Lady Queen," asked an old woman. "My time has passed, and I'm of no use to anyone now. Master planned to buy a younger slave at the auction then kill me so he no longer had to feed me."

"Once off the oshar, dear woman, you will have long centuries ahead of you. There will be so much to learn and to share. There will be hundreds of ways for you to contribute, so many new things to enjoy.

"The road ahead of us will be a hard one, but the elders, young children and their mothers, as well as the infirm will be sent to a place of safety. People will meet them there and care for them until the King of the Borni has Elfhome ready to receive them.

"The young and strong I'll take with me on the long hard march. There is a reason for this. You must become one with the forest, my people. We will take our time as we journey forth, time for you to adjust to life in the trees. Tanis!"

The young warrior appeared with his companions. "This man is Tanis, captain of my personal guards. Tanis and his people were once breed slaves. They've made this journey from slave to forest warrior, and they'll help all of you to do the same. They are the living proof that it can be done, even as I am.

"I, too, began life as a slave in Magdan. I'm sure a few of you recognize me. I, too, awakened to my true self, became one with the forest."

Another voice spoke up. "Lady, will you teach us how to serve you as queen? Can you tell us what that will be like? Are we all to be your servants?"

"Yes and no, good woman. You will be expected to serve me in that all Elves do as I direct them, but for the most part, as they will tell you, I require little personal service. Tanis and his companions serve as my personal guard by their own choice. They insisted I need a guard." There was some nervous laughter at that.

"I swear to you all that I'll do whatever I can to help you and keep you safe. However, I do have a passion and a purpose, and in pursuing that passion my warriors may be called to face danger with me. The taking of Magdan is an example.

"My passion is to free all the Elves from slavery. To this end I called upon my warriors to assist me. Because of this they faced danger. Follow me and one day I might call upon you too."

Mearith strode up beside Ariel. "You should also know the queen has a bad habit of facing the danger herself, for she won't send another to a place she wouldn't go herself. Good people, to serve Ariel is to serve all Elfkind. The queen asks none to wait on her, but she does ask for assistance in greater tasks.

"My name is Mearith Waleen of the royal house of the Borni. My brother, Evanseth is the King of the Borni. We both willingly acknowledge Ariel of the Bornani as Queen of all Elfkind and serve her as she directs. If we, as Elves, are to survive, we must accept Ariel as the one true queen. Our mages have foreseen this."

"Are there more questions?" asked Ariel. "No? Well then, I bid you enjoy your rest. If you think of a question, we will speak of it in the morning. Good night, my brothers and sisters."

Mearith took her arm and led Ariel away to a small fire at the edge of the encampment. They settled down for a meal and Arlon approached. Ariel smiled and indicated he should join them. "What's the count, Arlon my friend?"

"Lady, we brought out nine hundred and thirty-seven Elves. One has already passed away, Trelanth says her heart failed. We have about two warriors to one freed slave. Lady, I fear we will lose many more on the trek to Narthwood."

"Evanseth is preparing to receive the aged, infirm, young children and their mothers, as well as the pregnant women. The plan is to send them through to Sanctuary until Elfhome is ready to receive them."

Arlon nodded his approval as he chewed on a piece of traveling bread. "That's good news indeed, my Queen. It lightens our burden considerably."

Ariel sighed deeply. "Mearith, my heart, do you think they'll accept me? Will they come with us?"

"They will come, my delight, have no fear of that. Where else could they go? Back to the slave masters? Into the forest on their own? Into the farms or small villages to be instantly returned to slavery? No, they'll come with us. It'll then be our task to see them safely to Elfhome, and to blend them into our society."

Ariel nodded thoughtfully. Mearith nudged her and pointed, grinning. It was as she had suspected. Already they could see the Spiritpull at work as a few of the warriors sought among the freed slaves, following the Pull as it drew them to the side of their soulmate.

Ariel smiled with delight as she watched.

Several of the freed slaves were trying to talk among themselves, but one fellow couldn't concentrate. He was confused and frightened by the power of the emotion rising within him. He ached, burned for something, something that was near, but not near enough.

He felt it as it moved closer. Turning, he saw a woman, a warrior of the Borni, moving slowly nearer, as though searching for something, someone. A wild surge of pure joy welled up inside of him as she turned those questing eyes in his direction. She smiled and moved toward him.

Wide eyed, he watched as she approached, moving with the liquid grace of a forest hunter. She was beside him now, a frown creasing her perfect features. She was looking at his back. "You've been whipped."

Her voice was like sweet music, and it took a moment for the meaning of her words to sink in. "Many times. Most recently, on the morning you came for us."

The snarl slowly left her face and her bright smile returned. "Never again, my love, this I swear to you." She took his hand and raised him to his feet then stepped into his arms. "Come with me, and I'll keep you by my side and keep you safe always."

"I will happily go wherever you want to take me," he breathed, getting lost in her eyes.

She grinned with mischief as she led him to her campfire and companions. "I will remind you of that statement many times in the years to come."

A dozen others were found and led away into the warrior's camps.

The next morning another meal was shared then Ariel asked them for their decision. All but a small handful chose to accept and follow her. They knelt facing their new queen. "Hail Queen Ariel, Queen of all Elves."

The shout rang through the forest and Ariel beamed her delight. "I accept you, my brothers and sisters. You are of the Bornani now. We will remain here until I receive word that all is in readiness for the elders, children and infirm. Once we see these folk to a place of safety we'll begin the long march to Elfhome.

"I'll now ask those of you who have chosen not to make the journey to leave the camp now." Roughly two dozen rose and left the camp.

The day was well along when they found their way back to the main roadway. "Where do we go from here?" wondered one of them.

"Let's go south," replied another. "I for one don't want to go back to Magdan. I know all too well the fate that awaits me there."

The rest agreed. They walked south until darkness fell then they tried to make a camp. "What are we going to do? We've been without oshar for three days now. I'm starting to feel strange."

"As am I," agreed another, "but the queen said we won't die, we'll just change. I remember Ariel. She was a spoiled master's pet, but she ate only oshar like the rest of us. She's still alive, so I believe her."

"Maybe we should have gone with her."

"You mean trade one form of slavery for another?"

"I don't know. You saw those warriors. You remember the stories of the Borni. They looked like they're having good lives."

"Yes, and Bort, that woman came and took him away. That was the compulsion, I've seen that look on a man's face before. The queen saw and she smiled. If that had been master, Bort would have been killed on the spot."

"Yes, one of the warriors said they're allowed to choose for themselves who mates. We should have gone with them."

"Too late for that now," grumbled another. "Since we have no food we might as well sleep."

They awakened the next morning cold and hungry. There was a soft rain falling. Miserable, they set out once again, heading south.

Suddenly there was the sound of hoof beats behind them on the road. Turning they saw a dozen riders approaching fast, and then they heard the shouts. "There's a bunch of the slaves. Get them."

They tried to reach the forest, but the riders were too fast, they weren't going to make it. And then the stallion screamed. The ground trembled under the thunder of mighty hooves as Ariel, astride Grimm, broke from the trees and charged at the oncoming riders.

Mearith's horse was faster, and she slammed into the riders first, but Grimm was bigger and stronger. He thundered into the lesser horses like a battering ram, knocking several to the ground and sending others fleeing. He reared and lashed out with his hooves even as Ariel loosed the arrow from her bow.

With flashing sword, Mearith slew man after man while Ariel dropped others with her bow. The few who remained mounted fled from the madness and Mearith gave chase while Ariel remained to defend the Elves. Grimm continued to prance and snort, still spoiling for a fight.

At length Mearith returned and both she and Ariel dismounted. "Why did you come back?" asked one of the rescued.

"Queen Ariel doesn't abandon her people," replied Mearith. "Personally, I'd have left you on your own, but Ariel says to give you one more chance. So, what'll it be? Will you loyally serve Queen Ariel and accept her protection, or do you still want to go your own way?"

As one they knelt before Ariel. "Lady, please forgive us and accept us. We were wrong to doubt and fear you."

"My brothers and sisters, I didn't free you from one slavery just to bind you to another."

"The queen gives more than she gets, good people," said Mearith, relaxing at last. "She asks for instant obedience and complete loyalty, but she bears the burden of all our safety in return. You have chosen well.

"Now, some of you help me strip these corpses of anything useful."

Ariel gave a wry smile as she watched Mearith teach the people what to take from a battle. They got weapons, a number of cloaks, six horses, and some feed for them. There was little food in the saddlebags, but Ariel and Mearith shared what they had as soon as everybody had retreated into the trees and set up a small camp.

They settled down for the night, but Ariel grinned as she saw a few bewildered faces. "What did it say?"

"Lady?"

"You heard a voice on the wind. What did it say?"

"I don't know, Lady. I heard the voice, but there were no words I can understand. It's the madness, isn't it?"

"It's not madness, my friend, the poison of the oshar is leaving your body. The voice you heard is the voice of brother wind. He speaks to you in the language of our ancestors."

"The forbidden language of the dark magic?" he asked fearfully.

"No, it's the language of the Elves, the true language of the Elves. You've heard some of us speaking it before."

"Lady, did you hear it too?"

"I did, yes. It said, welcome home, Bornani."

The next morning they set out to rejoin their main party. They kept to the trees and took their time. Ariel started their language lessons and Mearith began teaching them wood craft. By nightfall they had all managed to find some things to eat and could speak a few words of Old Elvish.

Everyone was in the midst of the awakening, completely enthralled with all the new sights and sounds, scents and tastes. Late the next day they arrived back at their encampment to find it abuzz. All the newly freed slaves were well into the awakening. Ariel grinned with delight.

"The Queen," shouted a voice and everyone dropped to one knee.

"Arise, good people. Tell me. What is all the confusion?"

"We are having a mass awakening, my Queen," replied Trelanth as she approached smiling. "I thought it best to remain here until you returned. A great number have already fully awakened, and they're tending the rest as they pass through the process.

"Arlon has taken the bulk of his forces to watch the road behind us."

"Then all is as it should be. Are the Geni watching?"

"Yes, Lady, as you instructed, I'm allowing them to watch us."

"We'll let them observe for a while longer then we'll act," sighed Ariel as she dismounted and pulled off Grimm's saddle. Grabbing a fistful of sweetgrass, she began to rub him down. "Have you seen any sign of an organized pursuit?"

Trelanth sobered instantly. "I have, my Queen. The rider has reached Shotar and now rides with an armed force as they return towards Magdan."

Ariel stopped rubbing the stallion and stood up. "How many?"

"Two hundred horsemen, three wagons, and at least fifty slaves."

"Only two hundred warriors? The king of the Geni must not have believed the man when he spoke of the number of Elvish warriors. Fifty slaves, you say?"

Mearith turned from grooming her horse to face Ariel. "Ariel, we have nearly a thousand people to escort. We dare not lose our focus here."

Ariel arched an eyebrow at her. "You're willing to pass by three wagon loads of supplies and fifty camp cooks?"

"We can't take those wagons on that journey."

"We could carry the contents."

"Ariel, my beloved, I beg you, reconsider. Don't put a thousand at risk to rescue another fifty. Stick to your plan. We'll come back for the others another time. We need to see to the safety of these people first."

Ariel's shoulders slumped. "You're right, my heart, but it truly grieves me to leave a single one behind."

Mearith gathered her lover into her arms, "I know, my delight, I know, and I share your thoughts on this, but we must be patient. In truth we'll be lucky to get all these people to Narthwood before the snows fall."

"You're right, I know. Forgive me, dear heart. Thank you for guiding me and keeping me on track. What would I ever do without you?"

Mearith chuckled and hugged her tightly. "You'll never have to find out, my delight."

As Mearith released her, Ariel turned back to Trelanth. "Has there been any word from the king?"

"Sanctuary is ready, Lady Ariel. However the king thought it best to allow everyone to awaken before sending them through the portal."

"Do we have the time for that?"

"We do. The king's men will need another four days to get this far. We may be lucky and they may stop and occupy Magdan. There's one Geni who rides with them."

"Oh, has he tried to locate us yet?"

Trelanth was grinning. "He has, yes."

"And?"

"He sees a large encampment of former slaves with a few warriors, as does the mage who seeks us from Shotar."

"Is this one a match for you, Trelanth?"

"No, my Queen, he isn't. His skills appear to be equal to Dorgon."

"Interesting," muttered Ariel as she fed a treat to Grimm.

"Lady?"

"I wonder. Give me your thoughts on this. Why is it the Geni were able to defeat my ancestors, who were mighty in magic, but are now as weak in their magic as the Elves are under the influence of oshar? Could it be that they didn't completely destroy us at the breaking of the world because they couldn't?

"Could it be that they too burned out their magic in the battle to defeat the High Born?"

"It's possible," said Mearith, "but I wouldn't count on it."

"I won't," replied Ariel.

"Nor will I," agreed Trelanth. "This one could be playing a game or not, but I'll proceed as though he were a mage of elder days."

Ariel smiled and patted her shoulder. She led them to a fire where L'ark and his new companion were resting. They arose as the queen approached.

"Relax, my friends, relax," said Ariel. She sat as did her companions. "So, L'ark, tell me, how is it you can perform your duties as Arlon's second with an appendage attached to your side?"

Tereen looked worried, but L'ark just laughed and pulled her closer. "I was tasked with watching over the camp, my Queen. So far I have managed to survive it."

"Tereen, you remember me, don't you?"

"Yes. You were Ariel who became one of the Watch. I remember you played with my daughter as you both grew."

"Yes, that was me. What became of Telee?"

"Master sold her to a farmer in a village just north of Magdan. I never saw her again."

"Lady Ariel?" L'ark was looking at her intently now.

"Take two of the horses we acquired. Stay out of sight, but get it done. Be wary, L'ark, for they will all be watching now, and fearful. Rejoin us when you can, you know they way."

"I do, yes, Lady."

"If the task takes too long, go to Marc at Fugitive. I will return there in the spring." He nodded thoughtfully. "L'ark, take another warrior with you. Telee will need protection as she awakens, and an extra pair of eyes will be useful."

"Yes, my Queen. We will leave at first light."

Ariel smiled then rose to her feet. With Mearith at her side she moved slowly through the camp, speaking to as many as she could as she went. Mearith smiled as she followed along.

When they settled down for the night Ariel relented and answered the unspoken question. "My beloved, Tereen was ever good to me before master forbade me to see them. Telee was her mother's delight, and she loved her mother dearly. Do you think they will be able to find her?"

"L'ark will find the girl; I have no doubt of that. How long it'll take is another matter. Thank you for suggesting he go to Marc rather than face the long march late in the year."

Early next morning Ariel got the call from Evanseth. They spoke, then Trelanth made certain there were no prying eyes watching. The portal appeared and Evanseth stepped through with Belia. After the greetings they watched as the elders, infirm, pregnant women, and mothers with young children were assisted through and no one noticed as a teenage boy with a bad limp held back. Evanseth and Belia were the last to go then the portal vanished.

Ariel sighed as the portal vanished. "We're one step closer. I'm getting anxious to get on the road."

"As am I, my delight. The year grows late and we can't travel with speed, at least not at first."

Ariel turned to Trelanth. "Are eyes watching?"

"No, Lady. No eye can see us now."

"Can you show them something false?"

"I can, Lady, yes. What shall I show them?"

"Show them the newly freed slaves with about a hundred Borni warriors as escort. Show them traveling through the forest along the road south."

"As you desire, my Queen." She sank to the ground in a cross-legged position and began a series of deep breaths. Ariel and Mearith stepped back to let her work undisturbed. Soon they heard her chanting softly. They left her to it and walked away.

A while later a messenger arrived from Arlon. The roadway was clear, and none had discovered the trail that led to the encampment. All was well. Ariel sent him back with another message. They would set out for Narthwood at first light.

The man vanished back into the forest. The day wore on slowly for Ariel. Her mind was racing, and she itched to get going. Eventually Trelanth came to her. "It is done, Lady."

"Excellent. Help us now, most are through the awakening. Help us get them ready to go. We leave at first light tomorrow. When we do, I want to remove all trace of our having been here."

They spent the rest of the day helping the last few through the awakening and preparing to break camp. There was much excitement now as the journey was about to begin. Most of Arlon's men returned in the night, ready to help break down the camp and disguise the glade where it had stood.

All were awake and excited as the day lightened. They grabbed a quick meal then gathered up what there was to gather. They set out, heading back towards the road. As they came closer Ariel noticed Trelanth looking worried. "What troubles you?"

"Lady, the soldiers must have ridden through the night. The Geni is no longer with them, but they soon will be here."

"Dammit, I'd prefer to keep the folk out of a pitched battle right now. They're not ready, and neither are we as long as we have them with us. How much time do we have?"

"Not a great deal, my Queen."

"Can we cross the road before they reach us?"

"I believe we can, if we hurry."

Ariel looked at Mearith who nodded then urged her horse to greater speed. Ariel began to hurry her charges, but there were so many, all strung out along the narrow track through the forest.

They reached the road, and it was still clear. Instead of turning southward, they crossed the road and open field beyond, disappearing into the trees on the other side. It took a long time to get them all across the open area and into the forest on the other side.

In the end, all the Elves had vanished into the trees and along the path Mearith had found for them. Only Trelanth and two other mages remained behind. They worked their magic and soon all trace of the original path and encampment were gone.

Carefully they crossed the road and field, erasing all sign of the Elves passing. No sooner had they reached the trees than the soldiers became visible. Ariel and the mages sat on their horses just within the trees and watched as the army hurried by.

Ariel watched the camp Elves struggle to keep up with the soldiers. "I'll come back for you, my brothers and sisters. I promise you, I'll come back for you." She turned her horse away and trotted down the forest trail, the three mages close behind. They were safely in the forest now; the long march had begun.

FAR AWAY IN SHOTAR city, the Geni king raved. "Find her, dammit. I don't want excuses, find her."

The mage rose from his scrying pool and faced him. "I can't, for she'll no longer let me see. The great Queen of the High Born has returned. She called and they came, from where I can't say, but they came. Their queen has arisen, and the Elves are in the forest once again."

The End

A uthor's note: And now for a peek at the second chronicle...

The Road Home

(second edition)
by

Prudence MacLeod

Copyright July 2016
All rights reserved

IN THIS, THE SECOND chronicle of the Elves of Elendor, I will relate some of the trials and dangers faced by the Elves as Queen Ariel led them to a new home in the haunted forests of the north. Many were the dangers and rogue magics that had to be overcome on that long trek across the mountains, and many were the heroes who rose to face them.

The Long Chain of Fire

Ariel, Queen of the Elves, sat on her charger and gazed at the long string of people slowly making their way along the forest trail. The numbers of Elves seemed endless as they passed before her eyes. Only now was she beginning to understand the magnitude of the task she'd set for herself.

Beside her sat her companion, a centuries old warrior, an assassin without equal. The warrior had known, of course. From the first moment she'd seen Ariel asleep on that rooftop, she had known what lay ahead. "Well, my delight, are you pleased?"

"I'm terrified, Mearith, my heart. My only thought has been to set them free, but now I begin to see the magnitude of the task before me. Only now do I begin to see what I've done to them."

"Done to them? By setting them free?"

"Look at them, my heart. So many of them are terrified, and they're in no fit condition for this journey. The air will soon grow cold, and we have no cloaks or boots for them, no weapons either. How are we ever to get them over the mountains in winter?"

"Well, it's not winter yet. With luck, we'll escape that fate and be in Narthwood before the snows catch us."

"Do you truly believe that?"

"No, I don't. However, I believe someone else may have anticipated some of our needs."

"Oh?"

"Dear heart, Evanseth's greatest strength has always been his ability to see the upcoming obstacles, and to prepare for them. I think it's time we sent out some runners and scouts. We need news of what lies ahead, and we need news of Fugitive.

"If I know Evan he'll have left supplies for us at Fugitive, at least as much as he could spare. We need to know what's there and how much more we need to acquire before we reach the mountains."

Ariel nodded, deep in thought as the seemingly endless chain of Elves passed before her eyes. "As usual you've seen what I didn't and have taken the appropriate steps to prepare. I'd be so lost without you, my heart. You should have been the one to be queen, the one to lead us to freedom."

"No, my delight, you're the queen. You're the one with the vision, the ability to inspire all to your cause. Under my leadership, they would falter, the dream would fail, and all would pass away into the mystery of time.

"Ariel, my queen, my heart, it's you and you alone who can lead the Elves to freedom, bring us all back from the brink."

"I do hope your faith in me isn't misplaced."

"It isn't, have no fear. Ariel, may I ask something?"

"Of course."

"When you sent L'ark to seek out his companion's daughter, you seemed to feel quite strongly about that. Could you tell me about it?"

Ariel sighed then straightened in the saddle. "Tereen was ever a second mother to me. Telee and I were inseparable as children. We often played a game of freeing the slaves. We swore that we would both find a path to freedom and the first to achieve that would seek out and buy the other so we could both be free.

"Master overheard us talking about it one day, and I got the beating of my life. It was explained to me, at the business end of a whip, that I was an Elf, a slave, born to obey, to be owned. I was forbidden to see them ever again or they would be bought and killed before my eyes."

"But you didn't forget your vow to free your friend."

"Not for a single moment. Do you think L'ark will succeed?"

Mearith grinned. "He will succeed, my delight. Both L'ark and his brother L'mak are of the Southern Clans, no more tenacious creature exists. You may yet meet your childhood friend on the road to Narthwood."

"I do hope you're right. Come, let's find the end of the line and make sure everything is well there."

"I'll go. The queen should ride at the head of the column." With that, Mearith leaned towards Ariel, kissed her cheek, and then trotted off towards the end of the line. Ariel turned her eyes forward and set out.

As she reached the front of the line she found her general waiting for her with her personal guard. "Arlon, why have we stopped?"

"The day grows late, my queen," replied the general. "The way ahead is difficult, and the people are tired. I thought it best to face the rocky terrain ahead after they've rested and eaten."

Ariel nodded and dismounted. "That's good thinking, my friend. Make it so. Tanis."

"Yes, my queen?"

"You were scouting towards the open roads."

"I was, yes."

"What news?"

"The roads are empty, my queen."

"Empty?"

"Yes, my queen, nothing moved, no horse, wagon, or traveler, could be seen."

She stripped the saddle from the horse's back and pulled up a handful of sweet grass. She began to rub him down and he nickered his delight. "Arlon, Tanis, advise me now. If we could travel the road, even for a single day, we would avoid the rocky terrain ahead and gain a great deal of speed. What think you?"

"Well, you're absolutely right about the speed and distance, Lady," replied Arlon. "It'll take all day to cross the rocky hill ahead, with a gain of less than half a league. By taking to the roads we could manage two leagues in the same amount of time."

"Could it be a trap? Could there be an army in hiding, just waiting for us?"

"Possible, I suppose," replied Arlon, "but I doubt it. The only place to hide an army hereabouts is in the edge of the forest. We would know if they were here."

"Unless they were on the other side of the road," grinned Tanis.

Arlon clapped a hand on his shoulder. "Yes, my young friend, unless they were on the other side of the road."

Ariel smiled at them both. "What do you think, Arlon, is it worth a look?"

"Oh yes, my queen, it is indeed worth a look."

"Tanis."

"My queen?"

"Why are you still here?"

"I'm already gone, Lady," he called over his shoulder as he sped away, the rest of the guard falling into step behind him. They could run free for a while, with an army around her, the queen would be quite safe.

Mearith returned to her as the campfires were lit and food prepared. All the Elves had passed through the awakening and now, as they took their rest after a day of travel, they relaxed back to listen to the voices of the forest.

As darkness fell, Ariel climbed to a vantage point and looked back along the trail. Many of the campfires were visible to her, but not from the road below them. "What troubles you, Mearith, my love?"

"It's like a chain of fire," she replied, as she too gazed at the long line of campfires. "Invisible from the road below, but the light cast by the chain is not. If anyone bothers to take notice it wouldn't be so hard to puzzle out."

"I can't ask them to go without the basic warmth of fire. At least not until we get them better clothing and warm cloaks."

"I know, my delight, I know. They've not been off the Oshar long enough for their bodies to naturally generate the necessary heat. You or I could easily go weeks without cloaks or fire at this time of year, but not these poor people."

"Is there nothing we can do for them?" asked Ariel. "I was fortunate enough to have you to help and guide me. Most of these folk have no one."

They gazed at the chain of fires for a few moments then Ariel spoke again. "Mearith, what do you estimate our numbers to be?"

"Our numbers?"

"Newly freed to Borni, what is the ratio, do you think?"

"We have about fifteen hundred Borni, with nearly a thousand newly freed to care for, roughly speaking. What do you have in mind?"

"As I said before, I had you to guide me. Consider this, each newly freed could be assigned a Borni warrior to be a guide and mentor for the journey to Elfhome. The guide could teach language, wood craft, and fighting skills while on the journey, as well as provide assistance at time of need.

"That would still leave five hundred Borni to act guards, scouts, hunters, and protectors on the journey. The newly freed would still be part of the greater group, but have a special guide as well. What do you think?"

"My queen, how I do love the way your mind works. I'd never have thought of that, but it's an idea with great merit. I like it. Shall we run it past Arlon and Trelanth?"

"Let's do," grinned Ariel.

The general and the mage listened attentively while the queen outlined her idea. They both nodded in agreement. "Several have already been chosen by the Spiritpull," said Trelanth. "Those would be natural pairs."

"Agreed," said Arlon. "Actually, I like it, my queen. We'll be able to travel faster this way and lose fewer folk along the trail. The only problem I can foresee is if we meet heavy opposition. Most of our troops would be hampered until the newly freed could be moved back out of harm's way."

"Tell me truly now, Arlon, are we likely to meet such opposition in the forest?"

"No, Lady, we're not. Only when we're on the open road could we be so confronted."

Ariel sat lost in thought for a while, staring into the fire. Finally, she looked up again. "Mearith, tell me of the way ahead. If we abandon the trees for a day we can get around the cliffs ahead. From there could we continue on the other side of the road, or should we return to this side?"

"Once around the cliffs it would be best to return to this side for a time. Should we cross too soon we could be pushed against the great swamps that protect the privacy of Fugitive.

"At our current rate of travel, we need a day to pass the cliffs, and eight more until we reach the best place to cross. If we can use the road to skirt around the cliffs we can cut one day at least off that timeline."

Ariel's eyes suddenly hardened. "And if we took to the roads and marched there on to the crossing place?"

Mearith met her gaze squarely. "That would take only three days in total. However, all stealth would be lost. The ruse of us heading south would be lost. The Geni would know where to find us, even if we made it back into the forest.

"They could then oppose us in the mountains, especially near the ruins of Elanda, the place where the High Born fell. There is still much old and twisted magic resting there in the broken places of the palace grounds."

"We need to move with greater haste," sighed Ariel. "We watched from the trees as over a thousand men at arms rode south. I believe the ruse worked and they have sent all they have to spare to capture us.

"Trelanth, what think you? Is it worth the risk?"

"That I cannot say, my Lady, but this I do know. Many who journey with us now will not survive if winter catches us in the mountain reaches."

"Mearith?"

"She speaks truly, my delight."

"Your opinion?"

Mearith sighed then spoke. "We should take the risk. It's a gamble, but we're running out of time and alternatives."

"Then we await the return of Tanis. If he reports the roads empty of travelers, then we take to the roads. Arlon, see that every newly freed is assigned a warrior to mentor, teach, and protect." He nodded then rose and moved away to the next campfire.

The night was well along when that task was completed. All along the chain of fire the warriors approached and introduced themselves. They spoke for only a moment then covered their new charges with their own cloaks before settling down to sleep.

They were all awake before the sun arose the next morning. Everyone was making a meal of cold rations while awaiting the return of Tanis. Seeing the queen was awake, Arlon approached.

"It's done?" she asked.

"It's done, my queen," he replied. "We've tried to pair them as best possible. The strongest were paired with the weak and the mothers with children close, those who didn't go through to

Sanctuary. The most likely warriors were paired with the most adept at weapons, and so it goes.

"I've done my best, my queen, but in truth, many who should be here to mentor are with the king."

"It's all right, Arlon, you've done well and put more thought into it than I had. Thank you for that."

At that point Korath, a member of her guard, came trotting into the camp and dropped to one knee before Ariel. "I bring news, my queen."

Ariel smiled at her earnest young guardsman. "Rise, Korath, and share the news."

He was grinning with delight. "Lady, when we reached the road last night we heard people approaching. It was twenty soldiers herding a hundred slaves along, headed for Magdan, replacements for some of those we freed.

"We slipped in close to their camp and listened. Lady, most able-bodied soldiers and sell swords have gone south to hunt us. Shotar has retained barely enough to guard the city. All merchants and travelers have been warned to stay off the roads."

"That is welcome news indeed, Korath," said Ariel as she gripped his shoulder tight, "but what of the slaves you saw?"

"Tanis should be here with them in a few minutes, my queen." He was grinning with delight.

"And what of the soldiers who guarded them?" asked Mearith.

"The bodies have been dragged into the trees and hidden, Lady. The oshar they carried in a wagon was dumped out and the wagon left in the trees as well. The horses now carry the food, weapons, and clothing of the soldiers."

Ariel laughed with delight. A moment later Tanis arrived with his new charges. They were soon integrated with the rest of the group. Arlon wasn't smiling now.

"Arlon?"

"Forgive me, Lady Ariel, the boy did right, to be sure, but we now have a hundred fewer warriors to guard our passage. Are we still going to risk the roads?"

"We are."

"Then may I suggest Trelanth and her mages reach the road first and leave it last?"

"That is precisely what we had in mind," smiled Trelanth, as she and her fellow mages approached.

"Then let's get moving," said Ariel, as she threw the saddle on Grimm's back. "Tanis, take the guard, escort Trelanth and her party."

He saluted and led the way into the trees with Trelanth at his side and the others close behind.

The road was completely empty of traffic, nothing moved. Like a silent tide the Elves poured out of the forest and onto that poorly paved surface. The wagon Tanis had abandoned was brought back into service to carry three injured and a half dozen or more younger children.

Every Elf with a horse carried a passenger, either child or elder. The queen rode her mighty charger up and down the long line of Elves with a crippled boy clinging to her waist, for some reason he had not gone through to Sanctuary with the others. As she stopped on a small rise to watch she heard a soft voice behind her.

"Queen Ariel?"

She tilted her head back a bit to hear him better. "Yes?"

"You should kill me now, and throw the body into the trees."

"Why would I do a thing like that?"

"I'm crippled, Lady. I'm useless, and I'll endanger the others by holding them back. I thought I could keep up, but now I see that's not true."

"Who said this to you?"

"No one, Lady, it was my own thought."

Ariel patted the hands around her waist gently. "Then you need a new thought. What's your name?"

"I have none, Lady."

"I see. Have you learned the old stories of our people?"

"Some, Lady."

"Do you know the tale of Kern, the lame horseman?"

"I do. He was lame on the ground, but with his horse he was a mighty warrior."

"That's right, what else?"

"He became the Great Queen's horseman, the man who tended and trained her horses."

"Indeed so, that's the tale of it. Now, young sir, Grimm seems to like you. I name you, Kern. It is now your task to learn as much as you can about horses. It is said Kern of old could talk to them and they to him. I command you now to learn as much as you can of horses, and if you do well, you will become the keeper of my horses. Will you take on this task for me?"

"Oh, my queen, I swear I'll do everything in my power to learn," he enthused.

"Elves and horses work well together, Kern. I knew nothing of horses, but I was alone and sick, and someone had left a horse for me. I spoke to her and begged her to take me to the others in my party. This she did willingly. Never show anger or abuse to a horse, and they will serve you well. Remember."

"I will, my queen, I promise."

"Then come, Kern, we must find you a horse of your own. Until then you will ride with me and tend to Grimm for me." With a laugh of joy, she touched her heels lightly to the big war horse's flanks and he surged ahead. She brought him to an easy canter and headed to the other side of the road.

Ariel smiled and turned aside for a swift ride through the open fields and back again, she'd felt the arms around her waist tighten and the shudder as the boy sobbed in relief. He would not be killed as useless, as his master had threatened to do. He would have a life, a task, and a name given by the queen herself. When she felt he was ready, she turned the big horse back to the head of the column.

When darkness forced them to stop and make camp, she showed Kern how to take off the saddle and rub down the horse. She smiled with delight as he talked softly to the massive beast. When Ariel turned back Mearith and Arlon were grinning at her. "What?"

"It seems you have a new groomsman, my delight."

"I have. This man is Kern. Kern will ride with me until we can find him a horse of his own."

Tanis grinned and winked at the boy. "My Lady, we acquired several horses just yesterday. There was a likely looking mare in the bunch. She looks like she'd be happier with a rider instead of carrying a pack."

"Was there a saddle, Tanis?"

"Yes, Lady. We brought it in the wagon. Shall I ...?"

Ariel grinned. "Why are you still here?"

With a laugh, he was up and away. A short time later he returned leading a lively young mare who fairly pranced along beside him. He passed the reins to Kern then began to show him how to care for the horse.

"It was just one year ago, Lady Mearith was teaching me these things. We all have much to learn, but you're the lucky one. You'll get to spend every day with horses."

Ariel was smiling at them. "Ariel?"

"He wanted me to kill him, Mearith. He thought himself a liability, that he would slow us all down and put us in danger because of his lame leg."

"So you named him Kern and gave him a horse."

"I did, yes. Do you disapprove?"

"Oh no, my delight, never that. Once again you rise above all expectation."

For that night and the next two, the chain of fire glowed along the roadside of the Shotar Highway. Scouts ranged well ahead and guards watched closely from behind, but they traveled the road for three full days and encountered no one.

By the end of the third day messages were being sent from the front of the column to the rear and it was Kern on his horse who carried them. Tanis had been right; the young mare was the right choice for the boy.

None of them could have known she was bred for racing, and had been on her way to the new governor of Magdan as a gift. The boy and the horse bonded instantly and, as all true Elves, he had a natural affinity for horses.

Ariel was astride Grimm, trotting alongside the column when he approached at a gallop. He didn't dismount and kneel as she'd forbidden it because of his lame leg. Kneeling was painful for him. "Ho, Kern, what news of the front?"

"They've arrived unhindered, my queen. Already they enter the forest again. Lady, there is an Orc waiting there to speak with you."

"Drakkat is there?"

"Yes, Lady, that was the name."

"Then let's go." She urged Grimm into a gallop, but Kern raced ahead to let them know she was coming. She arrived to find Drakkat waiting with Mearith and Arlon.

"Drakkat," she shouted, as she leaped from her horse and hugged him. "What brings you here, dear friend?"

The big Orc just grinned. "I bring the supplies as ordered by that arrogant Elf, Evanseth. He dumped the lot in my lap and ordered me to bring it to you, then walked away. It took every horse we had plus what we could borrow from Marc just to get it here."

"That is welcome news. What have you brought me?"

"Cloaks, boots, tunics, leggings, and the like, plus a healer."

"A healer?"

"It is I, Lady Ariel," smiled a young Elf, as she approached and knelt.

"Beren, rise and embrace me. You've decided to travel with us?"

"Yes, Lady," replied the girl, as she released the queen and stepped back. "I've learned much from Meg, and much more from Egma."

"I thought age had robbed Egma of her wits?"

Beren laughed. "Lady, Egma believed me to be her youngest daughter, and she tried to teach me as much of the healing arts as she could. She has more to teach, I'm sure, but I felt the people on this journey would need me more as Meg will remain with Marc in Fugitive."

"It was well reasoned out, Beren, and I'm thrilled you're here. We do have great need of your skills. Back along the trail there is a wagon with folk who would surely benefit from your attentions."

"Then, with your permission, Lady, I'll be about the task." She gathered up her bag of supplies and stepped away, but Ariel's voice stopped her.

"Beren wait, Kern can get you there far more swiftly." The boy moved the horse closer. Drakkat grabbed the girl and tossed her up behind the rider.

"Hang on tight," said Kern. As soon as her arms gripped him he wheeled the horse and sped away, Beren's sudden shriek lingering on the air.

"Boy's reckless," said Drakkat. "I like that. So, what'll I do with all this gear that's wearing down my horses?"

"Arlon, have someone take inventory and distribute what Drakkat's brought us to the most needy."

It was long past dark when the last of the Elves were safely in the forest and settled down by a campfire. "All right, Drakkat, what else is on your mind?" asked Ariel.

"Hmm," muttered the big Orc, a smile coming to his lips. "We've had word from the mountains, Lady. The news isn't good. A small band of Dwarves found their way into Fugitive a few days past. They bring tales of strange things, and of Geni disturbing the lands near the Ruins of Elanda. What they searched for, the Dwarves did not know."

"I can guess," muttered Trelanth. "They know what's happened and they fear reprisals for past deeds. Ever the unworthy see retribution looming and seek to forestall it."

Drakkat chuckled at that. "It's true, the Geni have no honor, and what you say is most likely."

"But?"

"But this camp holds an untold wealth of slaves. Our queen has impoverished many, including many of the Geni."

"I care not for their motives," sighed Ariel. "At this point I would prefer to avoid them if possible. Mearith, your thoughts on this?"

"It will add many days to our journey, but there is a way, another path we could take. It will lead us to a hidden valley deep in the mountains. There's a river and forest there, and if desperate we could winter there safely.

"The place would be vulnerable as a permanent home, but as a waystation it'll serve well enough."

"Could we establish a permanent waystation there?"

"We could. What's on your mind, my delight?"

"If the weather turns against us there are many among us who could benefit from resting there for the winter. Would this be possible?"

"Yes. Are you suggesting we take them there?"

"Only if we must, but in future I would like to establish several waystations between Elfhome and Fugitive. These stations would be manned by Elves well skilled in woodcraft, easily able to foresee the advance of enemies and avoid them as well as warn all Elves of the danger.

"Ah well, thoughts for another time. For now, we need a way to get our people to Elfhome safely."

"There is something else you might consider, Lady Ariel," said Drakkat.

"And that is?"

"The Geni have sent most of their forces south, thinking you went that way. Strike them hard while their guard is down."

"Explain."

"You're pressed for time. A few mages and treasure seekers are poking about in your path. Strike hard and fast, destroy them, and pass through. You'll be long gone before the Geni can recall their forces. Yes, they will watch that road carefully in future. That's the time to establish the way points."

"My people are weak, Drakkat, and the warriors with us are dedicated to protecting them. I would not risk my people so soon, besides, if the mages are disturbing the old magics, ..."

"Actually, I believe Drakkat's right, my delight. Do not fear the mages, for I now believe these are not the mighty magic users of old. What think you, Trelanth?"

"I think I'd like to see what these mages are about, poking through the Ruins of Elanda."

"When we passed that way with Evenseth earlier this year I was disturbed by that place," said Ariel.

"In what way, dear heart?"

"It called to me, Mearith, my heart. I heard it whisper my name, call to me to return, to embrace what once was, to rise again as before, Queen of the High Born. I felt the stone that rides at my breast respond to it."

"Another test?"

"Yes, and not one I want to face with so many newly freed to care for. Perhaps you and I, with Trelanth and the guard, I might, but with so many ..."

"My queen, if I may."

"Speak, Arlon, advise me in this."

"Lady, you told me to focus on getting the people to Elfhome as quickly as possible. Each day we lose on this journey is precious, for the year grows late, especially in Elfhome. The world is colder there, as it will be in the mountains. I believe Drakkat has the right of it."

Ariel sat quietly for several moments, staring into the fire. No one disturbed her thoughts. At length, she sighed and squared her shoulders. "Trelanth, are you aware of any prying eyes upon us?"

"There are none, Lady Ariel."

"Prepare then. When the sun rises, the people will begin moving toward the Ruins of Elanda. Mearith and I will ride ahead with fifty warriors chosen by Arlon, Tanis and the guard will accompany us as well."

"And me too?" asked Trelanth.

"Yes, you and your mages. Our people will be safe enough, for we'll be the focus of all attention, if there is any."

"Perhaps there may not be, Lady."

"Trelanth?"

"Ethor is excellent at masking spells. He may be able to hide our activities from all within the city of Shotar. Only those we encounter might be aware of us."

"Excellent. That would truly please me."

"I'll meet you on the road, my delight. I think I should have a look at this path first hand before we go charging in."

Ariel just nodded as Mearith rose and trotted into the forest. "Drakkat, of all the people here to advise me, you've traveled the most in the world as it is now. Have you ever been to Shotar?"

"I've been in that city many times, my queen."

"We estimate they sent over a thousand men south to catch us. How many more warriors might they have in the city?"

A wide grin spread across his face and he chuckled. "Enough to defend it, perhaps, but not many more."

"Drakkat, old friend, from a warrior's perspective, what's the overall state of affairs in the world?"

"In the world? Well, from what I've seen over the years, this part of the world is ruled by the Geni. They rule by threat of force and magic. They keep the only standing army of professional soldiers, mostly humans and orcs. This army is spread out through the five cities."

"Like Magdan."

"Yes, Magdan is one of them."

"How many men do you think this army of theirs has?"

Drakkat was silent as he thought about that. "Perhaps fifteen thousand soldiers plus slaves and supply handlers. Most of them are stationed in the two cities to the south and west. The one guards against the raiders from the sea, and the other from the creatures of the south."

"Tell me of the sea raiders."

"I know nothing of them, Lady. I've seen their ships, but that's all. They seem to be both Orc and human, perhaps deserters from the ancient wars were their ancestors."

"And the southern threat?"

"All I know is what I've heard in the streets and taverns. Wandering tribes of Geni who were left behind when the Geni led their forces north so long ago. There are also Ogres, Giants, and other creatures that evolved from the ages of Geni magics, twisted, evil things, fit only for killing."

"Their numbers?"

"Unknown, Lady Ariel, but not so many that they would dare come north in force."

"Hmmm, Arlon, you were here when the world was broken, yes?"

"I was, my queen."

"Tell me of that time, the numbers of peoples."

"Lady, in those days the numbers of Elves, both Borni and High Born, were as the trees in the forest, many thousands beyond count. The Humans were few at that time, but the Dwarves were many as well.

"First the free Orc clans came from the south, driven from behind by the Geni forces. Drakkat's clan was one such. They tried to forge a new home for themselves, and allied themselves with the Humans.

"Once that alliance started to carve out a territory from the forest, we took notice and began to push them back south, but the Geni forces came then, hundreds of thousands of them and more, as there were of us.

"The great war ravaged the lands and diminished their number as well as our own, but they kept coming. The land was different then, but in the end, it was broken by the Geni. The magic of the High Born was too strong for them, and so they broke the world to release the demons."

"What happened then?"

"The High Born twisted the cataclysm so it consumed all. As the vast forests sank into the sea, swallowing most of the armies as well as the demons, the Borni left this realm."

"Arlon, speak to me of the numbers, the numbers of peoples now as compared to then."

"From what I've seen since returning, Lady, it's a sad thing. We Elves are so few compared to what we were, but the Geni seemed to have fared worse. It's my guess the High Born gamble was successful in destroying the armies of demons and invaders, but in so doing they exhausted themselves and were vulnerable.

"The Humans seem to have grown greatly in numbers and the Orcs appear to be recovering. The Dwarves fared much worse as their mountains took most of them beneath the seas when they sank."

"So, from what you tell me, am I to understand that, compared to the world before the Breaking, this land is somewhat uninhabited?"

"Yes, Lady, the great cities of yore are gone. Those that have arisen are but villages in comparison to what was."

"What are you thinking, Lady Ariel?" asked Drakkat.

"If I understand this correctly, it wasn't just the Elves who were decimated by the War of Breaking. With the addition of the Borni, perhaps the Elves are as numerous as the rest in comparison. If this is true, what would be the Geni's natural reaction, if they did discover us in the forest so near the city?"

Everyone close looked up at Drakkat's great bellow of laughter. "Those sniveling cowards would hide in their city, bracing the gates against a possible attack from the Elves.

"If there is an attack from them at all, it will come from magic."

"My thought as well, old friend. Trelanth, what say you?"

"The reasoning is sound, my queen. I will prepare the mages; we'll be ready for whatever they try."

"Prepare then, my friend, for tomorrow we march. Three days from now promises to be an interesting day."

Don't miss out!

Visit the website below and you can sign up to receive emails whenever Prudence MacLeod publishes a new book. There's no charge and no obligation.

https://books2read.com/r/B-A-ZKBBB-DXPZC

BOOKS 2 READ

Connecting independent readers to independent writers.

Also by Prudence MacLeod

Children of the Goddess
Lady Blue
Fallen Angel
Lady Justice
Lady Shadow
Lady Seeker
Watcher and Warrior
Shadow Ascending

Children of the Wild
Immortal Tigress
Children of the Wolf
Vampire's Lair
The Hawk and the Wolf
The Oregon Incident
Race the Wind
Heir to the Throne

Elvish Chronicles
Rise of the Queen

Forgotten Worlds
Suvi
Echo of the Past
Survivors
Ship
Fleet
Unite
IGEN
T.E.N.

Nova series
Novan Witch
Assassin of Nova
Beyond Nova
Claimstake
Red Nova

Watch for more at https://www.prudencemacleod.com/.

Telling a story is like knitting a sweater. Start with a ball of possibilities, pull out one small thread and begin. With luck and patience you will create something quite wonderful.

About the Author

On a far off windswept island Jennifer Crandall sits with her dogs and cats creating fantastic stories for all to enjoy. She publishes as JL Crandall, Prudence MacLeod, and Jenni Leigh.

Read more at https://www.prudencemacleod.com/.